CW00504606

Acknowledgements

I am grateful to all those that recounted their memories of Teddy. I have included most, if not all, be they good, bad or downright wicked.

Special thanks to Vin Ferguson for his constant encouragement for me to start, and to keep on, writing. He wanted to know the story of Teddy and the conflicts and challenges that went into shaping the angry man.

I would like to thank the Liverpool Laid Back Writers Meet Up group and especially, the organiser Mark Horne, for all their supportive comments, critiques and shared wisdom over the last few years.

TEDDYS TALES

Chapter 1 The Wake

Wakes can be sorrowful or joyful affairs, often reflective, always opportunities to learn more about the deceased. Teddy's was no exception. As family and a few friends gathered in that December afternoon and evening, the reflections began at 382. This was the last home of Teddy, he had lived there for 10 years with Mary. It was a parlour house, double fronted ex-council property. This was his dream dwelling, the culmination of years of machinating and manipulating his contacts in the local council. Flirting, bantering and the odd bribe, had all gone in to realising his dream of having a house on the main road. An arterial route into town, with a bus stop just a couple of hundred yards either way. It was his rich man's house, on show for all to see the barra boy had made good.

The renovation was not complete. It had started with removing the old Georgian style small windows and opening them up to wide "picture" windows. A signature feature of one of his latterly straight occupations as a joiner. He had perfected this approach over the previous years in the Dovecot council estate. A poor area by today's measures, but back then a desirable Liverpool suburb. It was there that the main transitions took place. Leaving the grey life of the fence and developing a respectable above-board lifestyle. At the same time the changing dynamics of his life were being laid down. On approaching his dream dwelling the front garden was more mausoleum than green space. He had flagged over the garden and made a drive in for his car. Raised beds flanked the path with geraniums, pansies and dwarf roses. The frontage had been rendered with "Snowcem", a white finished render that was unusual for the area, just one house had been done previously in all of Dovecot. Teddy had seen it some years before, and that was the flag he wanted to show to all and sundry, that he had made it. The icing on the cake was an outside light, in a carriage lamp style, on the left of the doorway.

The attendees were spaced out at 382, the older ones seated comfortably in the long lounge on the floral covered three-piece suite. No one had yet sat in *his* chair in the bay window, a hard-backed dining chair, long estranged from its table and three companion seats. The kitchen was a long narrow galley version, despite the ongoing building work it still accommodated several mourners. These were younger in the main and all had a drink in hand or on the nearest surface. Lastly the garden, though cold, had a circulation of smokers gathered in twos and threes dotted across the patio.

All avoided the building materials and debris. Carelessly discarding cigarette butts under foot or flicking them across the damp grass.

Teddy was in the parlour. The room was cold. The five gas-fire radiants, unlit, grinned out from their restraining wire braces at the walls. Central heating had not yet arrived at 382. A wallpaper pasting table, covered in a sheet, bore the open coffin. It was centre stage in the bay window. A steady trickle of mourners, usually accompanied, paid their respects during the wake. Some with wet eyes, others sobbing, and some eyes were dry and gazed unwaveringly at the man in the box. He had shrunk over the years, not the osteoporotic vertebral collapse of older people, but in body weight. His massive arms and barrel chest no longer evident. Arms down at his sides, scarred knuckles, from a multitude of fights and hard work, just showing. The shorter right leg not that obvious in repose. His comb-over now just a wisp in place. Hitleresque toothbrush moustache a faded echo of its former darker glory. Lined brow and hollow cheeks were still recognisable as him. The silence was calming. No longer the portent that often preceded a temper tantrum or violent outburst. Teddy was a complicated man. He had lived a life that had shaped his body, mind, and relationships, and not one of which was done by halves. It was full on or fuck off.

The doorbell rang with the Avon two tone. Another mourner had arrived bearing condolences and a bag of beer cans. Frances a nephew on Mary's side shook hands with Tony and said, "Really sorry to hear about your Dad." "Thanks. Come on in. Your John is in the kitchen, Mum is in the living room with your Mum and Aunty Molley" said Tony. Frances made a fuss of his Aunty Mary, as was his usual greeting but, with added clinginess to emphasise the graveness of the situation.

"Aunty Mary, how are you? I couldn't believe it when I heard it. It is just such a shock" as he clung on to Mary's hand with both of his. Frances' mother chirped in for her sister's delayed response.

"She is only just getting her head around it now after two days. It took me by surprise when your Dad dropped dead too, but I was a wreck for weeks after that. And with four young kids."

"I am alright really thanks Frances, it's like your Mam said, a shock. I thought he would go on forever, creaking gate and the like", said Mary.

"You never know the minute!" added Annie, blowing Woodbine smoke in an upward direction to ease her sister's none smoking status.

Molley had been quiet for a while and tried to change the subject to the funeral in two days' time. "Mary have you spoken to the lads about the priest? I don't think it's right not to have a priest at a funeral." On this interjection Frances made an excuse and headed for the kitchen.

"He always hated sky pilots Molley, and said when he goes, he didn't want one of them anywhere near", offered Mary without any conviction in her voice. Her face showed the turmoil she felt inside, the tremor in her hands emphasised the pain she felt trying to keep everyone happy.

"I know. He was never the same with the church after our Tommy and all that fuss, but it is his funeral, and he was a Catholic", offered Molley.

"I agree Mary, we are all Catholics and it's just not right to not have one at a funeral", exhaled Annie. Her face the image of indignation.

"I am at my wits end with all of this" sobbed Mary. Tony had been slow to re-join the kitchen mourners. Seeing his Mother's concern he said.

"Mum, I will have a word with Leo. You're not to worry about it." Tony was the voice of reason, despite being 24 years old and the middle child, in this high expressed emotional household. He had left home just a couple of years earlier. Leo was the apple of Teddy's eye, before Sharon had eventually come along. He was two years older than Tony and only showed the highly charged Kelly emotions occasionally, but when he did, they were full on too. Leo and Tony were atheists. They had both echoed Teddy's wishes that no sky pilots were to be at his funeral, it was these comments that had caused Mary to go along, so far, with the apocryphal plan.

Carlo was holding court in the kitchen, he was the life and soul of any party, even wakes. He was recounting funny stories of his Dad and joinery jobs they worked on together. He never seemed to grasp the gravity of any situation. He was the most like his father, in terms of looks, out of all the four Kelly lads. His curly hair and moustache were latterly caricatured by stand-up comedians, but in 1979 it was the standard scouser look for some. When he laughed his curls would bob about his brow emphasising his prankster eyes and wide smile. He was the youngest of the Kelly boys and only Sharon was younger than him. Tony addressing Carlo asked.

"Where's Leo?"

"In the garden with Frankie."

Despite the weak sunshine it was cold that afternoon, but it didn't stop the smokers on the rear patio of 382. Leo was sucking on his Embassy, he smoked the same as his Dad. Tony approached them, ignoring the smoke, he stated.

"Leo. We have to have a re-think about the priest. Mum is really upset about not having one."

"No way!"

"Listen, we know how he hated the idea of religion and he didn't want any sky pilot anywhere near his funeral but, he's dead and he will not know anything about it. However, Mum is the main concern now, not him, and she is really upset at not having a priest at the service." Leo's face spoke for him. It was shouting against Tony's suggestion of dropping Teddy's own funeral plan, which to Leo was a betrayal of his Dad's long standing and often repeated instructions. Teddy first announced his atheistic funeral direction shortly after his first heart attack. He never went into any reason for his desire. It was always taken as red that he did not believe in any religion and as such any lip service, as he saw it, was a massive contradiction. Leo's body language re-enforced his disagreement to the idea, he turned away from the suggestion and shook his head, lifting his free arm towards his little brother.

"Tony, no!" He hadn't drunk too much at this time and so his manner was not aggressive. "He always said no sky pilot and that's what he should get, *no* priest!" Tony pressed his case.

"Leo, we know, we know. But its Mum who we should be thinking about now. She is finding it really difficult. All the other women are saying it's not right and that there should be a priest. This is coming from all sides of the family. Aunty Molly was just going on about him being a catholic when he was younger. She said he was an angelic altar boy in St Francis' Xavier."

"That was years ago."

"Maybe, but they all think 'once a catholic always a catholic', despite what you might say." Tony let the thought hang with him for a few seconds. Was his body language starting to quieten?

"Well if you let them have a priest I am not going to the funeral." The thought of a family feud at this time put Tony under pressure. Feuds were common with the Kellys. Often, they were short lived, but some smouldered on for years. If Leo did not go, that would drive a wedge between the immediate family and would only worsen Mary's anxiety. But if there was no priest, she would fret over the immediate women's family counsel and their comments flowing now. Tony hid his growing frustration with his big brother. Despite being a few inches taller and broader than Leo he was still the little brother. They hadn't had a fight for several years now. The last one was resolved by Mary. Unlike Teddy whose answer to everything was, or had a threat of, violence, she had spoken calmly to Leo. She explained that it hurt her whenever her boys had a real falling out and that is was wrong for family to fight. In this case it was Leo that she found wanting in the dispute. And as punishment she was not letting him go out that night. At this time Leo was 18 or 19 and the thought of being grounded was anathema. He had declared he was not going to be kept in like a kid, he was a man and was going out. To this Mary had simply and quietly said that if he didn't, they were going to, and here she chose her words carefully, *fall out*. The thought of his mother being at odds with him cut right into his heart. Leo, though still a young man then, was a tough nut. He was fearless. He had stood up to numerous bullies, often beating them senseless when push came to shove. He looked out of the window, looked at his Mum, reflected for a few seconds, and sat down on the sofa for the evening.

"Leo it's a long time we since we had a falling out, and I don't want one now, with all of this" his arms vaguely drew in the ensemble, "but we have to think about Mum and how she is feeling."

Leo replied, "Let me think about it for a while." A beak through? Thought Tony.

"Hey Leo, your Dad was a funny fella", Frankie the family historian chirped in to defuse the tension. "When we were playing cards, he would say 'Hail Mary full of grace send me down a lucky ace', and then deal." This spread a welcome tone to the garden gathering. Tony moved away to chat to one of the other cousins and her partner. Frankie continued to chat whimsically about his uncle Teddy and earlier times. Leo lent a half hearing ear to the tales while stewing over Tony's words and helping his thought processes with copious swigs from his beer can, punctuated with exhalations of Embassy smoke.

Maureen, the eldest Kelly, was looking down at Teddy. She was asking herself why he was such a bastard in life. Her training had encouraged her to think about people from their perspective in order to understand the drivers behind their behaviours. She took in his shorter right leg, the lined face and the shrunken physique. He had not been a tall man by any means, maybe 5' 7" at best. She imagined him as a child before the illness. Playing in the dirty streets of Islington at the turn of the 20s and 30s decades. She saw a gorgeous, dark curly haired boy with flashing brown eyes. It was summer, the gang of kids were all barefoot as usual, the game was cowboys and Indians. They were all running about with their left hands out in front and slapping their right thighs with their other hand. All riding horseback, often stopping to shoot Winchesters from a kneeling position. All the boys were skinny, most wearing baggy trousers with big turn ups to their ankles. All were smiling. She thought about the influences that would change them, and Teddy in particular, in the coming months and years. What made this gorgeous boy with the flashing eyes and big smile turn into a monster, or so it seemed, from her experience?

Chapter 2 The First Blow

Teddy finished his meal of stale bread and dripping fat. Gulping down his tap water, from a cracked, and handle less cup, to slake the salted taste. He had an urgent mission with the local kids. As he went down the concrete stairs of the Bidder Street tenement, he was living the scenario to come. He was a Mexican bandit, part of Pancho Villas' gang raiding across the gringo border to steal much needed horses. He imagined he had 2 cartridge belts over his shoulders and 2 colt pistols, one on each hip, worn low, gunslinger style. It was a mission he and his friend Jimmy had made many times in the streets. Jimmy was just like Teddy, (apart from the black round rimmed glasses) a bit short for their age and with the same dark hair and brown eyes, and hence the bandit roles. They were Pedro and Pancho the Mexican bandits. They always had each other's backs, providing cover when the gringos were attacking, and encouraging each other onwards when they were charging forward.

Joining the other kids in the street, Teddy started arranging the boys as usual. He was charismatic, a natural leader. The other boys usually went along with the plays he suggested. Teddy was a show off. He loved the limelight. It was just as easy to be seen, or feared, as the hero or the villain. Occasionally, when a play was not going to his plan, one or more of the boys would argue against the plot. This would spark an angry outburst. Teddy would mimic his father, learned behaviour, Maureen later called it.

"What the fuck do you mean?" Squaring up to the boy, Teddy would intimidate the dissenter. A Mexican stand-off would ensue. Each boy knowing that if he made the first move, pain and a black eye could ensue. This was all that Teddy usually needed, along with his swaggering demeanour, to keep control as the director of their film, and the cock of their street.

Sometimes the gang play fights would be real. The kids from a nearby street would swoop down and steal their wooden rifles and pistols, often using superior numbers to make good their raid. This would require real leadership from Teddy to get their weapons back. He would outline what they were going to do. He never hesitated in his address to the assembled posse. They would ride in, chase down anyone with one of their rifles or pistols and give them a good clap around the head for their crimes. At the same time take any of their own stuff; sheriff's badges, bows and arrows and the like, as punishment. If any of the group wavered or showed signs of fear, Teddy's warlike persona would give them the courage they lacked for the clash to come.

It was the Canterbury street kids that took their hard-earned sticks away this time. So, Teddy addressed his gang of bandits.

"We are going to run in from both ends of their street, shouting and screaming to scare them. Then we run each of them down and grab our stuff. If they have something good, take that as well. If you can, give them a slap, and keep running. It is a raid, just like Pancho Villas, we take no prisoners!" The other kids were excited at the prospect of getting their makeshift toys back and giving the Canterbury kids what for. It was a microcosm of mob think. All feeling bigger than their eight to eleven, or so, years. The plans continued, mostly going over the same ground again, till Teddy was sure his bandits were pumped enough to make the raid.

On cue, the Bidder Street boys ran into Canterbury Street wailing and whooping, more like red Indians than Mexican bandits. The panic in the Canterbury kids' gang was instant. They left their sticks on the ground or dropped them to take flight easier. There was much screaming, more from fear of a beating than an actual one, there was one voice that could clearly be heard above the shouts. Teddy was swearing at the kids he was chasing, this made them accelerate even faster, the rush of adrenaline made him growl louder and his face showed pure delight at the extent of his prowess. Catching a kid, Teddy got him in a headlock and berated him for the attack on the Bidder Street gang. The kid was crying out for his big brother. "He isn't here, and you are getting slapped!" Teddy administered 2 or 3 slaps in quick succession to the boy's head. No damage was done, only pride hurt. Teddy looked round to see Jimmy fighting off 2 boys at the same time. He needed help! Releasing his victim, Teddy ran over to Jimmy. In a flash the 2 attacking boys were running off down the street. It was just the roar, and stream of invective from Teddy that made them hesitate, they were not going to win this encounter with Pedro and Pancho!

As the Bidder Street gang were collecting their toy rifles and pistols, nothing more than splintered pieces of wood, a shadow appeared cast from the evening sunshine. It was the big brother of the slapped head kid. To these boys he was a monster. Older by 2 or 3 years, he went to big school, and so tall, lamppost tall.

"Hey you Kelly!" Teddy stood up to his full height. He could not show fear in front of his gang. The big brother was a good 4 to 5 inches taller and much broader than Teddy. The Bidder Street bandits looked on. A mixture of fear and excitement brewed in their midst. What would Teddy do? Run away? Not his style. Get a good hiding? More than likely.

"You hit our kid, you fucking little bastard you!" The monster looked invincible. Older than Teddy but, was he tougher than Teddy? Still standing tall as he could, Teddy stared back at the big brother. "He deserved it. He stole our stuff, so we got it back, and he got slapped. That's fair."

"Fair my arse!" He butted the shorter, younger Teddy, sending him staggering backwards, to fall on the ground. He swaggered round to the other Bidder Street kids, "Any of you little *gets* come around here again and you will get the same. Understood...." He didn't finish his question due to the forearm lock across his throat. Recovering his balance, ignoring his pain, Teddy was overcome with a rage that burned. His eyes were still blurred from the tears created in the collision of heads, not from a kids normal crying. The fire inside him was 1,000c. He wrestled big brother to the ground, using his own body weight, which was slight, as a lever. Only easing his grip on the throat to make it easier to hit him. The punches landed quickly, all bar a few hitting their mark. His nose split open flowing blood down his face, the right eye already swollen into a ball shape, and closed over. Big brother was squirming all over the ground trying to wriggle free, but Teddy sat over him, pinning him down with strength made in the heat of hades. Teddy became aware that his right hand was really hurting. It was bleeding, his blood mingling with big brothers on his knuckles now. He glowered in big brother's face.

"Don't you come anywhere near me or my gang again or I will kill you! Do you hear?" Big brother could only gurgle, that was taken as a 'yes', by Teddy. "Alright lads, let's go, and leave this fucker here." Standing up Teddy felt 10 foot tall. He could feel the admiration of his gang engulfing him. He felt good. He would feel like that again in the future.

The chat was euphoric. All the Bidder street bandits crowded around Teddy, saying how they saw their leader beat the shit out of that gringo, the federale. Terminology was relative. Punches were made into thin air to emphasise the re-telling of the fight. Pancho Villa himself couldn't have done a better job. Teddy was patted on the back as they made their way back to Bidder Street, and their bandit hideout. The recognition of his feat, beating the monster big brother in a fist fight – for real! It was an achievement, and then some. The power was intoxicating. Filling his chest with a warm glow, beating a military band's tattoo with his heartbeats. Teddy was feeling invincible. His grin was wider than ever, brown eyes shining, and his dark curls were bobbing with each step. He was the epitome of the returning hero.

Rumours spread around the streets of the David and Goliath clash. How little Teddy Kelly had beat the shit out of the Canterbury Street's big brother monster. The fight was lengthened, more violence thrown in, more tears – on the big brother's part. How other kids were ready to jump in to save their leader, if he needed it. But he was doing well on his own. Talk of a retaliation raid on Bidder Street was mentioned.

Big brother walked away from the scene of his humiliation. His pride hurt almost the same as his face. He couldn't let anyone know that a little kid had just beaten him up. So, his side of things began to take shape in his mind. There were lots of them. He still went over to the gang brandishing sticks and clubs, no regard for his own safety. He was going to put them straight, not to pick on single kids with a gang. That was it. Yes, that would explain how a lad as big as him had come off the worse, despite going in with such noble intentions. As he repeatedly went over his story, it became truth. He was about to go up the stairs of his tenement block when a dark suited figure emerged in the stairwell. Father Riley had been visiting his usual parishioners.

"Hey up John, what on earth has happened to you?" Struggling with tears of pain and humiliation, big brother recounted the story. Father Riley had placed a comforting hand on his shoulder while listening to the truth, as big brother told it. "And it was definitely Teddy Kelly, from Bidder Street, that was the instigator of this attack?"

"Yes Father."

"Now you go and get cleaned up John. I will see you at mass on Sunday. I will have words with young master Kelly when I see him." Big brother went up the concrete stairs to his landing and a cat's lick wash, in the Belfast sink in the kitchen area. He was feeling better already. Heaven, and Father Riley, were on his side.

Neighbourhoods are similar the world over. A casual question enquiring of someone's whereabouts was all it took to start the ripple of a rumour. Once initiated, it would spread out across any layer it touched. In time the contagion of this one had reached crisis point. Teddy, like many kids in his neighbourhood was an Altar boy, as the oldest he was expected to help the church, in thanks for their blessings, despite actual blessings being thin on the ground. After mass that Sunday Father Riley asked Teddy to stay behind. After removing his ceremonial gown, Teddy wondered what could Father Riley want with him?

"Now young Teddy I have heard a very worrying tale about you and your lot. You ganged up on one lad from Canterbury Street and beat him up really badly. What have you got to say about that?" Teddy was taken aback. He still had embers of the glow that engulfed him and his great victory. The images in his mind were still very clear.

"That's not what happened!"

"Now then Teddy, I saw him. He was bleeding all over his face, his nose was broken, eye nearly burst. He had to go to the infirmary to get patched up. Now don't tell me that you and your gang did not beat him up with sticks and clubs."

"We didn't! He hit me first. He butted me right in the face and knocked me down, for nothing!"

"Teddy?"

"It's true! He hit me, just for giving his brother a little slap for pinching our rifles. You don't go and butt someone for that. He was the bully, not me."

"You know that lying is a sin. You have to confess your sins Teddy."

"Sod that! I did nothing wrong. He butt…"

The slap landed squarely on Teddy's head, taking the indignation right out of his argument.

"Don't you curse here! In this house!" His face the picture of biblical thunder itself.

"Sorry Father." Teddy had never thought of raising his hand to a priest, at that point in his life anyway.

"And you should be young man."

Teddy walked the few streets back to Bidder Street, dejected, wondering how could Father Riley get it so wrong?

It was a couple of days later that Teddy's Dad beat him. His friend from the bookies told of Teddy and his gang beating up some kid. It was so bad that he went to the infirmary for stiches and to get his nose re-set. His Dad didn't seek the full story, it was an adult that told the tale, and so it must be true. Teddy was the bully, and with a gang, beat the kid. The thick belt with the dulled buckle had come off as his Dad grabbed Teddy by the scruff of his collar.

"Don't you go 'round beating up other kids", each word delivered staccato as the belt landed across Teddy's back, neck and arms in punctuation. Teddy screamed more in fear of his father's beatings than the actual pain. His mother called for clemency, but none was forthcoming. "Now get to bed!" Teddy raced into the bedroom and hid under the coats and thread bear blanket. If he was lucky that would be the end of it. He lay in the light of the summer evening. Wondering how the tale of his bravery had become so distorted and turned back on him? The indignation was hurtful. Listening to the kids in the street, still playing out, still playing Mexican bandits. He hated not being in control.

Chapter 3 The Dice

It was just a chill, that was what his mother had said. He was rarely sick. A runny nose, and snot encased sleeve, was the worst that had befallen him previously. This felt different. He ached all over, he was hot, he was cold, he was sweating, he was sick.

Despite having an extra coat over him as he lay in the bed, that he shared with younger brother Tommy, he was cold. The cold was arctic. The sweat evaporating off him made the chill worse. His mother had given him Beecham's Powders in lukewarm water. That tasted awful, it made him retch, he had to drink the last dregs of the potion, for his own good. He had wild dreams. Father Riley was in there, doing something, he could not make out what. His Dad was a devil lashing him with a whip made of barbed wired. His mother an angel, white wings, calm smile she was saying something, but no sound came out of her mouth.

Eventually the fever passed. He was weak. Not just tired, weak. He could not get out of bed on his own. After another week like this his mother had sent for the doctor. They could not afford the expense, but she felt she had to spend it. The doctor arrived, Gladstone bag in hand, trilby on head. He examined the listless boy that was lying on the bed. He spent a longer time than usual on this house call. He went through the algorithm in his mind, testing each aspect of the boy's reactions and responses. Finally, he turned to Anne and said, "He has poliomyelitis, a bad case of it. He needs to go to the children's hospital now."

Anne was ashen, "Jesus, Mary and Joseph! Oh my god! Will he be alright?"

"Let's hope so. The quicker he gets there the better."

The ambulance arrived. It was a horse drawn carriage, not changed much in the 70 or so years since it was first introduced by Reginald Harrison at the Northern Hospital in 1884. It was the first ambulance service in Britain. On arriving at the Liverpool Children's hospital, Teddy was quickly found a bed. The next few days were similar in routine. Doctors arrived, looked at his notes, asked a few questions, felt his head, listened to his chest, lifted his limbs. Teddy was a little bit older than most of the other kids, only by a year or two. They all seemed to be similar to him, weak. The nights were usually quiet, only broken by coughing and wheezing noises from the beds.

A different doctor appeared. He was dressed funny, he had gowns on and a strange disc on his head. He examined Teddy. When he looked at Teddy's eyes the disc was positioned with the light and he could not see anything due to the glare. He felt faint. The other eye was next, faint again. He managed not to pass out, he took several breaths as quickly as he could manage. The doctor looked steadily at him. He picked up his hand, looked at the finger nails. He pressed a fingertip and let it go, peering at how long it took to regain colour.

"Tell me what your breathing is like."

"Just normal breathing" wheezed Teddy "My chest feels a bit tighter than usual today" he struggled to get these words out. The disc headed doctor nodded, he looked like he was deep in thought. He turned to the nurse in blue next to him. She was nice. She had a funny head thing also. It was a lace like triangular affair that kept her nurse's hat in place. She had a fancy belt buckle too. They had a brief exchange.

"Yes Doctor, I will arrange the transfer." She put a comforting hand on Teddy's arm as she spoke. Teddy was being transferred to Alder Hey Hospital. It was relatively new. Converted into another children's hospital, after the great war American wounded had left. Out near the West Derby part of Liverpool, actually in the area of Knotty Ash. That was far away by Islington street kids' measures. No one he knew had ever been that far from town before. A short tram ride to Paddy's Market was a long journey to them.

There was a park that could just be seen out of the window, Springfield Park. It was a sea of green. Teddy hadn't seen that much grass in one place before. It mesmerised him. There were trees too, big poplars that went right up to the clouds, giant oaks that spread out like so many green topped domes. He only saw these for a few hours. On arrival at Alder Hey he was being assessed. There was the usual stream of doctors, some were women doctors, he hadn't heard of that before. End of bed discussions took place as if Teddy wasn't there. He heard words like; paralytic poliomyelitis, loss of reflexes, flaccid limbs. None of these were known to him and he could only wonder what they might mean. He was scared. Not of the words, he was watching their expressions. These varied from impassive to outright worry on the face of the blue nurse. She was a different blue nurse from the Children's hospital, but she had the same fancy hat thing and belt buckle. She also had several badges pinned to her dress, and a watch hanging upside down. Her arms were puffed out with white over sleeves. It was not long till blue nurse told Teddy that he was very ill, and that his lungs were not working well at all. This was making his breathing so laboured (he didn't know what that meant), he just knew he was really light headed and found it hard to breathe. She told him he was going to have to go into a state-of-the-art respiratory aid that would help him breathe and keep him alive. That worried Teddy. No one had said anything about dying before. As it happened, he should have been more concerned about the immediate future. The iron lung, as it was known, was a form of torture designed by the devil himself, so Teddy came to think of it. He had to lie on his back inside a coffin like box with his legs and head sticking out. His neck was girdled with a stiff rubber tubing to keep the pressure differential correct and allow his lungs to fill with air. The gaseous exchange took place only if the lungs could inflate. But the partial paralysis of his intercostal muscles meant that that was not happening, without help from the respirator.

He saw the world differently. A small mirror was fitted to the casing, positioned to allow the occupant to see more of their surroundings. It took a while for Teddy to accommodate to this altered perception. He could not see the sea of green, or the trees, but he could hear them. The wind would whistle through Springfield park. When the windows were open, which was most of the time, he listened to the song it made. It was a comforting song, even when blowing a gale. It reminded him of the river.

He loved the rhythm of the river. He would embark on a mighty trek with his friends. They would leave Bidder Street with a lemonade bottle filled with tap water and any food they could carry as their picnic. They would set off on foot. Working their way down Islington past the rear of TJ Hughes department store. Cross over Seymore Street, where they could see the Duke of Wellington's column ahead. Continue down Islington passed the County Sessions House, and on to the Walker art gallery, they had not been in. Once they had tried. Some older kids said they had pictures of women with no clothes on in there, no wonder they had their own coppers to guard the place. So, they tried to get past the guardian on the door, he wasn't a real copper he just had a uniform like one, he had chased them.

"Clear off you load of dirty little wretches! If you come here again, I'll have you down the bridewell!" They ran like the devil himself was after them, for what they had been thinking, that day.

Jammed in close to the art gallery was the Central Library. Magnificent columns encircled the rotund building. It was just possible to see daylight between the library and the Liverpool museum. This was another columned building that sprawled down the rest of William Brown Street.

On crossing the road, they looked at the tunnel works. It was going to be another first for Liverpool. They stopped outside the Ship and Mitre pub to smell the thick, stale beer air coming out. They tried to see through the etched window pattern to see who was in there. The braver ones bounced on the railing trap door to the cellar. They sped off when the door opened in case someone was after them. Dale Street was a major thoroughfare to the river. It had several more magnificent buildings, housing the magistrate's court and the Liverpool Council buildings. The boys walked on, it seemed to be the longest road in the city. It curved outwards a little to accommodate the Town Hall at the junction with Water Street. From here they could see the river. This quickened their step as they walked down the last hill to the water. One block from the end of Water Street was Martins' Bank building. The three steps to the entrance were flanked with carvings of slave boys, in chains, being comforted by a patriarchal figure on one side and a matriarchal one on the other. The boys never noticed the irony with their own position.

It was just across the strand and between two of the three Graces, the Liver and Cunard buildings, to the Pier Head. This was a great place for exploring. It had a floating roadway! Trucks, horse drawn carts and even cars could go up and down it to the ferry and ocean liner terminals. The boys would stare at the archways at low tide, see the huge chains that held the structure in place. Imagine that was where they kept the slaves in the olden days, dungeons. They would watch the ferries criss-cross the river. See the well-dressed passengers, usually walking round and round the top deck till it docked. Once securely tied to the landing stage bollards, the deck hand would drop the loading ramp and let the people get off, while forbidding the waiting passengers from moving forward, with just a stern look. The sounds of the river echoed in Teddy's ears.

They picnicked on the bench seats looking out at the river. Taking turns to swig water from the lemonade bottle, a casual wipe of the spout with a dirty hand was all the hygiene applied between drinkers. The meal was a cold piece of bread that had been dipped in beef dripping fat. The fat would encase the stale bread in a shroud like manner, curving round the crusts readying it for burial. It would be interred in the eager mouths of the boys, lips smacking to ensure every morsel was ingested to power their skinny frames. Teddy gazed at the posh people walking by. He was always amazed at how clean they were. He was always grubby. He could not explain why, it was just always the case. The clean people came in all sorts of outfits, depending on the time of year, he would watch them. Nearly all the men wore hats, not the flat caps of the workers, mostly bowlers and trilbies. Occasionally there would be a Hollywood hat come off the ferry, but usually these came off the liner terminal and up the floating roadway. These were just the same as the Saturday matinee movies, cops or robbers mostly. Teddy imagined which type a hat wearer was. If the overcoat was tailored, he was a gangster, if a bit worn, a copper. He would look for a gun bulge on the left side, imagination let him see them. He wondered what type of gun it was, Colt or Smith & Wesson. The ladies were equally fascinating. These all wore hats or bonnets. The more extravagant ones again coming off the liner terminal, but occasionally off the Wallasey ferry. Some were so wide they were worn on a steep tilt, so the women could actually see where they were going. He wondered how the adornments stayed on at such a slope. But his greatest envy was for the shoes. He only had a second-hand pair of Sunday boots that were still too big. He wanted the oxblood coloured brogues that his gangster types, who disembarked the liners from America, wore. He wondered where these people got the money for all this opulence. He had once seen a five-pound note when his Dad had a big win at the bookies. He had shown the note to him and Tommy, before going off to invest it in the Monument pub near TJs, and with the bookie's runners.

While lying on his back, all that time, he re-lived those treks to the river, again and again. His memory helped with the wind rustling or gusting through the park and into the windows of Alder Hey. They were the good thoughts. The darker ones came gradually at first, found a niche in his mind and grew. These were like his fevered nightmares. Grotesque for the time and age he was then. He wanted to know why he was in the box, struggling to breathe when out of it. Was it his fault? Had he done something to cause this blight on himself? Another twist of fate mixed in a powerful cocktail. Teddy was a little older than most kids that contracted Polio, he was eleven when it started, now he was starting puberty. That hormone storm stewed the dark thoughts into a black broth.

Chapter 4 The coat

Father Murphey walked the wards, checking the end of bed codes for his flock. If it was wrong, he might tip an acknowledgment with his head or a half wink if he made eye contact with the kid. He only approached beds with the correct code, a filled in spot next to the three religion options; CoE, RC or Jewish. He stopped to talk with Teddy.

"How are you today my child?" He waited for Teddy to focus on him in his mirror.

"OK thanks Father." He was still in awe of the church at this time.

"Has your mother been in to see you today?"

"She should be in later. She has to come after the wash house or she will miss out because of the big queue."

"Oh, I see. Have you been saying your prayers while in here?"

"Yes Father." This was only partially correct, he had been asking God why him, why this awful disease had picked him, and not any of the other Bidder Street gang, or anyone else for that matter? What was this 'effing disease anyway? He got no answers or response of any kind.

"We all have our crosses to bear my child and as Jesus said, 'suffer little children and come unto me', so we must trust in the Lord."

"Yes Father."

Father Murphey placed a hand on Teddy's head as he spoke.

"Bless you my son." He moved on to the next appropriately coded bed.

Bless me! Bless me! What fucking blessing is this? Screamed Teddy's mind. He fidgeted in the box, felt constrained and weak and gave in.

"Fucking bless me" he whispered out loud. The temperature of his hurt rising again. It had been doing this a lot lately. Every time he thought of his predicament, it built up. At first it was a slow build. Then with frequency, came speed. Now it would flash furnace heat in a split second, causing his heart to beat harder and respiration rate to race, resulting in him struggling to breathe. Then he would have to slow it down and try to rationalise the rage. It always landed somewhere definitive. If it had been stimulated by someone, like Father Murphey, the blame was his fault. If it came out of the blue, it was a situational thing, usually poverty. More and more it was God's fault.

He was envious of the clean people. His mother could easily have been a clean person and he later thought that she was one. She could make the simplest dress appear more than it was by adorning a ribbon, or scarf, in some way that transformed her. She always wore at least a little powder when out of the apartment. She was a Kennedy. She had married Teddy's Dad as she was expecting. The wedding was a small affair, the standard for the day in Liverpool working class circles. Her father, Bull Kennedy, kept a straight face during the ceremony at the registrar's office in Brougham Terrace. He enjoyed the pub drinks afterwards, while hiding his resentment of the match. He knew his daughter's new husband was not the type of man he classed as upstanding. He had too much of a liking for the bookies, and most Saturday nights was the worse for drink. But he had acceded to his daughter's wishes and accepted that the child needed a father.

She wore her pregnancy well. She carried herself with all the airs of the Kennedy's. Always chatting with the other women she met, and showing off her bump, accepting their best wishes graciously. She still wore the Kennedy jewellery at this time, simple, but a little more expensive than most women's trifles. Her father had adored her. She was the apple of the big man's eye. Bull Kennedy was a foreman in the electrical cabling business. This work was booming, despite the economic downturn, as more and more areas became electrified, being readied for the future. He was always in employment. He held the power over other men when it came to work. As 'ganger man' he could start or fire men at will. His gang was almost all of Irish descent, a notable exception was Taff, he was Welsh, but another monster of a man, and the only non-Catholic, he was chapel. Taff was such an asset to Bull that he was his right-hand man, again a rare exception in Irish Liverpool street digging gangs. The work was tough. All day digging out narrow trenches along pavements, laying thick unbending cable in the ground. The cable was run off huge rolls, the size of cart wheels, off raised axels. The cable was really heavy, and it took teams of men pulling, tug of war style, to unravel it along the trench. The men worked to the encouragement of various politically un-correct ditties, to spur their strength on. One went something like, 'Come on, come on! Said the Elephant John, pull like you'd pull a darkie off yer mother'! Sometimes a new dittie would appear, reflecting the news or politicians of the day. If the team had not heard that one before, they might fall about laughing in the trench. This would get Bull or Taff to berate them with all variety of curses and threats. Bull and Taff would laugh themselves when having their brews later, making sure to allow that new one out again. Humour and hellfire were good for the soul and strength of navvies.

The newlyweds had managed to get a room in the Kelly's tenement apartment. The Kelly's like most families were of the extended type. It was a matriarchal household. The women were Edward's older sisters; Nellie and Katie. They ran the household. The men were Edward's older brother, Spike, and himself. Spike was an exception for the Kelly's. He was a policeman. He was the tallest Kelly there had ever been, so they said. He went to work and came back, never, ever, talking about it. Edward, since the wedding had been working in a different cabling gang. Bull had got him the start, so he didn't have to see the poor shapes he made in the trench, digging or pulling. Anne had set about nesting for her confinement. Re-arranging the meagre furniture, all second hand, so that the baby could be managed. The crib was identified, like most in that area, it was a deep drawer in a cabinet. That would be pulled out to take the infant when sleeping and stowed away when it was being nursed. Her mother had knitted the usual essential items, cap and socks for the extremities and bodices for the trunk. Her confinement came on in the middle of March. The year was 1924. The midwife was sent for. A girl playing in the street below was shouted from the landing and sent for the midwife, in nearby Soho Street. She took her friend along for company, and they both ran, buoyed with excitement, round the few corners to Soho Street.

Teddy, as he was going to be called, was born on the 18th. He was a bonny weight for the day about 6 pounds, and healthy. Anne was delighted. Edward, when told he had a son, was equally proud. That March was just like any other. The days were getting lighter and the weather a little warmer. Ten days after Teddy was born his dad had a great win on the horses. The Aintree Grand National was always an exciting affair. Edward had put two shillings on an auspiciously named horse and rider combination. Master Robert was the horse and ridden by another Robert, Bob Trudgill. That surely was an omen, thought Edward. So, he put a hard-earned florin on him to win, at 25 to 1. He came in first! Edward was keen to wet the baby's head, so the Monument pub took most of the winnings and as usual the following week, the bookies runners sucked up the rest. Anne was upset. She had her eye on a second-hand baby carriage, a Silver Cross. There were not many Silver

Crosses in Islington. The winnings would have easily paid for it and some, but not now.

That was the pattern of Anne's marriage, and the early years. Disappointment. Sadie was the first of Teddy's sisters, followed by Annie, then Tommy. Despite the hard times, and her four children, Anne was still very much of the clean people type. She still wore a smattering of powder and had the ubiquitous ecoutrements to her wardrobe. This was managed by hiding the odd penny, and hand out from Bull, away from Edward. It was in the sewing box on the family mantle shelf, hiding in plain sight, no one suspecting of its treasure within.

Teddy looked forward to when his mother visited. She was always considerate, patient with his complaints, placed her hand on his head for solace. She could stay longer than most visitors due to the iron lung situation. Other kid's parents could stay longer too, if their condition was serious enough. After a while a pattern emerged. She would come that bit later every time and be followed into the ward by a clean person, a man. He was tall and wore office clothes, carried a trilby. His son was three beds along on the other side. He had something awful too, but his was worse, so he heard the nurses talking one night. He had something called a cute Luke Heemia, or so Teddy thought he heard. That kid often had nose bleeds that went on for ages. The nurses would always send for the blue nurse when that happened. She would supervise the relay of shiny kidney shaped dishes and white towels. These would appear from behind the curtain, stretched around his bed, and be hustled off to the sluice room as they called it. A flushing toilet sound meant the blood -stained dish had been washed and rinsed out ready for its return journey.

His mother would enquire of the boy's health when talking with Teddy. He could only say a little, nothing much really. So she started to call across the ward to the office man and ask directly how the boy was getting on. He would mutter something quietly with a grave look on his face. Teddy could see over that way in his mirror. He thought he saw facial language, but he was not sure.

It was only a few weeks later, one afternoon, that the kidney dish relay was running again. This time something even more serious was going on. He knew this because blue nurse's face was very different, and she was trembling. She started shouting for the nurses!

"Get the house officer now! Get Dr Weatherall!" The kidney dishes were not keeping up with the flow. The nurses came back without the toilet noise happening. There was no time to flush the sluice, just empty the bowls and bring them back. Then it was quiet. Blue nurse slowed down when she was walking. The other nurses only spoke with their expressions, these were grave. Dr Weatherall arrived and went behind the curtains. He was in there for a few minutes. When he came out, he wrote on the notes board at the end of the bed. Then with a flourish, drew down the remaining page a squiggly line and then underlined it. Replacing the board by its clip, he put the top back on his fountain pen and put it in his top pocket. He went to the ward office and then was lost to Teddy's eye line. The ward was eerily quiet the rest of that day. No raised voices, no chat of band music or dancing could be heard from the nurses.

The clean man arrived early that day. He went to the office to see blue nurse. He was crying. They talked for what seemed like ages. A woman had joined them. He could not see who she was, only her coat. She had her arm around the crying man. Teddy fell asleep shortly after that. He had got in to a routine, when he was tired of thinking he would doze off. Only to realise he had been asleep on waking, usually to some attendee at his bed head. His mother was there, she was early. She looked upset.

"What's wrong", asked Teddy. Fussing with his hair and water cup and straightening her blouse she said.

"Oh it's nothing really, I just heard some sad news earlier that made me a little upset, but I am fine now. Don't you worry at all. You need all your strength for your recovery." After a while she had to leave, kissing his head as usual she said, "Bye my little Mexican Bandit." Teddy felt more grown up than a Bidder Street Mexican bandit now. He was maturing quickly.

"Oh Mam", he protested, "I am not a kid anymore now." Teddy was still young, but felt his situation was more grown up than his years. He watched her go towards the office door, where his eye line just about stopped. Then he saw a flash of colour catch his gaze from within the office itself. What was that, He wondered.

Chapter 5 The Loss

Good news was on its way. Teddy had been in the iron lung for several months now, and his breathing was much improved. During this time his understanding of the hospital had increased. He now knew that blue nurse was the sister and in charge of the ward. She was a nice woman but had to keep her distance from the other nurses, as she was the boss. She would have her brews off the ward with the blue nurses from the other wards, where they would mostly talk about the patients and their parents. The other nurses were nice, in the main. Some loved to talk about dancing and would eagerly engage their companions in chatter about the latest numbers played on the radio, from the big bands. There was intrigue here too. He could tell by the hushed tones and closed heads when a juicy piece of gossip was afoot. The responses of the listening nurses varied a lot too. Mostly it was hushed giggles that ended the exchange, but sometimes it would be a shocked gasp and a look of disbelief, followed by a spreading grin or worried look. Teddy could not hear all of these discussions, but he could hear some. The ones that caused most animation were the tales of the nurses and the doctors. These all went the same way. They went to a dance, only danced with each other, then took a long way back to the nurse's block… Here the tones always went quieter, preceding the gasps of delight or, occasionally, horror. Teddy made a study of these expressions, he was later to hear it called facial leakage, these gave away a lot of the context of their conversations. One nurse was impossible to read, she was Chinese, from the other side of town from Islington known as China Town. This was the oldest Chinese community in Europe dating back several hundred years. Nurse Chan was nice. She didn't say much but she was comforting in her own way. Always competent and business like. If he needed someone to talk to, she would listen to him, a slight nod of her head was all the reassurance he needed from Nurse Chan. This went a long way with Teddy. It could stop the tears before they came or dry them up quickly if they started. It was probably just Teddy's imagination, but he would swear she did have a smile, even if it was just her eyes alone.

In his growing understanding of the hospital workings, he knew that a man in a white coat that came was not a doctor. He could tell by the way he spoke, it was ordinary, and he did not have a stethoscope in his pocket. He was the physiotherapist. His job was to help Teddy recover his muscle and movement again. He was not a nice man or a nasty man, but he was demanding in his expectations of

Teddy, when he was working with him. Teddy was now out of the box, as he called it, he could sit up in a chair. He was delighted at the news of getting out. This was short lived on his realisation that he could not walk, or even stand up. Tears and emotions of anger, anguish and resentment flooded his soul. The dark broth that had been simmering over the previous months, nurturing and teasing out the black seeds into growing shoots of negative emotions, had done its work. Testosterone levels had grown to make visible the transition, albeit still early days yet. The young boy was becoming an angry young man.

He learned, with the help of the physio to stand up for longer and longer periods. He did this till he had to fall back in his chair, to recover his strength in his left supportive leg. Sweat would appear on his brow as he directed his anger to convert it into more supportive strength. He learned to use his arms to let himself down gently onto the chair, instead of flopping down heavily. He was given crutches to walk with. He soon got the hang of them, and before long was venturing further and further afield. His sense of humour came back quite quickly, considering. He would flirt with the nurses, not the blue one of course, with her he would appear deferential to her status. She could make things good or bad for Teddy. He would show the other kids his withered right leg. It was thinner than the left, all the way from his hip down to his foot. It was also shorter. The growth spurt driven by the hormonal changes had left the right leg lagging, due to the lack of nervous connections for muscle movement. This differential was to be maintained till he was fully grown. One day his physio announced that he would be able to walk without crutches, just the aid of special leg braces. He called these callipers. They were iron spindles down each side of his leg held together with leather support sections that went round his leg. The spindles were secured into a special boot heel. This helped to transfer the weight from his hip down to the ground mostly bypassing the weakened knee joint and limb. Teddy had once seen a kid with these before. He had joined in with the rest of the boys in the name calling back then. They followed the kid chanting 'leg irons, leg irons.' Till the kid had turned on them and lashed out with his arms. Teddy knew what the future held for him back in Bidder Street. He was not going to have any of that.

With time, walking with callipers was easier than with crutches. His range was much greater now. He could go all the way downstairs onto the long sloping corridor to the front entrance. He would even walk around the gardens along the Eaton Road side of the hospital. The tram went along Eaton Road, turned right on East Prescot Road and then headed back to town. He longed to get back to town and his friends. He had not seen any of them since his hospitalisation. It was on one of these walks that he first saw them. He was curious. How come they were there and talking to each other. No sound came his way, they were right over the other side of the gardens and perimeter wall. He was on the entrance steps and had a good vantage point. They were at the tram stop. Their body language was familiar to him, but what was it saying? Serious faces. Hushed conversation, something was up, he just knew this from watching the nurses. She put her hand on his sleeve and left it there while she spoke. He looked distracted, no, worried. Teddy had to walk up and down the entrance steps, to let people gain access to or leave the entrance area, his head never moved, eyes never left them, like a cat watching sparrows. As the tram appeared from the direction of Everton's training ground, they hugged and kissed. It was a quick kiss, but it was a lip kiss. He got on the tram heading for Old Swan. She turned and made her way to the entrance. Teddy spun around and went back up the hill corridor to the stairwell and up to ward B3.

His mother was visiting. Teddy was sitting with a couple of younger kids, who were playing with metal toy cars.

"Hello, my boy, how are you getting on with your walking? The Nurse said you can be discharged soon. Then we can go back home. Would you like that?" Teddy was sulking, so didn't say anything. He was thinking. Should I speak of it? He thought that he best not. He had not been beaten since his admission and he valued that. Slowly accepting his chosen position on the matter, he said.

"I am OK. I can walk a fair bit now, without having to stop, even all the way down to the, the sweet shop."

"Oh I have brought you a sweet. Here you are, an Arrow Bar just for you. For being such a good boy."

"Thanks Mam." He opened the thin bar's wrapper and started to chew on the hard toffee contents. His mum fussed him as usual. She told him about the boys on the street. "Have you seen Jimmy?"

"Oh yes. He was asking of you. I said that you were soon to be going home."

"What did he say to that?"

"He was delighted. He can't wait to see you again and fill you in on all the kid's adventures!"

"Has he been down the Pier Head?"

"I am sure he has. And he will tell you all about it when you get home."

Teddy spent the last few days, between physio and exercising, thinking of how he and Jimmy were going to go back to where they left off, all those months ago. He relived, again, the treks to the Pier Head. The tales they told each other of the poor African slaves, kept chained in the floating roadway dungeons. The clean people off the ferries, the gangsters off the liners. The leggers they got from the art gallery copper and whoever came out of the Ship and Mitre to chase them. He felt the air rush passed his face, his curls bobbing on his forehead, the pumping of his legs as he ran as fast as he could. He knew that feeling was never going to be the same again, but he still loved reliving it. A bitter, sweet memory. Black broth again.

Father Murphy engaged Teddy in conversation in the play area of the ward. He had heard he was due for discharge and wanted to press home, some biblical meme or other for him to carry back to normal life. Teddy was polite, but disinterested. Father Murphy could see this and sought to enlighten Teddy, with just how fortunate he was.

"You know, my son, that you are a very lucky boy?"

"How's that Father?"

"You have had a very serious illness and, yes you have been in hospital for quite some time, but you can still walk! Many of the other kids with polio can't even do that. They are going to need a wheelchair for the rest of their lives, and someone to push them around all the time! Where as you can do everything you did before. You will just need to catch up a bit on your schooling, till you are fourteen, then off to the big wide world and a job. You will get married and have children, and these will be Catholics of course, and you will bear your little cross with grace."

Fuck that! Thought Teddy. He was not going to take anything Father Murphy said as being real anymore. He had seen that heaven and hell were the same thing, just seen from different sides of the floating roadway. If there was a God, why the fuck did he invent a fucking disease like fucking polio?

He knew if he spoke about his thoughts it would generate one of two responses from Father Murphy; a beating for blasphemy, or worse, a theological one-sided discussion that Teddy would be out of his depth with. He was not going to have either. He now *knew* there was no God, not like they said there was. He just had to keep this new faith when challenged in the future. He nodded a lie to Father Murphy and underlined it with a pursed lip face. Father Murphy was content with his ministration, this sheep would return to Father Riley's flock at St Francis Xavier's. Putting his hand on Teddy's head for the last time said.

"Bless you my son." He curved round the ward like a good shepherd does, not realising that one had got away.

Teddy had now lost physical ability, he had lost his Catholic faith, he had lost all belief in any type of God. His greatest loss was still to come.

Chapter 6 The Tunnel

Teddy had spent many afternoons with Jimmy and others from the Bidder Street gang, catching up on what he had missed out on. Their gabbled tales of being chased, getting a legger was the colloquial expression, by various characters or other street gangs, excited him. He would re-live the hare and hounds' escapades in his mind, running alongside Jimmy, to escape overwhelming odds; bigger kids, more kids or the cocky watchman. The cocky just had to catch them while they were up to no good, he would shout as loud as he could, and that would be all the fright required to send the kids off like the grand national starter gun. He still felt the air rush pass his face while listening to these tales as he ran too. He knew he would not feel that rush from running ever again. This thought had started to eat at him. Small nibbles at first. The bite size increasing and growing in hunger the more tales he heard, but he could not stop himself asking for more and more tales of the leggers. It was as if he wanted to hurt himself by listening to these stories, let the anger bite into his very heart, have a real fight with the invisible forces that had brought him so low. He had been the General Pancho Villa, leader of the Mexican Bandits, he had authority, respect. He was looked up to, despite his small stature.

Now he was a kid with leg irons who could no longer run with his gang. For now he was still their leader. They listened just as avidly to his embellished stories of the nurses in Alder Hey, he added artistic license to make them more outrageous. The boys were starting to take an interest in girls.

Teddy found himself taking more and more interest in the revenge beatings of when one of theirs was caught and roughed up. He was outraged by the injustice of several kids picking on one boy and wanted to know how the punishments had been metered out. He kept a mental tally of the un-paid events, noting the main culprits, he was making a list, a black one, under the influence of the same coloured broth.

A source of great regret for Teddy was that he had missed the opening of the Mersey Tunnel. This had been a grand affair by all accounts. The King and Queen had come to Liverpool! They had set up a big tent across from the tunnel entrance. They had the movie people there, they were from Movietone News! The film was going to be shown in every cinema in the land. It was going to highlight Liverpool as an outgoing great city. The tunnel was joining both sides of the mighty Mersey docks and the

A41, to London and the south, to help speed up the transport of goods from overseas to the nation. The organisation for the event was huge. Every policeman in Lancashire and Cheshire was drawn in to help police the crowds. These were supplemented by, and to add to the pomp and circumstance, various military bodies. There was the Royal Lancashire Rifles. All stood to attention with fixed bayonets. Bearskin wearing guards from Buckingham palace were there too, so they said. The fixed bayonets stirred some in the rear of the crowds with mixed feelings. It was just over 20 years ago that soldiers with bayonets and live rounds had been used to quell disturbances in Liverpool from the general transport strike. But these feelings were dulled by the outright pride of most onlookers at the feat of civil engineering that had taken place right here, and underneath Liverpool and the Mersey river.

The engineers had planned to dig from both sides of the Mersey and to meet in the middle, deep under the river bed. This was not the first under river bed tunnel, that honour went to Isambard Kingdom Brunel, he had dug one under the Thames at Wapping and Rotherhithe, but this was going to be the deepest and longest for the day. It was a natural extension of another tunnel under the Mersey that had been dug, in 1885, to take the railway, joining Liverpool and Birkenhead. That was another first, longest and deepest electric railway. The navvies had broken through from each side, in the middle of the river, deep under-ground away from any landmarks. They had been out from the engineers plans, but just by about one inch. A great achievement to add to the growing folklore of the Mersey Tunnel. The seventeen men that had died in the construction of the tunnel were not mentioned.

Looking closely at the assembled crowds there was a clear pattern of outfits and class of onlooker. Behind the police and soldiers were the best dressed adults and only few children, equally best dressed. These were several layers deep up the gradient of William Brown Street and the gardens of St Georges Hall. There were even five or six rows of people outside the Ship and Mitre, which bordered the tunnel entrance at the start of Dale Street. As the camera swept around the flag waving admiring horde, over the expanse of William Brown Street up towards Lime Street the clothes changed. The further up the hill the more common the clothes became. The faces were all equally excited but reflected the un-equally dealt hands by the croupier of life at that time. Flat caps replaced Trilbies and Bowlers, head scarves were swapped for the summer bonnets and wide brimmed ladies statement hats. At the periphery, up the lampposts, on the lions outside St Georges Hall were many kids. They had to climb to get a vantage point, safe for the time being from the policemen and their shouts of 'get down, the king doesn't want to see unruly kids.' They knew the coppers couldn't get them for the swell of the crowds.

At the outer perimeter, all morning there had been a selection process going on by the police. They would assess the people, and those with VIP invitations went down near the tunnel entrance, the middle-class types were allowed to go next closest. This was to ease the sensibilities of the King and Queen, who it was deemed by the constabulary, did not want to see any signs of the poverty that lived cheek by jowl with the middle class in Liverpool.

King George the Fifth referred to the 'mud and darkness' faced by those who had toiled in the tunnel. He handed his speech to an aide then moved to lift the curtains that covered the whole of the four-lane highway entrance. The switch was electric, a sign of the modernising times. On pressing the lever, the huge curtains were raised to great cheers from the crowds. The King and Queen got into the waiting Royal Rolls and traversed the river through the tunnel to Birkenhead. The newsreel footage showed the convey of royal and civic dignitaries emerging at the other side, just down from the famous covered market. The same strength of police and military were evident, corralling the segregated crowds there too. This footage was testament to the greatness of Liverpool and the West Lancashire community of merchants and money men.

Jimmy told Teddy that the gang had tried to get down early that day, it was just five minutes-walk down from Islington, but the coppers were out even earlier. They had stopped every kid from Islington, the Canterbury Street kids were barred just like the Bidder Street bandits. It was easy for the constabulary to see which kids to block, if they had no shoes on, or their clothes were threadbare, the King was not going to see them. Teddy was angry at this news. 'The fuckers,' he thought. They had just as much right to see the ceremony as the well-off people. It was their tunnel after all, not the King's or the bloody Queen's. It was not all bad news to Teddy though, Jimmy told of the street party they had. Nearly all the streets had some sort of celebration in the summer sunshine that July day. In Bidder Street all sorts of tables had appeared from within the tenements, covered in table cloths or just bedsheets. The food was simple, scraped together to look more than it was, copious amounts of tap water for the kids, bottles of stout for the adults. Music came blaring down from the windows above, people started dancing. To start with it was mainly women dancing together, waltzing or foxtrotting. They were soon joined by the men, keen to show off their steps with the ladies clasped in close, in dance hold. Bosun Billy had started to do an American dance with a lady in a flowery dress. He had seen it in America when on shore leave from the White Star boats he worked on. The lady in the flowery dress had spun round and round, even showing her drawers, said Jimmy, and she didn't even care! The crowd were going wild and more and more people started doing the dance, or their interpretation of it anyway. The party went on till it was well dark that night. Gossipy stories went on for longer.

It was about this time, after Teddy got out of hospital that work started to pick up. The dark time of over three million people unemployed was gradually changing. There were more jobs to be had for the people of Liverpool. However the same filters and barriers were still in place. Suburb people tended to get office and shop jobs, townies the muddy and dark ones. If you were really lucky you got a job in Blackler's department store. They had loads of girls serving in their three-storey shop, the young men were trainee managers mostly. Blackler's was the shop of the clean people and those that aspired to be well off. If you got a job there, you were set for life. Good wages by the standards of the times, and you even got paid when you were on holiday! Every summer the staff went off to a secret destination for a day trip outing. These were great fun. Mostly they were young women, aged fourteen upwards. They would have relay races, sack races and play games of rounders. There would be a picnic lunch and treat bags for them. This was the way to look after your staff. They would return to work on the Monday feeling refreshed and well cared for in their employment. It was a dream job.

This was in contrast to the reality for many. Their path was drawn out for them by the forces that kept the system in balance. Background was key. What does your father do? That was the killer question asked by the teachers in schools. Depending on the response and the catchment area, the path was drawn out for most people. Labourer, porter, or driver if you were a lucky young man. Waitress, cleaner, young wife and mother were the usual options for girls. The unluckier souls were drawn down a darker tunnel. Destined to toil through the mud of poverty and to live in the darkness of the law's shadow. No escape out of that tunnel, or its tributaries, of recurring prison, prostitution or, if lucky, a visit from death himself and a sweeping blow from any one of the many edges of his scythe: consumption, poor nutrition, street fights or simply being hanged by the keepers of the system.

These were some of the thoughts that swirled round in the cauldron of Teddy's mind in the formative days after getting out of hospital. He had pondered for many hours on the future he had waiting for him when he escaped the lung, if he ever got out. He did not want the life that was being sketched out by the invisible hand of the system. A poor kid, with little schooling (hospitalisation was no excuse for poor education), disabled when it came to manual work. He was going to make a different path for himself and maybe for others in a similar situation. The Left Book Club had given many people ideas above their station. Talk of communists were always about, but the written word lived longer than chat. It was permanent, it could be hidden from view and danger, taken out and read, recited verbatim by true acolytes of the cause. It was a tack that Teddy was sailing towards even then as a precocious young man-boy. How much was powered by socio-economic theory and how much by resentment for the haves verses the have nots was unknown, even by Teddy, at this time of change.

Chapter 7 The Bullfight

Everything looked the same as before. The grubbiness, the kids, the games, but it wasn't. While Teddy had been away the hand of change had been at work in Islington. The hand usually worked slowly, the changes it made in people and things were gradual. People, especially, are comforted by sameness. Change works at a speed that makes it hidden to normal sight. So on the surface no change, but Teddy saw it. The Bidder Street kids had moved on. The Mexican bandits were now Chicago gangsters with Tommy guns, not Winchesters. The language was older, more cursing. Fucks became the seasoning of most conversations. More people had jobs, not a great many more, but more than before. All the kids had grown in size. One in particular had put on several inches in height and his face had become harder in lines and outlook. He had never forgotten the humiliation of his beating by, the then mobile, Teddy Kelly. Although he had the sympathy vote at that time, he knew it was his side of that story that accounted for that. He knew he had been overpowered by a younger smaller kid. Now the hand of change had reshaped the odds. He was going to right the wrongs of the past, his brother's slapped head, his humiliation in front of those Bidder street kids, the lies he had to tell Father Riley to cover for his lack of fighting skills. Now, in his mind and body he was more dominant than that little bastard.

He chose the theatre of conflict well. It was the corner of Bidder Street and Sim Street, this enabled more local kids to see the exchange, and to pass on the tale to a wider neighbourhood. He got his kid brother's mates to hang around this corner, to 'see the show.' He knew how it would play out. He had been watching Teddy Kelly from afar, planning this retribution to maximum effect. Teddy was getting angrier in his rows with other kids, not hitting out, but still in your face angry. He was going to taunt him, make a show of him. He had to be careful not to mark him, he had to keep the high moral ground that he had prepared with his lies previously. On cue the Canterbury kids started a chant going when Teddy and a few of the Chicago gangsters strayed to the end of their street. "Hop a long Cassidy, hop a long Cassidy!" This was a character from a Western movie that everyone had seen. The boys aped an exaggerated version of Teddy's swaying gait as they chanted. This caused Teddy to rage instantly. He moved forward as quick as his uneven legs would allow, arms swinging wildly to counterbalance the increased effort.

This was to become a warning sign in the future, if he moved like this, you got out of his way, sharpish!

Big brother walked around the corner as the chanting kids were easily out dodging the grasping arms of Teddy. They were squealing in delight at the name calling, and that they could easily out manoeuvre the limping avenger.

"Hey you Kelly!" Called out Big brother. Teddy took his eyes off the closest target to him and looked round to see a fight in the making. Body language was classic. Alpha male calling on the underdog to lie belly up in front of the pack or face the consequences.

Teddy's rage continued to burn on this turn of events. He was unaware that his normal response had changed so much that he would not be able to cope with such an encounter as this. He moved forward, stood as tall as his left leg would allow him, right big toe just contacting the ground to steady him.

"Hey! Kelly. Are you picking on my little brother again, you fucking cowardly bully yer?" Teddy could not speak any sense at this time, he could not think of the sensible thing to do. To back down and let the situation resolve itself with words and taunts alone. He growled, and spittle emanated from his lips as his own invective stream signalled: a fight it was going to be. Fists were clenched at his sides, as they rose Big brother easily read it and stepped back a pace, Teddy's wild swing caused him to stumble and take several correcting paces. The Canterbury street kids roared laughing at this.

Humiliation was mixing with adrenaline, swirling the broth round and round. Teddy lunged again, nimble feet easily side stepped the attempt. His grin was ear to ear, he was playing to the gallery for the Canterbury kids. This continued several times more, with each dodge the Canterbury kids roared, 'Ole!' Teddy was the doomed bull in the ring. Or, was he? Not in Teddy's mind. He was going to flatten this fucker and stamp on his fucking head with his fucking callipered boot!

He caught a lucky blow to the ear of Big brother, causing him to cry out more in shock than pain. The Bidder street kids roared encouragement. This dance continued, drawing more neighboured kids, a swarm of flies to a freshly dropped dog turd. When Big brother felt he had the audience he wanted, he decided to start the real humiliation of his nemesis. He stood his ground, bracing himself for the effort to come, right leg back supporting his own weight. Teddy came forward for the kill. Big brother flat palmed him on the chest, pushing him on to his backside in the dust, the cheer was deafening, the bull was down. Teddy scrambled to get up, his right leg struggling to comply with the nerve signals. On standing Teddy rushed forward again. The matador blocked the attack and Teddy was back in the dust to more shouts of 'Ole!' Teddy had no energy left in his legs. The extra effort of his left leg was too much, and his weaker right was draining strength with every passing second. He sat in the dust, on his bum, eyes streaming tears of frustration, lungs gasping for air, dry mouth – no sound. Big brother had done it. He had tamed the bull, Teddy Kelly was not going to be a name around here anymore, he thought.

The odds were overwhelming. The forewarned Canterbury street kids were too many and Big brother was a monster now. Jimmy could not have intervened. He did help Teddy to his feet, after the triumphant crowd had made their way back, singing the praises of the avenging Big brother. Teddy gained some air in his lungs and swore to get that fucker. He stumbled along supported by Jimmy's shoulder, the picture of an injured bandit withdrawing from the field of conflict.

It was not just the Canterbury kids that were emboldened by the bull fight, Sim street and even some Bidder street kids decided that change had come, and that Teddy was a shadow of the leader he once was. He was deposed. Wounded beyond leadership status, relegated down the pecking order by several years. One day this change was said out loud. One kid started to chant, quietly at first.

"Hey! Hop a long Cassidy", and swing apelike arms about, as he mimicked Teddy's walk. The kid knew he could outrun Teddy. All he needed to get his adrenaline rush, was to keep out of Teddy's reach. He was joined by one or two other kids. This taunting gathered pace over the coming weeks. Soon more kids would join in, gangs of swaying chimpanzees chanting the taunts. Teddy was hurt. He felt sorry for himself at the loss of his prowess, his status in the gang. His solution to this pain and loss was to plan revenge. He still used biblical quotes in his thinking. An eye for an eye. In his version of biblical justice, he would have both of their fucking eyes.

The list was not written down on paper. It was scored into his very fabric with ink of red mist, the colour of rage. He soon learned that he could not use the gunslinger stand-off method any more, they would just fancy step away and humiliate him. He developed a stalking approach to revenge. He would appear not to have seen a target, his expression, schooled in facial leakage, gave nothing away. When the prey had become blasé with the proximity of the once great predator, they relaxed.

Teddy lunged when the distance between them was inescapable. His arms immobilised the victim in a vice strong grip. Any desperate struggle only made it easier to succumb them. The punishment was swift. Delivered in the same staccato style of his father, each word punctuated with a punch to the head or face, while the admonishment, liberally seasoned with fucks and bastards, was spat out. Over time the taunting stopped almost completely. The punishments were inevitable. If you skitted Teddy you would get a beating and a half, not straight away but ages afterwards, even when you might have stopped doing it long ago. The only taunts now were occult. You never, ever, said anything derogatory about Teddy Kelly that he could hear, or hear about. He was too angry in his response.

Changes were still happening all about them. Another feather for Liverpool was the opening of the first UK inter-city highway. Joining Liverpool with Manchester. It started out as Walton Hall Avenue and went all the way to

Manchester as the A580. The old canal routes that had brought goods to and from Liverpool were now too slow for the twentieth century. The horse drawn barges that plied the waterways were still operating but had become less frequent with the increasing efficiency of the internal combustion engine. It was this trade route that gave rise to a generic term used by Liverpool people to refer to outsiders, woolly backs. When the bargemen had to traverse a tunnel, the horse would be unharnessed and taken over the bridge. The men donned a sheep skin protective jerkin to stop the barge line digging in to their shoulders while they pulled the boat through the narrow tunnel path. Re-harnessing the horse on the other side. Over time the term was used to describe anyone who was not local. Naming people by another, often derogatory, term has been used the world over by politicians and newspapers. It was about this time that 'The Hun' was back in the papers. The rise of socialism and nationalism in Europe was gathering pace. Fuelled by the years of hardship across the world after the great depression and the slow recovery. Here in the UK a charismatic leader was drawing huge crowds. He was an accomplished orator, he could speak easily and emphatically without notes. His followers took to wearing black shirts. These were invariably young men who took to violence with little actual, or perceived, cause required.

Teddy had heard of this politician. He was a baron or something but also a Sir. He had been in both the Tory party and in Labour. Now he was setting up his own party, the British Union of Fascists. The BUF. Teddy was not sure about the politics, but he heard that he had a limp too. He had crashed his plane in the great war, the one to end all wars, and since then walked with a limp. This didn't stop him being athletic. He could swim for ages and still did sword fencing, in those white suits and meshed hats they wore. He read about Mosley. How he had overcome physical adversity by his strength of mind, while building up his strength exercising the parts that still worked. He was going to do this. He would build up big arms and aim for the strength of Hercules as his goal. He would no longer worry about the fact he could not run anymore, or that he would never dance. He was going to be a different sort of man. One that people could look up to for his resilience and strength of character, and not look down on, at his disability

Chapter 8 The Flirt

Teddy noticed he was seeing many things differently. He was maturing. The social settings of Liverpool and Islington were sharply focussed. Discrepancies in fairness, as he saw them, were everywhere. He sought out various gurus and commentators on the reasons and solutions to the working man's lot. Teddy would listen carefully to the history of discord found in Liverpool, often going back to the previous century, but mostly in the previous decades. The general transport strike of 1911 was told often. How Winston Churchill, the home secretary of the time, sent HMS Antrim into the Mersey, loaded with military personnel, to quell a possible rebellion. Liverpool had a great tradition of taking to the streets, congregating at the wide-open spaces around St Georges Plaza and William Brown Street. Thousands of citizens would gather to listen to speaker after speaker call out the injustices of the social settings. All manner of political parties would address these gatherings, Fabians, socialists, communists and the fascists. Teddy would weigh up the reports of what each had been about and formulate in his mind what he thought would be the best option for the future. He was growing up.

Politics was not the only thing that he saw differently. He saw girls in a completely new light. Previously they had not occupied his thoughts much at all. Now, he saw them for the first time as people of interest. The hormonal surge had plateaued, testosterone levels had become normalised. He had new thoughts and desires. Girls suddenly, to his eyes, started talking to him more than he previously recalled. They had a different way of engaging his attention than boys. They looked into his eyes with a steady gaze, till something made them look away, he was curious. Why did they do that? It was not the same reason they averted their eyes every time. Some would hide a giggle behind their hand, not a mocking sound, but a hushed excited one. Others would have an air of disinterest, often checking that their message had been received with a sideways glance. Teddy was hooked on girls. The much older boys had girlfriends. They would walk together hand in hand along the streets, looking only at each other. The faces of the young men appeared soppy to Teddy. What was all that about he wondered?

It did not take long for Teddy to develop his style of chat with girls. He quickly discovered that many liked to be shocked with outrageous remarks and braggadocio. He supplemented these with his eyes and very cheeky grin. Each exclamation of faux horror was another sign that he was on the right track with this girl or that one. He also used humour, again with a shocking element, to win over affections. It didn't seem to matter to most girls that he had one leg shorter than the other and walked with a swaying gait, arms often swinging too. They only saw Teddy the boy. The young man.

His world was getting more and more complicated. He soon learned that girls had a code of conduct like the manliness of the street, not based on cowboy values, white hats and black hats. They had a group think approach. Theirs was based on fidelity. One on one meaningful relationships. If you wanted someone else there had to be a clean break off first, then the start of a new one. He found this hard to deal with. He wanted almost all of the girls in Islington, regardless of their romantic attachments. He was not interested in long term. A week was long term! Long enough for Teddy to tire of the pursuit, or to take his fill of darkness cloaked fumbles. He liked being a man. There was, almost, nothing better than the warm glow of slowly walking a girl back to her tenement block after a long satisfying fumble. The ultimate goal was the real one. This kept Teddy's mind fully occupied for weeks and weeks. The swirling hormonal broth was less black now, pinker than rage red. Nature was just working the way nature worked, relentlessly.

One girl, Elsie Hughes, from Sim Street was a recurring challenge for Teddy. She would let him get close enough to flirt with, but always just out of reach. He went off chasing other targets for his charm but came back to Elsie frequently. Elsie was the eldest of 6 girls, her youngest sister was about 8 months old. Her mother always seemed to be pregnant. Carrying her belly out in front for all to see the good Catholic wife and mother she was. It was a couple of years after Teddy's illness began that his mother fell pregnant again. He hardly noticed the change in her. She had become different since his run in with polio. The many days she had spent getting the bus or tram to Knotty Ash. Waiting hours by his side while in the iron lung. Not knowing if she would lose him completely. Eventually getting home to the rest of the family and Edward in their own tenement flat. This all had an effect on her behaviour. She was more demanding of Edward. He had to be better dressed than his normal donkey jacket and flat cap, he had to wear a collar on his shirt on Sundays. She had led the way with her wardrobe. She had always looked well presented, but then she took this up a notch or two. Whenever she went to Alder Hey, she would be at her best dressed. Always wore powder and ear rings, necklaces too. Her perfume had changed. It had become more expensive.

She adored new coats and it seemed a new one appeared every few weeks, a sign of the easing economic times perhaps?

One day Teddy saw a coat with a green hue, at first it was just a green coat. Then it became a puzzle to him. Why was it bugging his memory? He explored his mind's eye of memories, could not find it. Eventually his attention moved on. He had Elsie to think about. It was while he was playing with new lines of chat to catch Elsie, that the call from his landing went out for the midwife. Elsie shouted for one of her younger sisters. She sent her to fetch the midwife, the same one that had delivered most of the neighbourhood kids, including Teddy.

Molly, as she was to be called, was a beautiful baby girl, the fifth and last Kelly in the family. Anne's pregnancy and confinement had been relatively easy, just a few extra visits to the women's hospital every week. She kept her sartorial elegance up for these trips too. Molly was the darling of everyone that saw her. Dark hair, the same flashing brown eyes as Teddy's and his cheeky grin. She was the most travelled of all the Kelly infants. Anne would take her on bus rides for the fun of it, often staying out all day. She went to the parks. These were a long way off from Islington.

Sefton Park was the largest public park in the land, it went on for ages. Teddy had only been there once. Molly was chalking up quite a frequency of visits. It was another sunny day that Molly got christened at St Frances Xavier's church. It was not a private affair as usual. Many families brought their precious offspring to be welcomed into the fold. Teddy had gone along to show solidarity with the family and not to upset his mother with his new-found atheism. The usual mumbo jumbo and incantations were given up, the congregation joining in at their set times to echo the magic words.

Teddy let his mind wander, while he idly scanned the large congregation. He recognised most of the families, even if he did not know who the uncles and aunts were that gathered with God parents and siblings of the offerings. He took a double take while changing direction with his gaze at the back of the church. Who was that? It was a very familiar face from Teddy's near history. He was a clean person evident despite being surrounded by Sunday best clad celebrants. Teddy let his eyes take in the face. Was he looking up the isle at Teddy's family side of the church?

Teddy wasn't sure. Who was he with? He can't know anyone from Islington. He knew the face of the man and he was from Old Swan. Teddy explored the people on either side of the face. They seemed to be indifferent to his presence, they would be thought Teddy. He was on his own!

The exit procession from St Francis' was orderly. The churches newest members led the exodus, surrounded by their extended kin, each family calmly taking their turn starting with the front most pews and working backwards. As Teddy slowly walked down the aisle, he watched for the face to see where he was looking. As the Kelly column drew level with the face's pew, he saw it. The long hours he had spent studying facial leakage language, while he watched the nurses in Alder Hey, had made him an expert. There was a hidden eye contact with Anne and the face. Teddy looked at the face. He had brown eyes, dark hair and a softer expression than the usual Islington faces. He had seen that face many times before albeit all bar one in the mirror of his iron lung. It was the Dad of the kid with that cute thing that killed him. The last time he saw that face was at the tram stop on Eaton Road talking with his mum.

He recalled it vividly. They had both looked worried, his Mum had put her hand on his arm, he even saw the coat she was wearing. It was green.

There was a party to wet the baby's head. The usual bottles of stout and glasses of port. Teddy had started drinking beer when he could get some. It only took three or four for him to get more than tipsy. He left the party and sought space to think. He met Elsie, she was keen to talk. They spoke for quite a while, soon Teddy was less tipsy and more interested in Elsie than his swirling imagination.

He soon forgot about the christening and the strange turn up of the face. Life went on in Islington as usual. Teddy alternated between flirting, fighting over past insults and continuing his education from the street gurus.

Chapter 9 The Education Gap

School term started in September as usual. Teddy had
missed the first two years of secondary school education
since the start of his illness and rehabilitation. He went to a
special school in West Derby, near to Alder Hey, for two
terms, aimed at the basics of reading, writing and
arithmetic, while they focussed on him regaining mobility
skills. He started back at St Francis Xavier's (referred to
simply as SFX) in the September of 1937 to complete the
last two years of mandatory education. This was a typical
inner-city secondary school of the catholic flavour.
Brothers of the order of St Francis were employed as
teachers. They brought their version of classroom control to
bear in the form of 'the strap'. A vicious implement that
was applied to the upturned wrists of the boys who fell out
of favour. The offending boy had to stand in front of the
class, justice had to be seen to be done, as a deterrent
administered behind closed doors was a wasted opportunity
for crowd control. Some boys were regularly in front of
class for chastisement, as it was referred to. Teddy was one
of them. His crimes against the sensibilities of the system
were many. At first these ranged from, submitting incorrect
arithmetical solutions (that were considered as elementary
by the Brothers) to spelling mistakes on key biblical

English exercises. The latter were considered by the Brothers as the worthiest for corrective treatment, as they were fundamental stories from The Bible. Teddy's classmates could set their timetable by his summons to the front of class.

At first Teddy cried, as they all did, on receiving the gift of chastisement. It was for his own good as was so often said by the sandal wearing and hooded robed teachers of the good book. As Teddy acclimatised to these lessons, he decided he would no longer cry, despite the pain, in front of the class. He would take control of the situation, as far as he could, to deny the twisted pleasure of his tormenters, and increase his standing in the eyes of the other boys. This was easier said than done. The strap was delivered with full upper body force by many of the teachers. Landing on the defenceless wrist, the sleeves were compulsorily rolled up, to a loud 'thwack' sound. Breathing was the key to his defiance. If he could slowly breathe out after each thwack, and prepare for the next with an inhalation, he could manage the pain. The ultimate defiance came with his eyes. Although he never spoke, he declared for all to see that the power was shifting. He stared his tormentor right back, before, during and after the punishment, right up to the point where the Brother would send him back to his bench seat. He had to keep the charade up as he swayed back down the aisle, of bench seat and desk arrangement, to his own. Where he would sit upright, full height, while he re-arranged his shirt sleeves. It was just as he was fixing his sleeves one day that he realised that he towered above most kids when he was sitting down. All the benches were the same height but when Teddy sat down his head was higher than most. He later discovered that his arm span was well over six foot across. Had something gone wrong with his development due to the polio, had both of his legs slowed down in growth, while his upper torso continued as normal?

He enjoyed the history lessons, these were stories he could get interested in. They mostly were devoid of biblical references, he had developed a real aversion to any reference to the bible or any of its characters. He was struck by the similarity of Roman inventions with modern times. Yes, the tools were different, but the fundamentals were very similar. He liked the sounds, smells and bustle of the markets in his imagination. How the markets were prepared overnight to avoid disturbing the citizens. The carts would be silenced by tying rags around their metal clad wooden wheels to muffle the clanking as they carried the goods from far and wide. He enjoyed how society was organised.

Citizens were called upon to do their civic duty in rotation, merchants taxes paid for common utilities. Craftsmen toiled and were paid for their labours, soldiers were paid in salt! The people he had much sympathy for were the slaves. These souls were enslaved through various routes. Spoils from far away wars, big men were ideal for heavy stone labour. Women as house maids and wet nurses for the wealthy wives of the merchants and dignitaries. Slaves from distant lands carried their own cultures with them as far as they could. Unfortunate Italian people that fell afoul of the system, or were dirt poor hungry, also could end up as slaves. Teddy found this parallel to his own time. Where the clean people were citizens and the poor were enslaved in different chains and roles within society. Policemen, bayonet fixed soldiers and gun boats in the Mersey, kept the natural order of things in place.

Practical skills classes were what Teddy enjoyed the most. He was not good at technical drawing, he was marked below average. Woodwork was what he scored highest at, grade B was the usual mark. He found the range of tools that were kept, locked, in the wardrobe type wall cupboards fascinating. They were arranged by cutting, chipping, gripping or hammering function. All on pins, nails or hooks, all in their very own place on the walls and doors of the cupboards. The organisation was amazing, far from the random hap hazard way that things were stored at home. He liked to learn of the various joints that were possible, the tools that each required and the smoothing magic of sandpaper. This took of any rough edges and made the finished work presentable. Some display pieces had been finished in French polish so that the colours and sweeps of the grain were highlighted beautifully. He decided then that he wanted to be a joiner. He never got chastised in woodwork.

Although he was numerate, he was far from the finished article with mathematics. He could use the main operations, multiplication, division and so on. Algebra was as confusing as Latin and about as much use to anyone he knew. Who went round talking about x this or y that? Useless waste of time he thought, unless of course x or y meant fuck. Fuck this or fuck that. Calculus was a term he never came across in school. He did take to printed books of tables that he referred to as ready reckoners. These had a variety of data that could be used to calculate larger arithmetic products. In those times electronic calculators were still a long way off. These ready reckoners were to be used by Teddy for various money-making schemes in the future.

Education is wasted on the young, so they say. Teddy
sought his education by another name and route. He
enjoyed listening to men who could tell how things were,
how they became this way or that way, what things meant,
the injustices of the world. He sat down as often as he
could, to rest his legs and catch his breath. He would
choose to engage his circle of street teachers whenever he
found them seated, on benches overlooking the Mersey,
low walls around Islington or even the roadside kerbstones
- feet and legs stretched out in the roadway. These teachers
looked alike, clad in suit jackets in warm summers,
overcoats in winter, all had flat caps on in any weather.
Most smoked thin cigarettes lit with Swan Vesta matches.
There had been a Swan match factory in Liverpool for
many years. They all had lessons for young Teddy.

Social injustice was a common one. It found a home in his
head early on and never left. Old sailors would tell tales of
the wooden ships that sailed from Liverpool all over the
world. He often repeated during his lifetime the adage he
picked up from these tales, 'That was when men of iron
went to sea in wooden ships.' He was enamoured with tales
of hard men and difficulties that were overcome with brute
strength or strength of character. He learned about trade
unions, strikes for better conditions for the 'working man',

how the few had all the money and didn't care about the working man starving, like they had in Ireland 70 or so years ago, when the blight hit the potato crop. How that scourge had caused thousands of poor Irish people to leave and come to Liverpool for hope of work, food and shelter. The social norms from that diaspora still in evidence around Liverpool.

People crammed together in squalid accommodation, so they did not have to sleep on the streets, stretching food a long way to avoid anyone starving again. Sharing out of resources for the common good on an extended family basis. If anyone in the family brought food or money home, it was shared or spent on the whole household. Admiring and grateful looks were the rewards for bringing home valuable or edible goods, money put into the pot was always rewarded with familial hugs and kisses. Usually the responsibility of the household finances was held by the matriarch. She would eke out pennies for essentials and the occasional treat, keeping the household treasure in a tin on the mantle shelf. It was a special moment when a kid got to see the tin opened and a halfpenny or two was handed out for a birthday treat. This did not happen every year of course, which made the occasion so much more memorable when it did arrive.

Teddy was particularly interested in Liverpool firsts. How this city of contrasts was much more that his immediate, Islington based view. The old guys he listened to would usually start off in a similar way, with a question for their student.

"Which city was the first to have a special doctor to look after the health of all the people?" Teddy soon learned that the answer to most of these was, of course Liverpool. The floating roadway, a fascination of his early Pier Head treks, was a first. It had been developed due to the huge rise and fall in tidal levels of the Mersey, these were more marked in the spring tides, or neap, as they old salts would say. The dockers umbrella was the first all-electric elevated railway in the world. Not only that it had the first all-electric signalling system, to avoid accidents, it had the first escalators in any stations. The railway connected all seven miles of the Liverpool docks front from Dingle in the south up to Bootle in the north. The docks received ships from all over the world. He loved to hear of these far-away places that had goods to sell and how they wanted finished goods from England.

An old boxer mesmerised Teddy with his accounts of fighting in the Navy. They had various bouts to see who the best was, and these were pitched against other naval outfits or even better the Army's champion. There was great excitement at these tournaments, military honour was at stake. The gladiatorial tradition of Rome was still very much alive and thriving in the twentieth century. Often these bouts were accompanied by rival supporter scuffles and fist fights. When this happened the Red Caps, military policemen, would wade in with their riot sticks aloft and beat anyone in their way with them. It seemed that violence was a ubiquitous and timeless component of life. All the way from ancient Rome through the centuries and across foreign lands, from despots to holy Brothers, people had, and were still, using violence as a tool. To control populations and individuals, to achieve great goals or small wins, to secure positions of power or privilege, to avenge past wrongs, or slights. For Teddy to compete in this uneven world, made more so by his disability, he was going to need to be better equipped to cope with, and to use this lever of, violence. As his last day at SFX drew nigh, at the age of fourteen, Teddy knew he needed to develop his own edge, his own tool kit, to make his way on the uneven playing field of life. His next move was going to be his own development. He had to build up his strength in his torso to compensate for his legs and lack of mobility. He had to become hardened to the trials and tribulations of everyday life. He had to have that gladiatorial belief that he was always going to be the last man standing, albeit with a list to the right.

Chapter 10 The Split

Molly was nearly two when Anne left. She abandoned the
other four children and vacated the family home in Bidder
Street. This was a major blow to Teddy when he found out
two days later that his mother's absence was not what had
initially been described as, a trip to see her sister. The truth
came out in drips. The traffic through their tenement
apartment was different. Auntie Nellie and Aunty Katie had
both called in. Uncle Spike made a rare appearance too.
Teddy could not hear the words spoken, but his study of
faces all that time while in the iron lung had given him
enough skill to know that there was something very wrong
in his world. His Dad had sent all the Kelly kids out to
play.

"And don't come back in till I tell you", said Edward. The
clear worry on the women's faces, the anger in his Dad's
countenance, the controlled, but still concerned, look on
uncle Spike. Teddy thought that his mother had died and so
had Molly. He thought up lots of possible scenarios how
this might have come about. Both crushed by a tram or a
bus, those accidents did happen. Or, there had been a train
crash, or run over by a car or truck. It was no use thinking
up all these possibilities, he had to know, to feel in control.
So he offered to make tea, go for tobacco, see if they

needed anything else, all to get closer to the words. He eventually settled on creeping up to the door of the living room to hear. As it happened, he could have listened from the kitchen as the voices were raised.

"The fucking bastard, bastard, bastard", cried Edward. Spittle dripping from his lips. His sister Nellie joined in.

"What on earth has got into her? Jesus, Mary and Joseph have mercy on her." Uncle Spike calmly asked a question.

"How did this start? When did you first suspect anything was amiss with her?" He had heard this line of questioning from the detectives in the Bridewell, he wanted to be a detective.

"It has been a while now. She started going further afield to buy things, so she was taking longer and longer to get back. She even bought one of those collapsible buggies to get on the tram and busses, to here there and everywhere. Sundays she started going to Sefton park with Molly, staying out all day. She blamed my ciggy smoke for the poor air in here. That Molly needed fresh air.

"Do you know this fellers name? Where he lives?" Spike displayed the same calm manner, but with real concern in his eyes.

"Yes, its Jonathan Burke, he lives in Old Swan. Oakhill Road. It's a dead posh house. The bastard!"

"What number?"

"Thirty-two. It's an end house on the block. It has front and back gardens, and an open view to the front."

"What does he do for a job?"

"I haven't found that out yet."

"Leave it with me. I will have a root around and find out all about this chump."

"Chump! Chump! He's a fucking bastard not a fucking chump!"

"Try to stay calm. Getting angry at this stage will not sort this out. We have to be measured in what we do in order to get Molly back."

"What in the Devil got in to her?" asked Katie. She was older than Edward and a widow. She lost her husband in the closing stages of the great war. They had only been married a year, no children. She never married again.

"Fecking hell", joined in Nellie. She avoided swearing, so fecking was not strictly a cuss word, but conveyed the emotion just as well. She was older than Edward too, never married. She was engaged once, but that man just disappeared of the face of the earth, so it seemed. She lost faith in men after that. The two sisters lived in a one room flat in the same street as Edward and Anne. They wore the ubiquitous black of the old un-married women of the day. Wrap around pinnys, secured on one side with a huge safety pin, hence the name, were always worn. For going out these simple garments were covered completely with a long black wrap around shawl. It went over their heads and over one shoulder to frame their pale faces. Regardless of how they came to be un-married they all shared a common descriptor in Liverpool, Mary-Ellens. The faces of these women usually gave some hint of their hard lives, most were heavily lined, sallow skin, hollowed cheeks. Their smile, if given, was often toothless. They sounded as if they were from a foreign land when they spoke. It was distorted with lack of teeth and shortage of breath, often drowned in excess spittle, they used old Liverpool expressions, mostly Irish sayings, to describe what they were saying. It was another language indeed to anyone young. When these women had a cup of tea, the form was the same. They poured a little tea from the cup onto the saucer and proceeded to slurp the liquid noisily through kissing lips.

"Let's all have a cup of tea", suggested Katie, "that will help us stay sane with all of these goings on."

Teddy was breathing as lightly as he could manage. If he was found it would be a beating for sure. He checked his escape route, into the lad's bedroom and a slide under the bed would do it.

As he heard his aunt make her way to the kitchen, he had to scramble quickly into the bedroom he shared with his younger brother, Tommy. Scooting across the floor on his hands and buttocks in a pendulum manner. He reached the bed and just disappeared underneath it as the door opened. Katie went about boiling the kettle on the black stove cooker combination. It took her a while to prepare the brew. She had the same system every time she made tea. Teddy could not see her from his hiding place, but he could see in his mind's eye every move. He let his imagination follow the tea ritual to keep his mind off being discovered, it helped his breathing and stopped him thinking about what he had just heard.

When the tea had been brewed and the pot placed on the tray along with cracked cups and saucers, Katie carried the offering into the lounge. Returning to close the door after she had set the tray aside. The voices could still just about be heard from his sanctuary site under the bed, so he decided for safety's sake to stay there. It was not unlike being back in the iron lung. Where he had to remain calm and not move, as he was constrained by the coffin like space, all he was missing was his mirror on the world. He did not need that to see the scenario in the lounge, his imagination was his eyes. His Dad would be in his chair, smoking, sitting forward on the front edge of the worn cushion. Flicking ash, left handed, onto the knee of his trousers and then rubbing it in with his fist to stop the ash from falling onto the lino floor. Taking sips of tea with his right, spitting bits of tobacco out that got caught in his teeth from the unfiltered hand rolled cigarette. This was the normal for Edward when agitated. He could see his gaze moving around the room while he sought answers to his conundrum, finding none, so filling the void of ideas with a mouthful of fucks, bastards and spits.

As he listened the conversation began repeating itself, going round and round the same things. No progress. So he let his own thoughts wander around the disaster of his mother leaving them, taking his baby sister with her, to go and live with some man called Jonathan Burke, in Oakhill Road, Old Swan. In a house, a house! Not a flat, or tenement, but a house. A house with a garden, no two fucking gardens he recalled hearing. He wondered how anyone from Islington could afford a house, even without a fucking garden? How much was the rent on one of those, he thought.

He had passed through Old Swan when he left Alder Hey, on the tram back to town. It was a bustling neighbourhood with shops on both sides of the road. There was a pub with a great big freeze over the centre of the double fronted building of a black horse. The pub was called The Black Horse. It was a grand building, not like the smaller ones all over town, one on every corner almost. This was set in its own grounds just set back off the road a bit, so rich people with cars could park them outside while they had a drink. There was even a bowling green at the back, with people in white trousers rolling big black balls across the grass. He recalled thinking that this area was the poshest he had ever saw. Further up towards town there was a huge cinema. Across the road from that was another posh pub, the Mason's Arms, it was like the ones you saw on biscuit tins at Christmas. It was painted in black and white just like pictures of the olden times, Tudor times he thought. As the tram negotiated the bend in the road there were two more pubs. The one in front was another Tudor one, but bigger, it took up the whole block. It was called the Old Swan. The one opposite it was called by a funny name, it began with Cyg, he could not remember the rest of the short word. He did note that the colour of the that one was not Tudor livery but a deep red, red from the engineering brick frontage.

The only other building of note he recalled from that return tram ride, was just passed Old Swan, it was a grand façade of red bricks, a different colour red from the funny named pub. It had white stoned window mullions and decorative freezes of the same stone on uprights. It was the newly opened slaughterhouse and meat market for Liverpool. His mother had told him when he asked what that building was. She said it was new, only opened a few years before. She knew lots of things about it. That it was built by Liverpool city council and cost £670,000, he did not know how much that really was, just it sounded like a huge amount the way she proudly said it. He had wondered at the time how she knew so much about this one building. He just thought she must have read about in the Echo or the Daily Post.

He was bought out of his revere by raised voices from the lounge. His Dad had become angry again. Spike was trying to calm him.

"Let me find out all about this feller. Once we know what we are dealing with we can sort it properly. If we rush in, it could backfire something awful and you might not get Molly back. If he is the sort who knows his way around solicitors, he could get an injunction, that could mean you would go to Walton if you put one step out of line."

"I know you are right Spike, I just can't stop being angry with this fucker."

"It is Anne you should be angry with", pitched in Katie.

"Oh now, don't be hasty", cautioned Nellie. She was a calm woman. Her approach to the world was shaped by disappointment. She knew the sorts of stresses and strains that people had to navigate to have a reasonable life. "We don't know what this charmer may have promised her. He may be a fly by night and she could come back, with Molly, before you can say boo to a goose."

"Yes let's take a break from all this 'maybe and possibly' and let me get back with what I can find out. Right Edward, you and me are going for a pint." As the two men left, he could hear them going down the concrete steps. His two aunts tidied the flat and closed the front door behind them. When he was sure they had got far enough away, Teddy slid out from under the bed he shared with Tommy. He went to the window to check his father had indeed gone into the pub, no sign of him, so it was safe to go back in the street. As he went out into the daylight from the gloom of the tenement, he realised who this Jonathan Burke actually was.

Chapter 11 The fall

Anne met Edward in the spring of 1923. She was working
in a clothes shop off London Road when a well-dressed
man entered looking for a blazer. Very few men ever
looked for blazers in this part of town. He was charming in
his speech and respectful of Anne in his questions. He used
the polite term of *Miss* when addressing her. In return, like
with all customers, she also used the polite address of Sir.
All the time this respectful ping pong was going on their
eyes met several times. Edward had a steady gaze, he
looked deep into Anne's eyes and held her there. On her
part she gazed right back, and then some. This was a
meeting of minds, of sorts. Anne was well dressed in the
manner of the Kennedy women, she had simple, pearl like
ear rings and a hard-combed back hair style, the norm for
respectful women of the time. This had the effect of
framing her face against the teak wood background, of the
floor to ceiling drawered wall behind her, the pearl ear
rings giving the sense of perfect equilibrium when turning
her head. She was beautiful in Edward's eyes. Everything
he had heard of this girl was true. The local men had
admired Bull Kennedy's daughter for her beauty, but none
had the balls to risk dallying with this monster of a man's
eldest girl.

His strength and fighting prowess were legendary, not just in Islington, but across the city wherever navvies were digging trenches, or squabbling. Anyone who displeased Bull Kennedy was soon to feel the hot breath of his roar, if that was ignored, the haymaker fist, or shovel, presented to their face usually made them see sense. Only occasionally did Bull ever resort to actual violence. When this did happen it was all over in a flash, usually one punch from that massive fist, sent forward at the speed of a rattle snake strike, was all it took to flatten the fool who stood his ground to face Bull. The observers would talk of the encounter in the pubs, on street corners, in the dole queue or outside the bookie's shops.

The reputation of the man was embellished with every re-telling of these stories. His physical stature was increased, six foot six and built like a brick outhouse, was the accepted exaggeration. When he went for a haircut his hair was so strong it would fly off like a piece of cable being snipped with bolt cutters. He could drink any man under the table and out of the pub door easily!

The electric company supervisor had heard of him, and he wanted him as the ganger man for the elite team of navvies. This team had to dig trenches and pull cables without any delay, the march of modernisation could wait for no one. It was barely a hundred years since gas was 'the future,' now it was electricity. So Bull Kennedy was the figure and face of the future of trenching in Liverpool. In reality the man was only human, yes, he was big, but not six foot six tall. More like Six foot one and broad like many men from County Mayo stock. The local gene pool favoured men that could dig peat from wet boggy land and hurl it up and, on to the cart in one smooth sweeping action. Bull's father came from Mayo. He arrived in Liverpool with other migrants hoping for a better life, one where hunger was a memory. Bull's early life was hard. He struggled learning to read and write, only becoming moderately proficient. He left school at twelve to dig ditches for gas mains alongside his father, increasing the family income in the process. He married when he was seventeen and had seven children. Anne was the eldest and the apple of his eye. He was driven on to seek better gangs to work in for more money for his growing family. He wanted his kids to have good jobs, to live longer than the Kennedy's usually did and to have families of their own, brought up in the Catholic faith of the old country. He was no different in his outlook from anyone with, *a bit of nouse*, as the local expression had it.

Anne fitted his expectation exactly. She had done well at school. When she left at the usual age of fourteen, she could read and write perfectly. Her mathematical ability went beyond the usual scope of the four main operators of arithmetic, the standard for secondary schools then. She could even do fractions! She was respectful of her seniors and betters. Never incurring the wrath of the nuns, like some girls did, so was never chastised in word or by strap. Anne loved the finer things in life. She saw them in the cinema and in the posh people of the Liverpool suburbs when they were shopping or socialising in town. In her heart she was posh. So she made great efforts to be so. Her accent was not as harsh as the local town people, more Woolton. She enunciated her words as best she could, mimicking the shop owners she worked for. She always worked in shops. She loved handling the merchandise. The feel of the expensive garments made her tingle with fantasies of her future.

The young Edward Kelly was flush. He was in the glory of a winning streak that had lasted for ages. It started with the National, he had put half a dollar, on Sergeant Murphy ridden by Tuppy Bennet. It came in by three lengths and at 100 to 6. Winner! This was the start of his winning streak. He thought he was a wise gambler, carefully spreading out his winnings into piles. Food and keep first, buying better clothes and then the remainder was invested in more form. He picked reasonable chancers, those horses with form good enough to have a chance of winning, and with the odds just in favour of a bigger pay out when they did. He did well for quite a while. Not winning every bet but he was well ahead when he met Anne.

He decided that he was going to chance asking this beauty out on a date. When the fuss and politeness of the blazer purchase was done, he asked.

"Now that you have helped me pick this fine blazer, I would be honoured if you would find in your heart to come with me, to the Adelphi Hotel for afternoon tea on Sunday?" She was pleased. Her subliminal messages from her eyes, reinforced with a gentle touch of his arm when he tried the coat on, had been received.

"Yes I would love to have tea with you." This was an up and coming young man he could really make something of himself she thought. That Sunday went swimmingly. She loved the grandeur of the great reception hall in the Adelphi. There were lots of huge chandeliers, large arched windows that must have been ten-foot-tall, all covered in fine lace curtains. The sofas and chairs all had plush upholstery and complementary coloured scatter cushions. The waiters all wore tail suits and dickie bows and had the best manners she had ever seen. She ate the sandwiches and cakes delicately. She had done her hair in a softer style than the shop norm. It was worn high on her forehead and fell in loose curls down to her shoulders, it was the usual Irish deep black. Edward was smitten. Anne was cautiously optimistic.

They met several times more at the Adelphi. Anne enjoyed the spectacle of watching the other people in the great halls of the liner and railway hotel. There were people from London, arrived off the train at Lime Street station just along the road, luggage left with the porters while they had tea. Well to do business men had meetings over drinks of whiskey and port. Their cigar smoke curling slowly upwards to dance among the chandeliers. The longest gazes were spent appreciating the ladies' outfits. These were amazing in her eyes. She could recognise some of the London fashion house's creations, she scoured every fashion magazine she could get. The ladies' shoes were always visible when they walked to their allocated places. The overly attentive waiters, working their tips, would gasp in wonder at the fine gloves they wore, the only safe comment they could make before being thought of as rude. Anne was in her element here.

It was summer time and the evening walks back to Islington were warm and balmy. This had become a routine, tea at the Adelphi, staying well passed the heat of the pot while they chatted and eyed the circus of characters. Slow walk back to Islington, arm in arm, up Coppers Hill, passed the post office sorting depot. Turning left into Seymore Street then meandering along to Islington and home. Occasionally they would deviate. Staying on Lime Street to walk passed the pubs and hear the hubbub from within. They passed the Grapes pub on the corner opposite the Adelphi. A fine house with a grand domed tower and raised facades. The other end of Lime Street, opposite the station entrance was a more modest pub, the Crown. They often walked through the station concourse, breathing in the smells and smoke of the locomotives, mixed with stale beer and expensive perfume: a curious mix indeed. This concourse had a strange power. One could escape the grime of Liverpool and go anywhere in the land on the railway. The journey back was completed by turning right on London Road and up the hill there to Islington.

Edward had had a big win and was going to push the boat out. He was over excited all through their tea, ebulliently talking about what he was going to do with his life, more wishful than realistic. He suddenly ordered two whiskeys to celebrate his good fortune the previous day. Anne was a little hesitant at first, worried if her Dad would smell drink on her breath. Reluctantly she sipped her drink as Edward raced onward with his charming chatter. Two more whiskeys followed. She was living the other side of the Adelphi life now, with the posh people. Soon it was time to make a move home. This time they took the scenic route again along Lime Street. They were giggling and cuddling closer than ever before as they walked. As they passed the Crown pub, they decided to walk outside of the station, so they could take in the Lions and columned splendour of St Georges Hall across the road. They reached the building site for the future Liverpool Empire Theatre, as it said on the hoarding outside. The sun had set, and the evening was closing in. Cover of darkness went through Edward's mind. "Let's go up here Anne." He indicated up Lord Nelson Street, this was just across from Nelson's column. As they walked a little way up the street there was a worker's access doorway, set back from the perimeter hoarding, a perfect spot for a kiss and cuddle. They stopped and embraced, kissing each other long and deeply, tongues fully engaged. Edward moved his hand from Anne's back and slid it up her left side towards her breast. There was no resistance from her. Buoyed by the lack of challenge and the Dutch courage from the whiskey, he massaged her breast through the layers of blouse and bra cover. She held him tighter, he pushed against her belly with his, she pushed back. He let his hand go up inside her blouse, then under her bra to the soft warm skin. She never resisted. He was going to try lower. Sliding his palm down her side till the band of her skirt, then round her back. The waist band was tight. He found the button. With one hand he slipped the top button free, moved on to the next one, then his exploring hand felt the super soft buttocks. Each one was stroked in turn, fingertips sending tingling through her skin. When he was sure she was relaxed with this level of intimacy he raised his stake to win or lose. She allowed his hand to come around and under. She felt grown up, a woman, she had a charming man sending her into an immobilising state of stimulation. It was only a small step from this, to that.

It happened quickly. She was partly sedated from whiskey and wetness.

Once they had re-arranged their clothing, they continued their way home. Still arm in arm, not quite as tipsy from either stimulant. Their goodnight kiss was a mere shadow of their former ardour, more peck than mouth kiss.

Chapter 12 The Confession

The pressure had been mounting for several weeks. Anne was pregnant, no doubt about it. This was before pregnancy testing was done with urine dip stick technology. It was a waiting game, with very high stakes. No way out for Catholic girls in England, not like the Magdalene laundries of Ireland – which was not a way out either for the girls, but a face saving for the families. She had told Edward. He was shocked. The usual inane words were offered by Edward.

"Are you sure!?

"Yes"

"No doubt about it?"

"No doubt at all. I am pregnant!"

"What are you going do about it?"

"What are *we* going to do about it. Don't you mean?"

"I, erm, erm, not sure what we can do about it?"

"You will have to marry me you fool!"

"How can I do that?"

"Now don't be stupid! You will have to see my Dad, and we will have to get married, quickly before all and sundry know about it."

"What will he say?" The apprehension building in Edward's mind, how will Bull Kennedy react to someone getting his pride and joy pregnant, the pressure was making him sweat. His arm pits were damp, getting more so with every thought he had of facing Bull.

"Let's hope he says good luck! And doesn't decide to flatten you for getting me up the duff!"

The sweat came on to his brow at this suggestion. He was thinking, no solutions came to mind. The beads began to coalesce and run down his face in narrow rivulets of liquid fear. He tried to pass the buck.

"It was you just as much as me!"

"That's not what I'll tell him if you don't do the right thing and stand by me Edward Kelly. I will tell him you took advantage of me after getting me drunk on whiskey, I didn't know what was going on till it was too late. He won't just punch you then, will he? You will be lucky to walk again, if he lets you live that is?"

Edward stared at his prize girl, the one that everyone in Islington had eyes for, she looked different now. She certainly sounded different. Anne was now in control, not him. She was deciding what would happen, when and how. Also how they were going to lessen the blow, when it came. And it would come. Chastity was expected from all girls then, not just the Catholic ones. Society had a poor view of fallen women. Once an unmarried girl was pregnant, she was no longer a girl, she was a fallen woman. Only swift action on her part, a whirlwind marriage for the young sweethearts, and a miracle of an early birth were to be the salvation of her, and her family name. Anne had chosen her tack carefully. Some girls threatened their boy with suicide if they did not marry them. She knew that would not wash with Edward. She had learned a lot about his character in the last couple of weeks since first learning of her pregnancy. She didn't realise he was so self-centred in his outlook. He only thought of Edward first, every time. What would that mean to me? How can I do that? What about my family, were words that he had used to weasel his way out of responsibility. So she had decided to use her father's scary reputation as the lever to escape the scorn and ignominy of her situation. Edward would tremble at the thought of her father beating the living daylights out of him, for touching his daughter, especially if she told it in the right way. The sweat coursing down his face told her she had chosen correctly. Anne let her work soak in a little longer before she again took charge and moved to the next phase, the meeting with her father.

She had prepared Edward and schooled him in what to say. They would arrange for a meeting, over tea on Sunday afternoon, after mass and before he went for his pint, in the Prince of Wales pub on London Road. He would be in his Sunday best, after church and his usual attire for the Prince of Wales, so he may not want to mess his suit up with blood stains. This comforted Edward a little, not that much really. He was scared stiff. He still hadn't told her that he lost his job as a labourer. The pressure was mounting on several sides. Edward felt trapped. He could see no way out, no matter which way he approached it. He was going to have to risk his life, as he saw it, with Bull.

Sunday mass went as usual, over an hour of it in total. Edward felt every mention of sin, damnation and redemption in his very fibre. The sweat was still there, his breathing rapid and shallow. They arrived at Bull's terraced house, the Kennedy's didn't live in a tenement. Tea was prepared by Anne and her mother, Edward was sitting uncomfortably on the front edge of his cushioned armchair. Bull was expecting a request for his daughter's hand in marriage. Suggestions of tea with a young man did not happen as a rule, the only possible explanation was he was going to ask for his permission to marry Anne. He was a little concerned with Edward's prospects, but he was working and did OK for himself, judging by the clothes he wore when not on the building sites. He had decided to play his part as the reluctant father, allowing his daughter to grow up and leave the family home to start a new life with her beau, and to wish them well on their chosen path. That was not how it played out.

He was incandescent with rage as soon as the words had hit his brain. The emotional mixture was explosive. How could a Kennedy girl get herself in this mess? What were people going to think. What would the priest say, his mother would turn in her grave if she knew? The anger was next to break through. It was this man's fault here. He couldn't keep his hands off his daughter or his cock inside his trousers. His next move was all in one sweeping action. He was off his chair and took Edward by the scruff of his neck, lifted off his feet Edward was pinned to the door in a vicelike grip. Held there by just one of Bull's hands. No air was getting passed this choking fist. The face of Bull was so close the engorged veins in his head were clearly seen through the misting of Edwards consciousness. There was a faraway sound. He could not make it out. It sounded like Anne's voice. His peripheral vision was fading to black as the hypoxia worked its way into his brain. Then suddenly he was crumpled on the floor, against the door. He was alive. His head started to clear, the distant sound rushed into his consciousness, it was Anne crying out for Bull to stop and not kill or hurt him anymore. She loved Edward and was going to marry him.

Edward felt the front door slam. Bull had stormed out, swearing and spitting threats of murder if any hint of scandal got out. He was relieved he could breathe again, he was alive, just. Anne had saved him from almost certain death, in his mind. The hardest hurdle had been jumped, the Beecher's Brook fence. Now it was just a matter of staying in the saddle till the finish line. He had not thought about the church at that point.

When Anne and Edward went to see the priest, they didn't expect the reception they received. He was Irish, like most Liverpool priests, he was best described as old school in his interpretation of a good Catholic marriage. He listened patiently and sagely to the young couple's request for a church wedding. It was going smoothly, Anne thought, till he took a long breath inward and then let out a long heavy sigh.

"Now then, it is not acceptable to the Church, or this priest, to see fit to allow a marriage to take place if the girl is in the family way." The shock on Anne' face was mirrored, to an extent, on Edward's countenance too. How did he know she thought? She wasn't showing, that much anyway. Who had she told? Anne went through the few people she had asked advice from, for *a friend* in need. It must have been one of them that had ratted to the priest that she, and not *her friend,* was in the family way. The conversation went on a little longer, but to no avail. He was not going to move. She was going to have to go through a civic ceremony to save her and her family name. He thought how easy it was back in Ireland to hide these fallen women away. They just needed to be signed in with the nuns by a man, any man. And, unless they were claimed again by a man, to make them respectable, they would remain in the Magdalene laundry system for life. Hidden away from the sensibilities of the congregation and the lie that dogma was supreme over nature.

When Anne recovered her composure and had control of her thoughts again, she was formulating her next set of moves. By the time the couple had walked back to her road, she had a plan. They were going to be married at the Brougham Terrace registry office, just around the corner at the top of Low Hill. It would be a scaled down version of the wedding she had planned, but it would still be hers. Bull had taken a week to calm down. He had decided to let the women sort it out and would have no part in it. As it happened, he did attend the ceremony and the small drinks party afterwards. A few friends and family wished the couple well and had brought the usual array of gifts for the newlywed's new home together. They had a room in Edward's family tenement flat. That was a start, she thought, for now. Still her future was rosy in her mind and expectations.

Islington life went on. The newly wed Kelly's settled in to a routine. The Adelphi life that she had envisaged them living was a far distant memory. The money he had to throw around back then was gambling winnings. His winning streak had soon gone west too. He rode the upward wave for a while, only to crash deep into its trough. It smashed his hopes and dreams to millions of droplets, and for them to disappear completely as the water reformed and all was level again.

Strains of managing as a couple soon emerged. There were crossed words at first, when Anne's expectations were tried. Edward had one idea of how a wife should be and she had another. The words soon morphed into threats of violence, only held back by the spectre of Bull in the background. She was disenchanted, well before her confinement. She was also trapped. No way out as she saw it. Her only comfort was in how she presented herself to the world and the Islington neighbourhood. In the winter and turn of spring in 1924 her trips out of the tenement flat were few, but she always wore her maternity wear with panache. She was married to a Kelly, but her genes were Kennedys through and through. The local women had long moved on in their gossip. The scandal of Anne Kennedy marrying Edward Kelly in a hurry, at the registry office, was history. She was not the first fallen woman in those parts, she was just one of many. The harsh words on the corners and the wash house were saved for the latest Trollope to come to light. Anne Kelly was going to make it, she was a survivor, she was a Kennedy.

Chapter 13 The Circus

Teddy was coming round to his new life. He knew his limitations with mobility, he would never play football, or get a legger off the cocky watchmen, he told himself he was more grown up than that now anyway. He was finding his way, coping with the rage, using laughter to diffuse stand offs, and trying to impress people in different ways. He found that though he could not walk, or stand for long come to that, he could do hand stands and walk on his hands. This became his party trick when it came to showing off. He spent ages perfecting his technique. Starting with simple headstands, supported with his forearms flat on the floor, extending his legs upwards, holding them there with his core abdominal musculature. Then progressing to using his hands as the steadying supports. It was just a short step to elevating himself high off the ground with his extended arms. He was spurred on by the attempts of others to try to copy him. This was achieved with varying amounts of success on their part. He soon left all challengers behind when it came to walking on his hands. This was going to be Teddy's party trick and he was going to be the best there was in all of Islington. The challengers all fell away when he had the idea of walking up the tenement block stairwell. The concrete steps were going to hurt if you fell on them.

Teddy was fuelled with show off payback, the recognition he would get when he managed this feat was going to go a long way in the street.

He practised in private. Sweat would pour down his forehead, soak his armpits but he carried on. He learned to roll when he was losing his balance, as in judo, so that he did not hurt himself too much. His arms became stronger and stronger. At first, they were sinuous in shape, he was as skinny as the next Bidder Street kid, as his effort increased, and his results became better his arms started to change shape. Biceps became prominent, triceps just as much so. His chest had been scrawny, now it was starting to widen as his back muscles were worked hard. Strength was becoming easy to him. He could open any tight jar lid with ease, or just a little extra breath of effort. On the makeshift see saw, a plank raised on a small pile of bricks, he could send two kids soaring upwards or hold them aloft with just his arms leaning on the other end. He was getting a herculean reputation.

When it came to walking, he was still easily recognised from way down the roads of Islington, he swayed from side to side, arms outstretched away from his body, it was more chimpanzee locomotion than a regular bipedal gait. He still used callipers, which raised a few smirks and still the odd name call. He would not let these go by unpunished, still the waiting game of retribution was played. With his increasing strength the admonishing punches were delivered with more vigour and damage. This helped to deter any other foolish kids from daring to be heard skitting Teddy Kelly. It was not long till Teddy decided that callipers were not helping him. More from the idea of being seen using them than any lack of improvement. He stopped strapping them on, he had long ago defaulted with physiotherapy, the trek to Knotty Ash and Alder Hey on a regular basis soon put an end to that. Without the support of the leg irons, as he still referred to them, he needed a different technique to support his walking. Pockets were the answer. If he held his hands in his pockets, he could lean his torso weight into his hips and transfer it down his leg. This did two things, it got round the issue of no callipers and it stopped the chimpanzee swinging arms. He was walking in a more normal manner. He felt much happier.

He had other circus tricks to impress. He discovered early in his floor crawling phase that in order to get around, without having to stand up, he could scoot across the kitchen floor on his hands and swing his body underneath him in a pendulum action. His left leg was good for extra grip and effort, but his right leg still got in the way. His solution to this was to tuck it out of the way. Across his lap as if he was about to sit cross legged was the usual. Then he learned that he could, with a bit of effort, tuck it around his neck, like a circus contortionist. This brought great laughs from his siblings and friends. He became a skulking monster spider coming to get his little sisters, they screamed in fearful joy as they ran away. It was still applause to Teddy and as such reinforced his need for recognition.

The hormone storm was still in the air. Teddy was now as much interested in impressing girls as he was the lads of the neighbourhood. They would enjoy his company as much as him. He would entertain them with ribald jokes, he never shied away from cursing or sexual inuendo, the more the girls were shocked the eager he was to go further in his outlandish language. He even started kissing some of them, initially as part of 'dare games' on the corner, then more in earnest as his taste increased. He became acutely aware of the dirt around him. He had always been dirty as a kid, he couldn't explain it, as soon as he left the tenement, he would have grubby hands and a smudge or two on his face. This was not going to impress girls he thought. He started to think about his clothes, which ones were best in terms of fewer moth holes and smell. What were other lads wearing around and about. The working teenagers were all well-dressed on Sundays, despite what overalls or other workwear they had during the week. It was Sunday attire that Teddy used as his yardstick. He had to use altered hand downs from his Dad as the starting point at first. He asked aunty Katie to take them in or turn the trousers up, make the jacket a little looser, sew a button back on. He was grateful to Aunt Katie, she always did what he asked. Her reward was to gaze at his young face and his flashing brown eyes, that were inseparable from his smile, when he paraded her work back to her, before going out to impress some young girl he had his eye on.

His envy of the posh people was still there. Why did they have such great clothes, coats, gloves, even in summer! The hats were still a source of amazement to Teddy, had been since his early days looking at the clean people, as he called them then. Most men wore flat caps in Islington. There were a few who wore trilbies, no one wore a Bowler. Those men came from the suburbs like Woolton or over the water off the ferry. He didn't want a trilby or even a Bowler, he wanted a gangster hat. One he could wear with attitude. He saw himself in a smart, made to measure suit, oxblood brogues and a fedora hat. His make do and mend outfits were only temporary, till he got a good job and had regular money coming in. He was going to be someone, soon, when he got just a little bit older and left school for good and got on with earning money. What use was school anyway, he thought. He could read and write and do sums, he had his ready reckoners for big calculations. He had listened to the street teachers, the men he heard all he needed to know about the world, of faraway places, seen from merchant ship sailors, of the injustices of the capitalist system that kept the poor, poor and the rich even richer. He knew that anyone who tried to change the system was pilloried and sent to prison, marked for life as an agitator, to be shunned and excluded from respectable society.

Teddy had got a Saturday job. Loading goods onto wagons at Lime Street station for onward distribution. He could lift heavy weights easily thanks to his circus training regime. All he had to do was lift them off the doorway of the goods car and turn around to stack them on the waiting wagon, that was parked adjacent to the train. It was hard work despite his strength. He worked alongside older lads and young men. These were favoured by the ganger man in charge as they were cheaper labour than married men with families. Teddy was a valued worker to Big Jim Metcalf the ganger man. He was young and keen to earn as much money as he could. He asked to work extra shifts, or part ones after school. Big Jim obliged whenever he could. Soon Teddy was doing more shifts for Big Jim by skipping school and going to work instead.

Teddy's final beating from his father came after a man had called to their tenement. He wore a dark coat and trilby and carried a suitcase. Edward had been in as usual, as he no longer had a job digging trenches for the electric company since Bull had died, he let the gentleman in to the lounge as they called it. He introduced himself as Mr Collier, and that he worked for Liverpool Education. He started by outlining that going to school was a legal requirement in the UK, and any child that did not go, or was not allowed to go to school, had to be investigated. That was why he had come to Bidder Street. His son Edward Kelly, known as Teddy, had not been to school for the last six weeks and he had been instructed to call to establish why not. He had seen that Teddy's record had polio disability listed and he wanted to make sure that this was not stopping his attendance at school. Edward listened carefully to what Mr Collier had to say. He was keen to avoid any serious consequences from Teddy's truancy, yet he had no idea that Teddy had not been going to school. Teddy didn't speak that much with him. He preferred to be out and about with the other lads than at home. He made up a story that Teddy's polio was making it hard for him to get up the hill to SFX, and also that it caused joint pain that lasted a few weeks. He assured Mr Collier that Teddy would be back at school regularly, once he had had a word with him, like Mr Collier said, about the importance of regular attendance at school.

As Mr Collier left the flat, he was shown out by Auntie Nellie, she had been cooking in the kitchen with her sister Katie. On closing the door she turned to her brother and asked what the school board was after? The term school board was not an official officer in Liverpool since 1901, but it was still widely in use. Edward said that Teddy hadn't been going to school for weeks and he was going to get what for, bringing trouble to the door.

Teddy never got much time to explain that he had been getting extra shifts from Big Jim, Edward just started berating him as soon as he got through the door. He had his belt off as usual and began whipping his son across the back and legs. Swearing as he struck, choking back spittle so his curses could be heard. When he stopped, he realised something was different. He had not heard the usual shrieks of fear. Teddy stood up after the beating and looked his father in the eye and said.

"Is that it?" When no response came from his father, he took it as done. He walked slowly out of the room to the shared bedroom. Edward then knew that he could no longer intimidate his eldest son with beatings. If he was to hit him again, he would have to risk a real fight, with fists.

Chapter 14 The affair

All the kids had been sent out to play and told not to come back till they were called. Annie and Sadie went off to the group of regular girls at the see saw corner, Tommy was off to his Lone Ranger gang. Teddy skulked off to see Jimmy. Once the apartment was clear of kids the adults gathered round a pot of tea to plan the next moves. Spike had done his homework and could report that Jonathon Burke was the assistant finance manager at the newly opened Stanley Abattoir. He lived in Oakhill Road Old Swan. He had lived there for 4 years, living alone with his son, after the death of his wife. She had died after a tragic accident with a tram in Lord Street 5 years ago. He did have a son from that marriage, who had been a long stay patient at Alder Hey hospital in Knotty Ash. Spike had learned that tragedy had struck this guy again, as his son had died from acute leukaemia, three months after being admitted to Alder Hey. He was from Irish Catholic stock that went back three generations ago to the famine. He presumed that Anne had met him while visiting Teddy, who she saw almost every day while he was in the iron lung. He had no actual details of their affair but assumed that it would have been relatively easy for them to retire to Oakhill Road after, or instead of, visiting Alder Hey. How long it had been going on was also unknown. It had been a couple of years at least. Edward was holding back his rage. He listened as Spike laid these details out, like a detective at a crime scene, matter of factly – no emotion. His mind was reeling trying to remember details of her long journeys to the hospital. How she often went shopping or visiting her family before returning home, to let them know how Teddy was getting on. More recently, after Teddy was out of hospital, how she had begun to take Molly on long outings to Sefton Park or further afield, staying out most of the day. She had been seeing him, him! His thoughts were dark.

Spike started to assess the situation.

"She has taken Molly with her, she obviously wants to start a new life with this guy. The question is are we going to allow that to happen?"

"No *fucking* way we are!" Edward had almost choked on emphasising the invective. He was hurting. A pain so deep it was hard to put into words, so he could only swear to allow this visceral turmoil to vent. His sister Nellie pitched in.

"Now Eddy, take it easy. We all need to stay calm while we figure out how on earth, we are going to get Molly back here safely."

"Yes we need to stay calm and focussed about this", joined in Spike. "As I see it this feller has no strong immediate family, only sisters. Cousins? I don't know about. So to me the easiest way to accomplish this is to pay him a visit, after dark, and explain that Molly is yours and there is no way he is going to get a ready-made family at our expense. If he wants Anne, he is welcome to her, I am sure you don't want her back do you?" Edward shook his head, words were still hard to make. "OK, he finishes work at 5.00pm and so would be home by 6.00pm easily. If we leave it till about 9.30pm or so, then we are sure to get them home together, and Molly should be in bed by then, out of earshot. The plan continued to be hatched in Bidder Street.

Anne had had enough. She realised this a long time ago. The thought had dawned on her only a year or two into their marriage. Edward was not the smart young man she had believed him to be. His courtesy shown early on at the Adelphi was just an act. He was a self-centred man obsessed with gambling and showing off his winnings to impress others. In reality he had little to show off with. His job was a common labourer, he did various jobs on building sites or anywhere where a few weeks casual work could be had. Moving gypsy style from one source of shillings to another. She had asked her father for help. Bull had been reluctant at first to help her. She had made her bed and now had to lie in it. But his heart softened when she cried on his shoulder and bemoaned how life was so hard without regular wages coming in. He reluctantly got Edward a start in a different gang from his, on the electric cable installations, so he did not have to look at him. He did not rate Edward by any normal measure of a man. He suffered him on account of his eldest daughter had chosen him, no matter how poor he knew her choice had been. Edward was till in fear of Bull. He avoided any direct antagonism of him. He kept his temper to harsh, hurtful words to Anne, never raising his hand to her, for fear of being half, or fully, strangled again by Bull.

Dreams of another life began to fill Anne's mind. At first, they were idle daydreams: dreams of a man, a real man, finding her attractive and wanting to take her away from the one she had mistakenly chosen to have a life with. This man was going to be handsome, really charming and very well dressed like a proper gentleman should be. This man was to be made flesh one afternoon while she visited Teddy. She sat at Teddy's head at the end of his iron lung in the ward, as usual her chair was facing inwards to the centre aisle, so she could look down on his face and he did not have to look in his overhead mirror to see her. Teddy had been more than usually sad with his fate that day. He had been crying a little, she could tell, so she soothed him with stories of how everyone was alright back in Bidder Street. How they were all looking forward to him getting out soon, so they can all play together again. He was still sulking somewhat and avoided her eyes as often as he could, even closing them to shut out his distress. On her part she tried all she could to comfort him, eventually letting him be quiet with his own thoughts. She looked around the ward, Teddy's home, as it was. The windows were tall metal framed and rounded at the top, made up of smaller panes of glass. She could see the park beyond the perimeter wall. There were tall trees at the far end and lots of fully leafed oaks filling in spaces in a haphazard pattern to the perimeter wall. She could just make out the tops of the swing section in the middle of the park, partly obscured by oaks on either side. The traffic could also be seen wending its way up and down East Prescot Road. Occasionally she saw huge columns of black smoke being pumped up from the locomotives travelling on the hidden railway below street level on the far side of the road. It was while she was watching the last wisps of smoke meandering slowly upwards that she first noticed him. He had spilt some water while pouring a drink for his son and exclaimed, 'Oh dear me!' This drew her attention. She watched as the man wiped up the water without fuss and swiftly placed the damp blue roll in the bin at the end of the ward. Walking back to his son's bedside she saw he was tall, at least 5:10. He looks like a nice man, she thought.

On subsequent visits she placed her chair so that she could be face on to his usual seat opposite. Teddy never noticed the subtle change. She decided she was going to get to know this tall, well dressed chap. It started with an innocuous question of how his son was getting on? He had a well to do voice, no evidence of the town twang scouse, he enunciated every word clearly. No matter what he said, she just felt she was lifted by every word to a higher plane of consciousness. Anne had to start concentrating on what he actually said, in order not to come across as inattentive. Their conversations were all about illness and the weather to start with. They shared stories of their respective boy's dilemmas. She had never heard of leukaemia before and was sad to hear that he was highly unlikely to recover. He always kept a brave face on, for his son's sake, as well as his own. He did not want to cry in public. This endeared him even more to Anne. How strong was this man in the face of certain death? She was going to make another move. She hurriedly said her goodbyes to Teddy when she saw him begin his routine of leaving his son. It just appeared to happen that they left the ward together. So they descended the stairs and walked down the hill of the main corridor to the exit, still chatting lightly. The murals on the walls were characters from well-known kid's books, aimed at making the hospital less clinical. As they emerged into the daylight down the steps they continued walking together, across Eaton Road to the tram stop. While they were waiting, she got to know more about him. He was widowed, losing his wife in a terrible accident in Lord Street. She made all the usual words of sympathy and regret, placing her hand on his arm for added empathy, leaving it that bit longer than necessary.

This became a pattern in itself, leaving the ward together and getting the same tram. He would get off just a few stops along at Queens Drive, he lived in Old Swan. She carried on to Islington, getting off near the Monument pub. Soon they started letting the first tram go past without getting on, while they chatted still. She took every opportunity to touch him. These were on the arm, shoulder and finally she took a little something that had become entangled in his hair, letting her fingers comb it while she removed the imaginary item. Her eyes were fixed firmly, but softly, on his. He heard what they said and rose to the offer. He asked.

"Would you like to come to my house for a cup of tea?"

Anne smiled for an instant in her triumph, it was a triumph. She waited a little before asking.

"Is that OK? I mean what would your neighbours think?"

"Never mind about neighbours. I don't care a hoot what they think." She was grateful that he didn't use a swear word to emphasise his feelings. She was certain he was a real gentleman, and worthy of her, she was a Kennedy after all.

It was just two cup of tea meetings later that they became lovers. She let him know there would be no resistance when he made the first move. This was all done without a word being said, so that he would always feel, that it was him who had the idea, and made the first move. She fell for him and his advances, not the other way around. It was a real comfort to Jonathan when his son died to have someone who cared for him in his grief. How cruel was the world? To take his wife and shortly after his only child. He struggled to keep his faith in the face of these losses. How could God have a plan to take away the people he loved for some greater good? His only benefit was this unhappily married woman, who had been sent by an angel, to help him through this.

The tipping point had come shortly after the death of her father. Bull had died suddenly. His heart had given out. He had been to the Prince of Wales pub after mass, and was laughing with Taff over something or other, when he just fell to the floor, dead. The shock was terrible. The whole neighbourhood came to the service at St Francis'. It was not long after that tragedy that Edward first raised his hand to her over a spending row. She tallied up all the wrongs he had ever done, in her eyes, wasting money in the bookies when there were clearly more important things to buy for the family. Not working hard enough to keep reasonable paying jobs and a steady supply of income. She mourned the loss of her father and her dream life as a single entity. The time had come to break free. Jonathan Burke was the key, and her knight in shining armour, that was going to set her free, she just needed a joker of a card to ensure it happened.

She planned a special tea event, as they referred to their trysts. She was going to get pregnant. That was the killer card in her mind that would carry them through the turmoil of divorce and fallout from Edward. The child would cement their relationship. She asked for a small drink of whiskey, to relax her as she was a little stressed, and suggested he could do with one too. After a couple of these and some teasing foreplay on her part, she was ready. As he reached for the condoms, she told him that wasn't necessary for this time, she would be OK. They made love for longer than usual, she thought that would increase her chances of getting pregnant. Her throat sounds when he came were reassuring to his ears, he had made her come too. To Anne these were triumphal shouts of success, and ultimately freedom. She relaxed into a post coital reverie of her future life. A life away from Islington and to the suburbs of Old Swan. She was going to escape.

A spanner got in the way of her plan that very night. Edward had taken his marital right, against her wishes. Now what?

Chapter 15 The Rescue

Anne had to keep her secret. She didn't know one way or
another who the actual father was, it could be either of
them. Her pregnancy went the usual way, the only change
was her desire for fresh air. So she had taken to riding the
tram to help with the nausea, and smoke of town. She went
to the parks of Liverpool, Sefton, Princes and Springfield.
Her plan with Jonathan was taking shape but she had to
broach the subject of them becoming a family gently. He
was not ready in his mind yet to be a husband again so
soon. She had to coax him round to the idea. It was going
to be a marathon, not a sprint as they say.

When Molly was born the die had been truly cast. She was
a dark-haired beauty. The darling of everyone that saw her.
Anne dressed her in new clothes, money she was getting
from Jonathan, and not the usual hand me downs that was
the norm for Islington families. Anne oversaw the painting
of the box bedroom as the nursey at Oakhill Road. The
plans they made were all set. She was just going to
disappear with Molly one day, out of the blue. No
explanation, no discussion, no fighting with Edward. It
happened just as she planned. She packed two small bags,
one for her and one for Molly. Only taking essentials as she
could soon afford to build everything back up again thanks

to her new man and his important job at Stanley. The tram ride was uneventful. Getting off in Old Swan she was reassured with the hustle and bustle of the thriving mini town centre. Walking down the terraced house streets with small front yards, before turning into Oakhill Road. She filled with pride at the sight of her new house, yes, a house! This was one of the new roads of Old Swan, as the area was expanding the new houses all had gardens, inside bathrooms and most had three bedrooms. They even had gardens at the back! Jonathan came home that afternoon to a wonderful evening meal and all the signs of their future happiness together.

They had only just started to get into a familial routine, relaxed that Anne had managed to keep everything secret from Edward, or so they thought. Their world was shattered, literally, as the front door was burst open around 9:45pm one evening, spreading window glass down the hallway. Edward and his brother Spike. They had charged in before they had time to wonder what had happened. Spike had Anne restrained by her shoulders, taking care not to hurt or mark her. Jonathan was being punched, staggering backward into the wall cupboard corner of the lounge. Edward was shouting and swearing at him, he didn't hear what was being said, he desperately tried to break free from the restraining hand while dodging the flying fists. Edward pushed him to the floor, taking out a police wooden truncheon and pointing it with menace at his face.

"You stay there you fucking basted yer!"

Anne was hysterical. She was crying and shouting at the same time, while flayling helplessly in Spike's grip.

"You leave him alone you fucking bully. Get out! Get out!" She shrieked.

"We have come for Molly. We are taking her home" said Spike calmly.

"You fucking are not!"

"Yes we are" repeated Spike in his policeman's 'don't even think about stopping us' voice.

"She isn't yours! She is ours, ours! Don't you touch her!" Anne was struggling even harder to break free, to no avail. She eventually stopped struggling. Gathering her wits about her she gained strength, she always felt that Edward was weak, and now she was going to goad him, hurt him back.

"You have always been a useless good for nothing man. Gambling and drinking away what should have been spent on the family. You are just like the rest of those fucking Kelly's, useless!" Spike slapped her across the head, just once. She bit her tongue.

Edward addressed the man on the floor.

"You stay there you fucker. If you move, I will break your fucking skull open and stamp all over your fucking brains!" He waved the truncheon for added menace in his face. He turned to go upstairs. Anne shrieked as loud as she could, she could not bear him taking their daughter, as she had convinced herself she was. Edward ignored her. As he left the room, Spike drew his truncheon and pointed to Jonathan to stay down. He did as the man with the stick said. Edward returned moments later with Molly, still asleep, in his arms, the truncheon having been returned to his pocket.

"We are leaving now. Any attempt to try to take her back and I *will* kill the both of you. Any more talk of who her father is, and I'll be back. And you two will be dead and buried!" He looked at the man, still on the floor in a bloodied heap. "Don't think I won't do it. I know where you live and where you work. If you want to have this fucking whore, you can have her. But don't go anywhere near me or mine again!" Jonathan nodded his agreement, he could not speak, his spirit was just as broken as were his jaw and nose.

They left just as quickly as they came. Anne ran to the door in the hall, only to be threatened away with a wave of Spike's truncheon and a stern warning expression. One more step, the face said, and we come back in and kill the both of you. She had heard stories of how the police frame people and cover up things. It would be easy to fabricate a break in gone wrong and two people ended up dead. She felt really scared for them both. She shut the door behind them. It was a clear choice, start over again with Jonathan, or die. She really believed that Edward would kill them both, or even worse the child. Anne took seconds to make her mind up. By the time she went back into the lounge, in the Oakhill house, her mind was made up.

After cleaning his face up as best she could, they went to the infirmary at Broadgreen Hospital, just a short way along Queen's Drive to get his jaw wired and nose re-set. There had been an accident, a collision with a car that didn't stop they told the clerk at reception. On returning home later that evening they sat huddled together, he couldn't speak clearly, only lisp his words through the wired restraints. She hushed his tear-filled tones with caresses on his head, telling him that they were going to be all right, and that it was going to be better to start again, as man and wife, to have a family together. Anne said that in all honesty she could not say for sure that Molly was theirs, she had really hoped that it was true, but no one could say for sure. For Molly's and both of their sakes too, they had to put this awful time behind them and look to the future.

On returning to Bidder Street Edward returned Molly to her bed with her two sisters. Covering them over again with the bed coats and blanket. She was where she belonged, with the rest of the Kelly family thought Edward. Back in the lounge his two sisters wanted to know what happened.

"It is better that you don't know", said Spike. It was impossible to read him, he was always calm and measured in what, and how, he spoke. Edward said

"She won't be back here that is for sure. And if she does, she will get such a fucking hiding no one will recognise her after that!" Nellie was aghast at the violence in her brother's promise.

"Jesus, Mary and Joseph! God forgive us."

Edward began laying out what the future would look like for them all.

"We should stay like this, all of us Kelly's together, looking out for each other. You two can move in permanently and help us to get by, and we will all pull together." His two sisters agreed to merge their households and share the costs and chores as one family from now on. Spike said.

"We need to tell the kids something about why she had gone. I think we should say she has gone back to Ireland to look after an elderly aunt. What do you think?"

"Yes that will do for a start said Katie, she had her Auntie Maggie still in Mayo. That is far enough away on the far side of Ireland."

"Good idea. And we can just let that role on and on over time. Then she can get consumption or such like and fade away properly", offered Spike.

"That's it. That's it", agreed Edward, "She can fade away gently in Ireland, no one is going to go there and find out. She is not coming around here again, ever."

So the story was set. The kids would find out in the morning, nothing too dramatic, just matter of fact like, that she had gone away to help. Edward didn't realise at the time, but he was never to refer to Anne again as the mother of his children. She was dead to him now and will be dead to his children and family in time.

Teddy heard the story as they had planned to tell it. He listened, along with Tommy and the girls, to the sad tale of Auntie Maggie in County Mayo who had none of the old family left to look after her, so she had gone to her aid. She would be gone for a while but will let them all know how she is getting on, by letter. They said the post in Ireland was a bit hit and miss and it might take some time to hear from her. All except Teddy accepted the yarn. The girls went off straight away to the see saw corner with their dolls and combs, Tommy joined his gang for a horseback chase, and Molly was happy exploring the lino floor pattern as she crawled about. Teddy limped away, deep in thought about his mother. He didn't believe a word they said. He knew the real story, as far as he could.

Auntie Maggie was hale and hearty and would live unaided for ever. His mother had decided to live with Jonathan Burke. This he knew as fact. In his final moments as a youngster, he had joined all the jigsaw pieces together. Starting with the coat in the hospital. He realised that the flash of green he saw in the ward office while looking in his lung mirror, was his mother's coat being taken off the chair. He recalled how they seemed to always come in and leave together. This had been going on forever he thought. All the time he was ill, anxious and scared, constrained for months in his coffin -like respiratory aid, she was seeing him. Jonathan Burke. He played the visual memories over and over again. He saw them at the tram stop. Her hand on his arm, he knew that was not right then but couldn't place why. Her touching him, stroking his hair! How she had tried to take Molly away.

She was willing to break up their family to go and live with that fucker Burke and leave the rest of them. Now she had left them all. For good, he knew. That could mean only one thing, she was now dead to him, for ever. He would not speak her name again and when anyone asked, she was going to have died, yes, she was now dead. That was the last thought young Teddy had. He was no longer a kid, now he was a young man, graduated to manhood at the death of his previous family unit. This story was to live with him all his life. He would tell his children, when he had them, that their grandmother had died, a long time ago.

Part 2

Chapter 16 The Priest Debate

Cans of beer had started to replace the tea at 382. Maureen was back in the kitchen and agreed the offer of a can of lager from Alan, her cousin on her mother's side.

"Here yah Mo, get yer gob round that, it'll take yer mind off it all." Alan was the eldest of Auntie Annie's kids. He had the slow drawl common in an old part of Liverpool, Smithdown Road. It had the effect of making the speaker seem dim.

"Oh thanks Alan, it's just what I need after seeing him like that in the coffin." She shook the image out of her mind with a slight head movement, pushing hair back off her face while doing so.

"Yer know he was a real character our Uncle Teddy. I remember when he lived in Earl Road when we were all kids then. He made us laugh. He'd take his false teeth out and come an' get yer like a monster, ha, ha." The laugh was slightly forced aimed at easing the concern on Maureen's face.

"He was a real monster when it suited him. Anyway that's all in the past now. We have to move with the times and get on with our lives." The painful memories were shooed away as she stated this. Her mind set on having a drink to help her relax. She had seen into the past whilst looking at her father in repose in the parlour. She had felt the pain of his early childhood and had an idea of why he might have been such a bastard in his behaviour while she was growing up.

Frankie, the family historian had burst out laughing. He was with Carlo and Leo and they were recounting some of Teddy's early escapades as they knew them. All three, two brothers and a cousin, on their father's side, were laughing now. Frankie had a good memory. He was the first-born cousin on Teddy's side and could remember Teddy from when he was growing up.

"Yer Dad was a case yer know" he had a similar slow speech pattern, with just about a discernible difference in tone, he grew up in Islington and never left till he was an adult. "He used to say really funny things". Carlo interrupted to pitch in.

"He always used to say, 'Honest to Krushov', 'not honest to God'".

"Oh yeah, he hated the church" re-joined Frankie.

"That's why we are not having any *fucking sky pilot* at me Dad's funeral" added Leo, taking a long draught of lager from his can. Tony overheard this and remained quiet. Now was not the time he thought. He turned to join the three of them.

"Hey Frankie, you will know all about why me Dad was a communist won't yer?" He asked.

"Well, he was always going on about it, and how unjust it was that all the money was held by a few people and loads of others were wanting food and housing and so on", replied Frankie. Tony thought that politics might be a safer bet of a topic for them. Frankie switched tack in his memory banks to dredge up some anecdotes. While Frankie was in full flow, the doorbell rang again, Tony went to answer it. To escape. It was his older brother Michael, the extravert of the family, he was larger than life and more outrageous, par for the course for a gay man.

"Who's here?" He asked Tony, not waiting for any response, just pushing passed him to enter the lounge. "Mother darling how are you, my love?" Mary opened her arms to hug him, she remained seated, he gave a histrionic performance of an embrace and kissing greeting.

"I need a drink" I'll have whiskey thanks Tony." Tony went into the kitchen for a glass.

"Is that our Michael?" asked Leo.

"Yeah, can't yer hear him?" replied Tony. Frankie was not sure if it was politically correct to remark on Michael's sexuality, he didn't know if he was out. Not that you needed to think about it, it was obvious.

"He's on the whiskey already" added Tony.

"Oh fucking hell!" added Leo, "He'll be a pain in the fucking arse in a bit."

"Hey Tony, go easy on his whiskey, he'll be screeching even more than usual today" said Leo.

Michael continued his kissing and embracing routine as he worked his way along the assembly of couched women.

"Auntie Annie, how are you?" Not listening to her reply, eyes on Teddy's youngest sister, "Auntie Molly! How are you feeling?" His hand was on her arm, this time he did make eye contact and appear to listen.

"Oh I'm OK thanks lad", Molly had a deep throaty voice and a slow staccato laugh. Tony brought the drink in and gave it to Michael.

"Oh fucking hell Tony, is that all you've got! That won't even touch the fucking sides!" Swilling it down in one, he returned the glass to Tony and said, "Now I will have a proper one, thank you darling." Tony looked sideways at his older brother and returned to the kitchen without a word. He poured another whiskey and returned.

"Now that is more like it my lovely little brother you" blowing a kiss.

Tony returned to the kitchen. He made eye contact with his cousin John, one of Auntie Annie's big family.

"Hey Tony! Do you know where I can get a hatchet from?" Puzzled by the question Tony thought for a moment then replied.

"Greenberg's is the nearest. Why do want a hatchet?"

Taking a slug from his lager can, allowing the liquid to slide down his throat, before he answered.

"Because I want to cut some fuckers hands off!" Tony was always amazed at the colour that surrounded the wider family.

"Oh, OK." Was all that Tony could think of saying? He did not want to get stuck into a long discourse about life on the Cantril Farm estate.

Frankie was recounting tales of the old times about Teddy.

"Hey yer Dad was alright yer know. He was dead strong, those arms on him. I remember when our hoist broke in the warehouse. Yer Dad just pulled on the rope and hauled the bundles right up. He had massive arms on him. My Dad used to give him a break once in a while, yer know, when Teddy's work dried up. He would have us in stitches. He was always making stuff up about anything, if it was in the paper, he had something to say about it and it was dead funny. I remember once I was having a sip of tea and he said something, I spat me tea and a gob full of butty all over the place!"

Frankie decided to change tack, "Hey yer dad was inside a couple of times yer know?"

"Yeah we know" replied Leo. "He told us lots of stories about Walton."

"Did yer hear about the cuddly toy?" Asked Frankie. Tony got tired of listening to all the old stories again and went over to chat with Christine, another cousin on his Dad's side, she was Molly's eldest. He engaged her in light conversation, not wanting to get into anything too emotional, he had a plan brewing in the back of his mind of how he might be able to persuade Leo to change his mind about the priest.

Mary had gone upstairs to the bathroom. Teddy's sister Annie addressed Molly in hushed tones.

"Do you think Maggie will know about our Teddy?"

"Oh fuck, I hadn't thought about her in years. You're right, she should know. He is, was, the father of her two, Maria and Edward." Responded Molly.

Annie Cotton joined in uninvited.

"I think she should know. Our Mary would agree too."

"Is anyone in contact with her?" asked the other Annie.

"I don't think so. I wouldn't know how to get in touch with her. The last I heard of Maggie she was living in Old Swan." Offered Molly.

Sadie, the eldest of Teddy's three sisters had a suggestion.

"I can find her. I live in the Swan. I'll ask Dezzy, the postman, he'll know."

"Good idea!" said Molly.

"He never ever told us he had other kids" added Michael, "but we knew. Our Sharon met his daughter once, by accident. She was in the Red House in the Swan and a woman came over to her and asked if she was Teddy Kelly's daughter. Our Sharon said, 'Yes, why' so this woman said, 'He is my Dad too.' So, our Sharon gets chatting to her to see what the goss' was. She told her loads of stuff, like how he went to prison, and that her brother was born while he was in there. When he came out, they only lasted a few months, before her mother chased him out the house for carrying on and bringing more trouble to her door."

"Oh g'way!" interjected Annie, she was aware of how her sister met Teddy not all the gory details about his ex though.

"Sharon might know where she lives, and she can let her Mum know about him" suggested Michael. He flamboyantly took a sip of his whiskey expecting a cheer or some form of accolade for his insightful contribution. None came. He carried on regardless.

"I wonder if he ever contacted them at all?" asked Michael.

The shrugs and blank faces told him no one knew.

Mary returned to the room, re-taking her seat on the couch. Her sister in law started the thread off.

"Mary we were just saying if Teddy's ex and her kids knew about him yet. Sadie here said she could ask the local postman and Michael says Sharon might know where Maria lives. What do think?"

"Oh yes she should know. Won't she see it in the Echo notice though?" Mary was not keen on having Teddy's ex and his other kids at the funeral. And, all the pressure over the priest was still weighing heavy on her nerves. She was looking for someone to save her from the anxiety.

Michael announced that he needed another drink and went into the kitchen.

"Francis! My dear old Pearler, how the Devil are you?" extolled Michael to his cousin.

"I am good thanks Michael" replied Francis, "Sorry to hear about your Dad."

"Oh he was just waiting for it to happen. Always fucking angry all the time. Remember when we came back from St Helens, pearl diving, and he went mad because he wanted size 14s and all we could get were 12s! Ha he was beside himself, all because he had promised to get 14s for the sisters across the road."

"What do mean, pearl diving hey Michael?" asked Frankie overhearing him.

"Oh that's what he called shoplifting, apparently in gaol they have silly names for things. They used rhyming slang too, like have you got any Tom. Was have you got any jewellery, Tom Foolery. He was just a fucking show off."

"Hey is that right? You were shoplifters, you two?" pointing to Francis and Michael. Francis shrugged his shoulders in his usual way of self-deprecation, a disarming mannerism he had developed, and smiled an apologetic grin, a hint of a nod confirmed their illicit past occupation.

"Well fuck me! Are yers still at it? I could do with some stuff!" he laughed.

Chapter 17 The First Barra

Teddy had been working on and off for Big Jim Metcalf for some time. He had carved out a niche with the unloading of freight wagons and the transfer to the waiting trucks. He now stood on the freight wagon and unstacked the bundles, offering them in a ready to pick up manner for the floor guy to transfer to the truck. His arms and upper body strength coupled with his weight transference were what helped him do this heavy manual work. He worked with Weasel Wally, he was what was commonly known as a 'head worker', someone who looked for the easiest way to get out of working, or if not, the least effort required to get something done. Wally even looked weasel like in his appearance, he had a long face and a perennial nose twitch that showed his incisors whenever the spasm occurred. He was the first to break off work, for the tea and meal breaks and the last to start again. He could weasel his way out of anything or, weasel his way into something that was considered a better option. It was a better option that helped Teddy to get an idea for making some more money. Big Jim had said a half ton of potatoes were to be wheeled across to Queen's Square fruit and vegetable market, to JW's. Wally was as eager as anything to do it. This puzzled Teddy, "Why the hurry Wally?" he asked.

"The early bird catches the worm" he replied with his trademark twitch for emphasis.

"How come?"

"Preparation is everything my young apprentice. If you're going to get an edge, you have to have a plan."

"I'm listening."

"I know I can sell a bag of spuds to Coxy for half of what he usually pays. So all I need to do is let JW think he's got all his bags, with a clever stacking trick." With this Weasel Wally started packing his porter's cart with half hundred weight bags of potatoes. On completing the loading he said to Teddy, "Now what do you see?"

"Twenty bags of spuds."

"And that is what JW will see, twenty bags of spuds."

"I still don't see it. How have you whizzed one?"

"That's because you haven't counted them going on, you are looking at the standard stacking of twenty bags of spuds on the cart, aren't yer?" Teddy nodded. The cart had to be stacked in a set manner to balance it, and also prevent the load shifting and falling off in transit. "Now for me ale money" he then threw up another bag of potatoes onto the cart, making it look like twenty-one bags. "Coxy will give us four bob for these."

"Two bob each then?"

"Ha! My arse. You get to learn my boy, not to share me ale money."

Weasel Wally pulled the cart loaded with potatoes across the yard, out the side entrance and away over to where Coxy had his fruit and vegetable barra, just outside the station.

"Hiya Wally! What have you got for me?" Hailed Coxy the barra boy.

"A bag of best King Eddies."

"Oh lovely, lovely. Three and six do yer?"

"Oh hey Coxy me awl mate, four bob it is. These are going for eight shillings at least over there."

"You drive a hard bargain Wally, Ok drop it here quickly." He pointed to the green baize skirt around his barra. As soon as the bag landed, he pushed it under the baize and out of sight. Only sharp eyes would have spotted anything untoward. Coxy shook hands with Wally and they parted company. Just before Wally assumed his position at the cart handles, he put the four shillings into his trouser pocket. They had been passed across, unseen, in the handshake. He continued the short journey across Lime Street down St Georges Place, into Hood Street and the Queen's Square market. The delivery was shouted out to JW, and Weasel Wally shooed away his labourer.

"Yer alright me lad, I've got these, you have a blow." The stack of twenty bags looked like twenty bags on the floor of JW's stall. Wally waved to JW as he started back up the short incline to Lime Street Station, knowing that the stack would be dissected piecemeal, one bag at a time. Whichever porter removed a bag he would not count the stack left. The clever ruse of stacking the bags to look like twenty, would not be noticed as they often moved about when being unloaded. Weasel Wally had been doing this for as long as he could remember.

Teddy started to have his own ideas on skimming stuff, literally. He thought of a way to make his own full bag of spuds. It started with the careful twisting of the bag's sealing wire, removing about four or five pounds of potatoes, resealing the bag and with a brisk shake about it looked like it had the requisite half hundred weight. Initially these potatoes went back to Bidder Street to his

Aunts for the table. Then he expanded his horizons and income. There were always extra bags at the depot, to re-bag any that had been split open in transit or while unloading. Teddy began to fill these, to about the 56 pound they should be, by guessing. He was not going to short change his customers. He decided not to brag to Weasel Wally what he was doing. He didn't want to use Coxy as his buyer either, just in case he mentioned it to Wally. Teddy sounded out Old Man Shanley. He had a barra on London Road, opposite TJ's department store. Old Man Shanley was delighted to have a bargain and Teddy made his money, it was a win: win for all, apart from the owner of the goods, who did not know he was out of pocket.

Teddy would chat to the aging barra boy, asking him how his business worked. Old Man Shanley was delighted to have someone interested and let Teddy into the world of being a barra boy.

"You have to get up very early for the market, it opens at five thirty every day, except Sunday of course. You have to know what people are buying, or likely to buy, in your area. Down at Lime Street, Coxy sells loads of expensive looking fruit to the posh people going by. Now here, I couldn't shift stuff like that, no one has the money for fancy fruit. You're lucky if you can sell a few pounds of apples, let alone a hand of bananas. Likewise you know how much people have to spend, so you only buy from the wholesaler what you think you can shift in the day. It's no good having to store stuff overnight, some of it goes off quick. I have been doing it all me life and have a good idea of what sells and what is likely to be wanted, if the weather is good or bad." Teddy liked to learn and would always ask supplementary questions.

"How do you know how much to sell your stuff for?"

"Well the usual is you add a third to the price you have paid and sell it for that. Now you have to know how many units you have in a wholesale size bag or tray. You have to divide what you have paid by the units you can sell and add a third, that is a bit easier when you first start out. It helps you see if people can afford what you're selling. Then when you get the hang of it you can do the sums at the full bag, or tray level, and see how much profit you will make on that. Then it's just a question of the gift of the gab, shouting out what you've got and how much of a bargain it is getting it off you, and not having to go all the way down the road for stuff." Teddy tried doing some mental arithmetic, using a bag of potatoes. He worked out that he could get eleven lots of five-pound sales out of a bag and the odd pound left over would be lost in little overweighs for customers. He liked the idea of being his own boss.

Teddy started adding coppers to the turn in, along with his skimmed vegetables at Bidder Street. His Auntie Nellie was always eager to get any extra money to help make do. She fussed him with cheek squeezes and pats on the back, he loved to be recognised for his ingenuity and manly contributions. Whenever he heard his aunts talking about money, more specifically lack of it, he would plan a way to get an edge, as Weasel Wally would say.

Clothes came back on Teddy's agenda. Now he had a few bob more to spend, he wanted to make sure he looked good. His Sunday best now consisted of a suit with a double-breasted jacket, collared shirt and tie. He had spent ages perfecting how to tie the biggest knot. He sought advice from anyone who had an impressive tie knot. He settled on the one that a girl had shown him how to tie it. She worked in a small outfitters shop near the back of TJ's department store. He was buying a tie and just mentioned that he wanted one that would make a good fat knot.

"Then you will want something like this" she offered him a tie from a different drawer. The colour was not what he wanted.

"I was looking for a dark blue one", he said.

"Yes, but I'm just showing you the style you will need if you want to make an impressive tie knot."

"Oh, OK, why will this make a big knot then?" asked Teddy curious as ever.

"It has a much longer reach here in the cut, see" pointing to the difference in the two ties. He could see that the one she suggested was longer 'in the cut'. He was picking up her vernacular, you never know when something might come in handy in the future, for an up and coming aspiring spiv he thought.

"Oh, I see. And how would you recommend tying it then?" He thought she might be stumped by this, she was a girl and didn't wear ties.

"What you do is take it, like this, around your neck, with the long side on the right, see?" He nodded, all eyes on the girl and her movements, mesmerised somewhat. "Then you wrap it across twice, like so. Pick up the free end and bring it up and under the knot so far, see? Then tuck it into the front fold of your knot, slide it up and down till it's neat and centred, like so." She had the tie perfectly centred on her neck, it looked a little weird as she had no collar, just a bare neck, but Teddy was taken with an overwhelming desire to flirt with her.

"Wow! I will need you to do that for me every Sunday morning" his smile was a mile wide and his eyes sparkled in synchronicity with it. She blushed, she had made a hit with this guy, and she was going to get a sale out of him too. "OK, that's looks really good. How about taking it off? Will it need unpicking?"

"Oh that's dead easy with this knot. You just pull it apart like this" she held the knot in one hand and pulled the neck side with the other, and as smoothly as a magician, she undid the knot and the tie was unravelled back into one long piece again, the knot had just disappeared.

"Well I need to learn how to do that. Let me have a go."

"Oh you will have to buy it first, in case you damage it."

"No problem. How much is it?"

"One and threepence" she offered. She was sure he would be able to afford and buy it.

"Sold by the lovely lady with the best and biggest tie knot in the world!" He handed over one and six and waited for his change. "Now then, we will continue the lesson." He copied her movements, placing the wide side to the right.

"A little longer than that" she suggested. "Yes that's about it." Teddy followed her lead till he had the big symmetrical knot. He wriggled it up and around till it was central on his neck. In the mirror, they were both looking into, his smile was once again wide, and he made eye contact with her again.

"You're a great teacher. Now the moment of truth." He started to pull the tie knot apart. He made no attempt to hide his delight when it completely unravelled, leaving no snags. He was now going to make a move.

"Do you fancy going to the Cinema on Saturday?" He left his eyes firmly set on hers. She blushed again and replied.

"I would love to."

The arrangements were agreed, and Teddy left the shop richer for two things, he now knew how to tie an impressive knot and untie it with a flourish that would be equally impressive, and he had a date with a fine-looking

young woman for Saturday. He started humming his
favourite tune at the time, '*If I were a rich man*'.

Chapter 18 The Equaliser

Violence was in the air. Cinema newsreels were full of German remilitarisation, Hitler's speeches were a regular feature and Mosley's Black Shirts made the screens too. The British Army were recruiting, promising all manner of skills to be had in exchange for a time in the armed forces. The Spanish Civil War was being waged. Pictures of Guernica's devastation and Luftwaffe Dive Bombers had created great concern. This violence was transferred, albeit much diluted, onto the streets of the UK.

Mosley's gatherings were often accompanied by running street fights between his supporters and those opposed to his values. Moral fabric was starting to degrade, according to the sermons, as was the state of organised religion. People were becoming more self-centred and less establishment orientated. In Islington these changes were echoed to varying degrees. The church still had huge followings and great sway on society. In Liverpool the Catholic church was a bastion of the old guard, thanks to the Irish cultural heritage and evident in bulging congregations at mass. Not everyone was of the same mind. As the rise of communist ideology gained ground more and more people had started to challenge the status quo, in discussions mostly, but also in refusing to attend church services, some had even refused to have their children baptised. The individual was becoming more important than the congregation.

Teddy had now completely forsaken any religious ideology. He had cemented in his mind that all the talk from 'sky pilots' and what was written, in any version of the bible was just a load of tosh. He had personal experience of just how unfair the world was. He could use infectious disease, family breakdown and societal injustice to argue his position. He was even angry about anyone who took the religious view as true, as in his mind, no fully-grown man can believe in all that shit.

Teddy was still fighting. He had to come to grips with all manner of prejudice and other people's belief in his inability to do the sorts of things all able-bodied men could do. It fuelled the rage. The name calling had on the surface gone away, but it was still there. A new and more hurtful name was being used, no longer hop a long Cassidy or leg irons, now it was spastic, or the more vicious spaz. Before it was mainly kids' that did the name calling, now it was young men, often as part of joke telling, aping the swaying gait, or just as part of the background aggression that was in the air. These men were mostly bigger than Teddy, certainly more agile. He needed an equaliser as he saw it. He looked around for anything that could be swung clublike or brought down with hammer force. Pieces of wood that were lying about, lumps of brick or stone off the ground all came to be a part of his fight back. Usually the threat of superior violence aided by the weapon were enough to diffuse the situation. Too often though, he followed through with punitive action. It may have been deterrent based but, knowing Teddy he just had to strike and strike hard. His anger had an unquenchable thirst for instant violence. He only calmed down afterwards, and his humour would return. The onlookers would recount their version of the altercation when Teddy was not around to hear, just in case they offended him.

After watching one of his favourite gangster movies he decided that he needed a permanent edge. He had seen how powerful the use of a cosh or blackjack was in Hollywood to increase gangster threats. He wanted one. His chosen tool for the job of equaliser was a short section of lead pipe, about eight inches in length and just about an inch in diameter. It weighed a couple of pounds at least. He dressed it in Sunday best inside a sock, so as not to damage his suit trouser pocket. For weekdays he had it slid into the 'ruler' leg pocket of his overalls without the protective cover. Teddy decided to give this tool a name. He pondered for a while on what to refer to it by, when he was bragging about beating this or that bully, finally deciding on Headache Stick. This was very amusing in his mind. He used the term often when bragging, revealing the sock cover on Sundays, or tapping the bulge against his leg overalls when at work, just to show that he was always, edged.

In terms of work he had now progressed to moving stuff with his handcart, his barra, as he referred to it. It was previously owned by Old Man Shanley. When the old man fell ill and could not work, Teddy had offered to buy it from him. The cost was ten shillings, which Teddy didn't have, so the old man had said he could pay him in instalments. It took Teddy about eight to ten weeks to scrape the money together by legal means. When the final amount had been paid, the old man was a little proud that Teddy Kelly was an upright young man and an asset to the community.

The hand cart was part of Teddy's life. He was always seen moving stuff from here to there around Islington. This work varied from moving entire households over two or three cart trips, to one off jobs shifting large items that were too heavy to carry any distance. When he wasn't moving stuff, he was helping a local joiner, known throughout Islington as, not surprisingly, Johnny the Joiner. Johnny was a calm, pipe smoking man in his late fifties. He rarely ever got excited let alone angry at anything. He had seen so much in his life. In the great war, he lost nearly all of his friends that had signed up to fight the Hun together, in the so-called Pals regiments. He lost his first wife to consumption as it was called then. Two of his six children had died in infancy. His rage against the world had dissipated long ago. Now he was at peace with himself and the way of the world. He could rationalise almost anything as not being worth bothering about, certainly not worth risking life, limb or liberty over. He taught Teddy how to work with timber, from rough support struts to more intricate window framing skills. He valued using older pieces of wood for economy, just removing any nails or spikes that were left in, so that the wood could be sawn through safely. Teddy loved to learn of new things and made a skill out of memorising everything he heard, he felt it would all come in handy in the future.

Shortly after the war started Johnny the Joiner and Teddy were in demand. There were lots of damaged buildings in the neighbourhood that needed shoring up or windows replaced. On one job the local rectory had suffered some damage. Johnny had been asked to help the church by fixing the window and door. It was a relatively simple job to do and took them a little over two days to complete. During this time Teddy got to see a bit about the life of the local priests while off duty. The housekeeper was a widow and looked about sixty if she was a day. She brought the two priests that lived in the rectory their tea and newspapers every morning. Sandwiches for afternoon tea, which they ate while discussing various matters between them. Teddy was amazed that both of them smoked cigars, big fat ones, like Churchill. They had a good life thought Teddy. Board and keep paid for, lots of gifts from the community for their help with incantations and crap, often given after funerals! The cigars they smoked were gifts. A local newsagent had a regular supply from Cuba, he knew a sailor that made regular banana boat journeys there and always smuggled a few boxes back every trip. The priests were grateful. They repaid his generosity one time by not seeing that his daughter was three months pregnant. They agreed to marry her and her beau in Church, and not to exile them to the registry office.

"Hey Johnny, what do you make of all this carry on then?", asked Teddy indicating the relaxed tableau on the rectory lawn.

"It's a case of live and let live. Why rock the boat when it doesn't affect you?" replied the sagely Johnny.

"They go on about sin this and sin that, and all the time they are living the life of fucking Riley, literally *him* in this fucking case", he pointed to Father Riley, his face upturned to the heavens, gently blowing cigar smoke skyward to commune with his imaginary boss.

"Now then Teddy. There is no point in getting excited over it. Just let them get on with it. They aren't doing anyone any harm having a smoke in their garden, are they?"

"It just grinds away at me" answered Teddy.

The house keeper reappeared at this point carrying a tray with decanter and two glasses. She placed it down on the table.

"There you go Fathers your afternoon tipple, to keep the cold away."

"Look at that Johnny! They're having fucking whiskey now."

"Yeah so they are", replied Johnny, "looks like a good one too, probably a malt."

"Fucking malt whiskey and Cuban cigars brought out to them like they were fucking Gods themselves! The Fuckers!"

"Easy now Teddy, you don't want them to hear yer now, do yer?"

"I don't fuckin' care what they think!"

"But I do Teddy, so keep your voice down" advised Johnny.

Teddy bit his lip and shifted his wrath inwards till the job was done. As they left Johnny shook hands with Father Riley and they were in the street before any money changed hands.

"What about them paying for the job?" asked Teddy.

"It's OK they will sort me out later" replied Johnny shifting the weight of his tool box to the other hand.

Teddy kept quiet, he didn't want to rile Johnny any further, it might backfire on him and getting work. He knew that Johnny would not charge the priests for the job, or the materials. Another perk of the job as superstitious sergeants at arms for the Islington parish.

As the pair walked back to Johnny's yard, Teddy pushing his cart with their toolboxes and remaining timber pieces onboard, they passed the newsagent's shop who supplied the Cuban cigars.

"Hang on a minute Johnny, I need some baccy", said Teddy parking the cart's support legs down. Johnny had his pipe in his mouth as usual, deciding to take the opportunity to actually light it while Teddy went into the shop. Teddy waited to be served. Looking around he saw where the newsagent kept the tobacco and cigarettes, behind the counter and the till. There were several columns stacked together by brand. He saw Woodbines and the popular Capstan Full Strength, along with the self-rolling tobacco versions like his own Golden Virginia.

"Pack of Golden Virginia thanks love" asked Teddy while he examined the layout of the shop and the door locks, returning his gaze to the tobacco shelving. Watching how smoothly the young girl picked up the pack and handed it over in exchange for the money.

Chapter 19 The Cheat

The war had been going on for about a year now. Liverpool was under sustained, almost nightly bombing by the Luftwaffe, mainly targeting the docks and railway depots, but spilling over into the residential areas too. The cost was huge. Damage to buildings and infrastructure was immense but dwarfed by the human costs. Dock and railway workers turned up every morning to an unknown scene, hoping they would get work for the day if they were dockers, and if they would be able to move trains at all. Some dockers got daily work removing explosion damaged building rubble, finding bodies of the cocky watchmen on some occasions. The lucky ones got to load and unload the ships as normal, if the dock was spared that night and the boat made it through the western approaches, dodging the U-Boats, to safety.

Talk was always of the people who had perished. Those that were dug out of the rubble, or parts of them, and those that appeared to be just sleeping. These had no visible injury whatsoever, no sign of blood, bruises or damaged clothing, 'not a scratch on them' was a common descriptor phrase from onlookers. Every house that had been hit had a small group of people, neighbours mostly, looking on to see who and what was brought out of the building by the work details. There was always a constable on duty to ensure nothing was removed by way of looting. Life returned to the new normal in Liverpool during the day, and went underground most nights, signalled by the wail of the air raid siren. The all clear signal was always met with sighs of relief by most and prayers of thanks from the Godly. Those that died often met the reaper by chance. They were sitting on the wrong side of the shelter when it was hit. Half of a family could be wiped out, leaving the others to weep and wail, or promise death and destruction in revenge on the bastards who bombed them.

Some sought shelter under their beds or stairwells in the hope that rubble might fall away in the blast. This worked for some and claimed others at random. Fatalism was one way of coping with the horror, compensatory control as in superstition or the way of organised religion was another. Priests would preach the 'mysterious way' of their Lord's workings. Some believed them and accepted it as His way. Others raged against this approach as being more evidence of hollowness.

Business went on as usual for some businessmen in the community. Sol Greenberg was one of them. His business was buying up bomb damaged goods from families of the dead and invalided, and re-selling them, to those who needed new stuff to replace their own broken or damaged items. He had a few warehouses dotted across Liverpool where he stored the goods, before sorting the best for department store sales for their second-hand goods ranges, the remainder for general public sale. He was confident that whatever he bought would eventually be needed by someone, he just had to wait for them to knock on his door. Sol also had a thriving pawn business where those in need of quick money would 'hock' precious items, in the hope they would be able to reclaim them in the agreed timeframe with the additional interest due. Those that could not pay the loan plus the interest had to come to terms with losing their goods. These would in due course be up for sale in the pawn shop. He had a sure-fire business model that saw him and his family in good stead. He never ever made a truly generous offer, he was certain in his knowledge that these people were desperate, and it was this lever he used to maximise his profit.

Teddy and Jimmy were in the Monument having a drink one Sunday afternoon. Their Sunday best signalling that the two Mexican bandits had come up in the world. Jimmy was in a light grey single-breasted suit, black shoes and trilby hat. Teddy wore his favourite double breasted one with his new tie, tied in the biggest knot he could manage. A broad brimmed hat adorned his head, it was a fedora, worn at the regulation tilt of the Hollywood gangster.

"How's your business Jimmy?" asked Teddy.

"Oh it's ticking over, not doing too much, just a little bit here and there to make ends do" replied Jimmy. He had a small scrap metal yard, inherited from his Dad. It only drew customers from the local neighbourhood due to its small size, but it was a going concern, just.

"I didn't mean the yard. I meant the night shift."

"Yeah that's doing OK too, again I only do bits to keep the bizzies from looking to closely." Jimmy had started out as a burglar when he was in his early teens. He was small framed and could squeeze into the smallest of open windows. He perfected an MO of second or higher storey entry, wherever there was an open window, or one with a poor seal that was visible from street level. He could scale a drainpipe like the organ grinder's monkey would appear on his shoulders from the floor. He was fearless of heights. He could move by hanging onto a gutter and then go hand over hand along, till he reached his entry point. Then with a few wiggles and fingertip grips wend his way into the building to pick his bounty. Goods were then sold to those in need of a bargain, usually in the very establishment they were drinking in.

"Do you ever need to move bigger items?" asked Teddy.

"I never take more than I can carry."

"Why is that?"

"I want to look like I am just walking home, or going to the bomb shelter, in case a bizzy stops me."

"Have you ever been stopped?" asked Teddy, curious as to how Jimmy would have escaped the law.

"I have an arrangement with one of the big bizzies. If he sees me, I give him the best piece I have, he says thank you and lets me go on my way."

"Neat!" admired Teddy. "How did you manage that, to get a bizzy to allow you to keep on going?"

"He stopped me one night. I nearly shit myself. He just appeared out of nowhere as I was closing the front door behind me. How he managed that I don't fucking know, you should see the size of this fucker, he's huge, even for a fucking copper" explained Jimmy. He continued, "Yeah he was just there, right in front of me. His hand went on to my shoulder as he said, 'You are out and about at a strange time my lad, what are you up to? And don't go telling me any lies or I'll have you in Walton for lunchtime tomorrow?' Well I was all jabbering on, about shite, when he said 'What have you got in your bag? Anything for me?' As soon as he said that I thought thank fuck, he's bent. So I showed him the pocket watch I had just lifted, it was the best piece of the lot. He said, 'Well that will do me nicely, thanks. Now you get the fuck home before I change my mind!' So, I said thank you constable and was off like a rocket."

"Does he still stop yer?"

"Yeah once in a while. I'll tell yer what though, he has given me a couple of tips on which shops are slack with upper storey windows and, what he would like to get out of them!"

"Get away!"

"Honest to God! he does!"

"Well fuck me!" offered Teddy.

Their glasses were getting low, so Teddy looked to the barmaid.

"Hey, love two more of these, when you're ready. Hey! Did I ever tell you that you are beautiful, and that if I had a girl like you, I'd sit up all night looking at yer?"

"Every day Teddy. I set my watch by it" replied the good-looking girl with the wry smile and stud earrings.

"Here yer are, and yer own my love" offered Teddy as he handed over a ten-bob note. Her face lit up with the show of wealth. She duly put a threepenny joey in her tip glass and when returning the change said.

"Thanks a lot Teddy", she gave him her biggest smile, showing straight white teeth and smiling eyes in the process. Teddy on his part returned the look and matched the smile, winked at her and pocketed the change. Turning to Jimmy he said.

"I'd love to take her out."

"If you do, watch out. She has been seeing some big fucker from Sim Street."

"Hey Jimmy, what are you doing tomorrow?" asked Teddy.

"Not a lot, why?"

"I have a big job on for Sol, moving three lots of stuff to Owen Owens with me barra. I could do with a hand. Fifty:

fifty! That's a quid each, for a quiet Monday morning."
Jimmy had little on that Monday so agreed to help him out.

Monday morning Teddy and Jimmy with the barra reported
to Sol's Islington warehouse. Sol indicated the load
earmarked for Owen Owen's department store opposite
Clayton Square. He gave them the name of the head porter
who they had to meet at the rear of the store in Horton
Lane. The porter would give them a receipt for the full load
once it had all been safely delivered, Teddy was to return
with the receipt to get their payment for the job.

The loading of the first lot of goods went to plan, secured
with the fancy haulier's knot Teddy had learned from his
time in Lime Street with Big Jim Metcalf. They set out
down the hill towards town. The load was not too heavy but
stacked high, so they pulled the cart behind them, both
acting as brakes when the momentum gathered too much
pace, boots singing on contact across the setts finish to the
roads. They were chatting about anything that caught their
eye. Shouting out hello to people they knew, whistling
loudly at any girl they came across, very few ever looked at
the two workmen who were whistling. Teddy knew that
girls were not interested in workies, only well-dressed men
with money, but he still loved to whistle anyway.

As the two worked their way into the narrow entrance to
Horton Lane, they were sweating and a little breathless.
The head porter came out to meet them.

"Are these from Mr Greenberg?" he asked officiously.

"That's right boss" said Teddy adopting the persona of the
dutiful workman in the presence of the superior.

"OK, unload it all here." Pointing to the reception section
of the goods inward entrance. "There should be more than
this. Are you bringing the full load?"

"Yeah that's right Boss. It will be two more like this, is that
OK?" He nodded that would be fine. They unloaded the
cart looking around the entrance bay for curiosity and
possibly a return nocturnal visit.

The other two loads went along similar lines to the first
one, nothing of any substance occurred. That happened
when they returned to Sol's with the receipt from the head
porter of Owen Owens. Sol was in good spirits, shooing his
own workmen hither and thither, calling out oaths of
despair and threats of damnation accordingly.

"Here you are Sol, the receipt from Owen Owens" said
Teddy as he handed over the chit.

"Oh lovely, lovely" said Sol. He was happy that this paper was as good as hard cash from the large department store. All he had to do to cash it, was to return to their finance office on the fourth floor, present the chit and take away his money.

Teddy waited patiently for Sol to pay them the agreed price of £2 for the morning's work.

"Oh yes, silly me" feigned Sol, "We said thirty bob didn't we?"

"No. It was two quid, not thirty bob" said Teddy, a red hue started to form in his abdomen.

"It was thirty bob! That was what I said, and that is all you will get out of me for that job" replied Sol with an air of finality about it.

"Listen you fucking robbing bastard!"

"Now there is no need for that sort of language. I will send for the constable if you persist with that tone." Sol was used to ripping off people, he knew by just how much he could sway an amount, less than agreed but enough to still make the 'take it or leave it' option just workable.

"It was two fucking quid!" insisted Teddy. He was now close to violence, his hand was hovering over his leg pocket, his weight shifting to more left sided than evenly, preparing for the forward lunge.

"Hey Teddy! Let's leave it at that" suggested Jimmy, real concern in his voice. "Don't let this fucker get you into trouble with the bizzies for smacking him. He's not worth it."

Sol took this as his cue for the offer.

"Thirty bob, take it or leave it, and if you are still here in thirty seconds, I'll set the dog on you both."

It was the law that Teddy had in mind, not the dog. He would crack its fucking skull with his headache stick, if it went for him. He really wanted to crack Sol's skull though, but even in his rage he knew that would end badly for him, and Jimmy, as an accomplice.

"Ok then you fucking robbing bastard, give us the thirty-fucking bob then."

They left pushing the cart in front of them.

Chapter 20 The Re-match

It was late September the bombing was continuing. The latest atrocity was a hit on Walton Gaol. This caused the death of twenty-two prisoners when high explosive bombs demolished a wing at the prison. It seemed that almost everyone who spoke of the incident had known of, or knew someone, that was related to one of these causalities, most of the prisoners were local to Liverpool.

Talk of the Hun and reprisal action was common, often fuelling actual fights over the extent to which the punitive action should include. Some took the view that their civilians should be bombed to bits too, while others thought only military targets should be pursued. Violence was again 'in the air'.

Pre-existing poverty, social injustice and the mounting loss of life locally helped to stew aggression. Often this was verbal, just reserved to name calling and obscene gestures aimed at those who were deemed responsible, but too frequently fist fights broke out. If the police got involved the combatants often spent the night at the bridewell and then up before the magistrate in the morning charged with affray. Most were bound over to keep the peace and fined, with a few sent to Walton for weeks or even a couple of months.

If any policemen were injured in these affrays then the punishment was severe, incurring six months incarceration, or even longer. Sometimes the settling of grudges held by officers with petty criminals were dealt with in this manner. Police officer injuries, as a result of an unprovoked attack on them, while they risked their life protecting property during this time of war, were fabricated. The accused would have nothing to counter the injured officer's evidence or their fellow officers' testimony supporting the assault. The magistrates never questioned the officer's accounts, and always found those charged to be guilty. One of those who died, on that September Wednesday night in Walton, was unjustly incarcerated in this manner. He was a father of four and married to a local woman. His crime was not to pay a corrupt policeman the bribe that was demanded of him, and he was even brave or foolish enough to suggest going to the station to report him.

Some policeman had a bogeyman reputation. There was the nose breaker, he always smashed in peoples' noses, with a horizontal swipe of the standard police issue truncheon, as a visible sign that they had displeased him in some way.

They would carry their twisted proboscis as a brand. One was particularly cold and calculating in his approach to petty criminals. His name was Palmer.

Anyone with anything to hide in Liverpool would have known of this policeman. He had a network of snitches, enrolled as a 'let off' for a trumped-up charge, that informed him what thievery and scams were afoot in Liverpool, mainly in and around the city centre. He was feared. This was the big officer that apprehended Jimmy, and removed the pocket watch from him, as he was making good his exit from that burglary job.

Teddy was getting more day work with his barra. The number of people who needed stuff moving while they went to stay with relatives, as their house or flat had been bomb damaged or completely destroyed, was increasing. He flitted between his own small joinery jobs, having parted company with Johnny the joiner, and the barra removals.

It was while moving a woman to her sister's terraced house that he passed a face from his past. He was standing on what was left of the corner. He was smirking with another man as Teddy pushed his barra over the setts to a metallic squeal as the wheels contacted the rippled road surface.

"Hey! Kelly, yer spaz!" he shouted. "Get off and milk it!" It was big brother and a drinking pal of his. They were laughing at the sight of Teddy struggling with his loaded barra. They made exaggerated actions of limping and cart pushing to mock Teddy. Big brother was still in a false sense of superiority over Teddy, he had enjoyed showing him up that summer afternoon. The street kids had spoken of the bull fight debacle for some time afterwards.

One can only imagine the hurt that this name carried when it entered Teddy's ears and tunnelled deep into his mind and soul. For when it eventually landed, in slow motion as it finally triggered the violence receptors in his core being. The explosion of movement was completely unexpected by the two antagonists. The drinking buddy was floored with a single punch from the advancing Teddy, he was removed as easily as pushing against an open door. The real target of his rage was the utterer of the hurtful name. Teddy now felt no pain, only rage and hate raced through his nervous system, directing his musculature to move faster than most would have thought possible. Big brother didn't see any of this coming. He failed to see the swift drop of the right hand to a leg pocket on his assailant's overalls, or the short piece of grey pipe that had appeared conjurer like in his hand. He did feel the pain though.

"Who the fuck are you calling a fucking spaz yer fucking piece of fucking shit yer? Here take this and fucking this and fucking that. Yer fucking shithouse yer!" The punishment delivered in the now stylised staccato fashion, punctuated with cursing to emphasise the heinous nature of the insult.

Teddy stood over the stricken man as he lay prone on the corner. His companion had recovered enough to know that he had to leave the scene as quickly as possible, his footsteps were a faint echo. Teddy was heaving for breath; large gulps of air were sucked inwards to help the compromised lungs to function and supply oxygen to the limbs and muscles that had just been deployed with such effort and resulting force. He wanted to keep attacking the man on the floor. He wanted to kick him. Kick him till his head fully burst open, but that wasn't possible with just one fully functioning leg. He thought about dropping down onto the road to keep hitting him, but his wrath was waning like his energy after such a sudden and forceful bout of movement. He returned to his barra, picking up the handle bars he pulled off. As he worked the cart forward, he steered the wheel over the prone arm of his tormentor.

"Don't you ever fuck with me again or I will fuckin' kill yer!" promised Teddy.

By the time he had arrived at his destination his breathing had returned to normal, as had his humour. He was met by the displaced lady and her sister. He unloaded her worldly goods, just about a barra full was all there were.

"Here Teddy are you having a brew and a sit down to rest yer legs?" offered the sister.

"Oh that'll be lovely. And have yer got a broken biscuit to go with it?" his eyes sparkling cheeky charm and his mouth grinning wide. The sister was a good-looking woman, younger than the displaced lady, she wore a flowery dress, these were the fashion at the time, and a wrap-around pinny over it. Her head was mostly covered with a scarf tied at the front. Teddy liked the look of her, of course he would stay and chat.

"Where's yer fella?" he asked nonchalantly sipping his brew of builder's tea to wash down the couple of custard creams he was eating.

"He's off fighting the Gerrys. The fuckers them. They are bombing us nearly every friggin' night now".

"Yeah, it's horrible isn't it? Every day I hear of someone I know of who has been killed or hurt in the overnight raids. They are supposed to be hitting the docks and we get it right up here in Islington too. They must all need fucking glasses them Gerry bombers!" His attempt at humour was only a little off kilter, bearing in mind her sister was now homeless due to ocular impaired bombers. They both raised a smile of politeness for Teddy.

"Here I will get this lot upstairs. You finish yer tea Teddy and chat with our Sis, I won't be long". Teddy welcomed the chance to be alone with this fine-looking young woman whose husband was away fighting the Gerrys.

"I'll have a drop more of that tea, if there's any left?"

The pot was lifted and while she poured the second cup, she steadied Teddy's hand so as not to spill any. The touch was electric to Teddy. He felt the warmth of her fingers and the touch was just heavy enough for him to imagine she wanted to tell him something. He looked deep into her eyes. She felt his gaze, not taking her own eyes off the filling cup or her hand off his. She spoke.

"Oh Teddy you are a flirt. You will get me into trouble with that smile of yours!"

"Would I get you into trouble? Never! I would always use a Johnny!"

"Oh get away! You are incorrigible!"

"What's that mean?"

"You are a very naughty man Teddy Kelly!"

"Only if you want me to be" offered Teddy. His eyes squeezed by the grin across his face.

"Here, do have another biscuit. That will take you mind off what you're thinking. You're a smutty man you are." Her face possibly said something different.

"Now I am only kidding, yer know that don't yer? Here give us a little kiss to show no hard feelings." He opened his huge arm span wide in welcome and she duly entered the embrace. They pressed up hard against each other. She had not been held this tight for some time, she melted into the large chest and felt secure in the strong arms that encircled her, she felt safe. Her head was on his shoulder. He lifted her face up with a finger to her chin, she looked at him. Her eyes said yes, this motion was seconded in her face. He leaned forward and kissed her on the lips, she kissed him in return. They explored each other's needs with their tongues, felt the heat of their bodies increase with the closeness. More blood flowed into, than could get out of, the vessels down below his belly causing Teddy to get hard, very hard. She felt the changes in their embrace and wanted more. She telegraphed her need by pushing her belly forward and urgently pressing against his with a slight but steady in out rhythm.

Taking his cue from her he lifted her dress hem up and over to reach the waistband of her knickers. Sliding his fingers inside and down over her buttocks he pushed them down just far enough. She encouraged him vocally but in hushed tones, she didn't want her sister coming down too soon. He deftly undid the buttons of his fly while still holding her close with his left arm. He freed his blood engorged and hard penis and positioned it ready to enter. She pushed forward. She needed to feel wanted and fulfilled again. Her breath escaped with a long sigh as she relaxed into the union. Teddy had hold of both buttocks and was leaning his weight backwards against the wall for support. His normally compromised right leg when walking had little strain on it. His own buttocks pressed hard against the wall to take all the strain. She was partly lifted up, taking most of her weight on her pubis, giving optimum pressure on her clitoris, she was oblivious of the surroundings. All she could feel was pleasure. It was good to be loved again. Her orgasm came swiftly, too quick for her to delay and prolong the painful ecstasy. Once she realised, she had passed the point of no return, she let the wave of nervous energy flow through her. She started to breathe in quick gulps, Teddy felt her body relax. He was certain she had come. Eager for his own orgasm, he pushed harder. She suddenly went stiff and pushed him away, their union unceremoniously interrupted.

"What's up?"

"No you can't come, not like this" she said re-arranging her hemline and underwear, patting down the creases. "You will have to come back, with some Johnnies. I am not getting pregnant when he is away" she said with finality.

The descending steps on the stair signalled a quick resumption of seated tea sipping.

"All set?" she asked her sister. "Did you have enough draw space?"

"Oh, yes thanks. You are a really good sister, you are the best!" replied the displaced woman.

As Teddy meandered back to his Islington base he was in top form. The fierce altercation now forgotten in the warmth of his encounter and the expectation of the re-match. I hope she takes her scarf off next time thought Teddy.

Chapter 21 The Priest

It was just one of the funerals that followed the direct hit on Durning Road bomb shelter near Edge Hill railway yards. The shelter had been packed tight with people hiding away from the bombs and cold. It was a Thursday evening and the raid was particularly heavy and prolonged. The whole city was targeted.

The bombers were aiming at the railway yards of Edge Hill. No one knows if they had mis read their bomb sights or were avoiding the anti-aircraft fire when the bombs began their fateful fall towards Durning Road, not far from the sidings.

There were women and children, older men and those infirm for the services or employed in vital industry, safely they thought, ensconced in the basement shelter. Those that survived would tell later how they came to be aware the shelter had been hit. Some had come round to sand and gravel in their mouths as they had been face-down in the debris. Blinking away the dust out of their eyelids, still not seeing anything as the lights had gone out too. Fumbling around in the dark, reaching out, calling names of loved ones, friends and neighbours. Relief when they touched a living soul, sadness when they found too many had perished in the dark and dirt of the Durning Road disaster, as it was to become known as. One young boy that survived discovered that his baby brother and the young girl, a friend of the family that looked after him, had died. They had been just across the aisle from where he had been sitting, no more than three feet away. He was only scratched, and they were dead.

Churchill described the hit on the shelter, that killed 160 people, as the 'single worst incident of the war' so far. It was not the last shelter or sheltering place to be hit. There were more people destined to die in dust and dirt when huddling together for safety.

The priest conducting the service of the Islington man, a railway worker at Edge Hill, duly went through the mass protocol, reading from the open book, saying the words - but not feeling them. One young man in the congregation was staring at him. His gaze was cold hatred. He had dealings with this priest when he was a schoolboy, or more correctly the priest had had dealings with him. He was still scarred from the *special treatment* he received from Father Maloney.

He had a routine of selecting quieter boys for 'the treatment'. The fear and guilt instilled in these boys prevented them from speaking out against the abuse or naming the person involved. Father Maloney was the number two priest, below Father Riley. He too was Irish. A young man of thirty-two. Flawed in his choice of sexual gratification. Confident in his position in the community and the protection of the Church. He had left a trail of boys behind him. Wherever the Church sent him he would follow his sick but effective modus operandi.

The two priests had joined the mourners at the Monument pub after the service. Both had a glass of whiskey, to keep the cold out. Various pious parishioners would approach them with handshakes of thanks for the lovely service Father Maloney had delivered, and for Father Riley coming to see the dead man off to a better place.

Teddy turned to the young man next to him, "What's up?" He had seen that the man had wet eyes while looking in the direction of the priests.

"Nothing, really" he replied. Teddy knew he was covering something. Whenever he found this his curiosity would press him on to ask further questions.

"Oh come on! I can see you are upset about something" he let his words sink in. "You can tell me, I'm Teddy, The Barra Boy" he said with his charming eyes encouraging the man to talk freely. "You can tell me anything. And if I can help, I will". He was expecting to hear of how sad he was at the loss of the dead man, what he did hear sent a wave of revulsion through his very fibre. The man was sobbing, trying to hide his emotion from others in the pub, while he told Teddy what had happened to him at the hands of Father Maloney.

"Oh hey! That's fuckin' awful, what happened when you bubbled him?"

"Nothing. Father Riley said I was making it all up, attention seeking behaviour he said it was. And that I was being sinful making up such terrible lies about Father Maloney. I had to tell no one else about *these lies* or I would be excommunicated."

"Take no fucking notice about all that shite. You should excommunicate him from his fucking head." The man smiled, a half-hearted one at that, but it was a smile at least thought Teddy. He ordered two more drinks.

"And one for yourself love" said Teddy handing across money to the girl with the stud earrings. They continued chatting, changing the subject to a lighter vein. Teddy made to leave the pub, adjusting his hat, ensuring it was tilted just right.

"You take it easy hey? Don't let that fucker mess with your head anymore, he's just a twat who deserves a fucking good hiding." Teddy winked at the barmaid as he walked to the doorway, she smiled and winked back too.

Teddy thought no more that day about the paedophile priest, just assigned the tale to the cannon of contradictory religious shite as he saw it. The story came back, much nearer to home, the following Sunday. His little brother Tommy had just come back from mass, he was an altar boy, just as Teddy had been when he was younger. Teddy recalled the conversation in the Monument.

"Hey Tommy. Who was the priest today?"

"Father Maloney. Why?"

"Does he ever talk to you on your own?" The question put Tommy at great unease. Teddy saw the change in his body language, he had become defensive.

"No! No." replied Tommy lying. He turned his head away from his older brother to hide his face, that told a different story.

Teddy knew straight away that something was definitely wrong here. He pressed Tommy.

"Does Father Riley do it too?"

"No he doesn't do it, it's just…" his phrase stopped when he realised that he had given the lie away.

Teddy was raging instantly. His mind whirling on what he would do to that fucker. Slowly he came to his senses. There was no way he would get away with beating the living daylights out of a priest, or was there?

He planned how it would go. The community, and the law, would never stand for the beating of a priest, even a paedophile one, so a public humiliation was out of the question thought Teddy. He had to do it differently. It was not long before he came up with a plan that would work.

Teddy spent a week watching Father Maloney's movements around the Islington parish. He had to keep telling himself not to rush in and beat his head to a pulp, he had a plan and had to stick to it. As he watched the clergy man move about the parish, he was building up more reasons to hate the whole idea of organised religion, cementing his belief with various mental vignettes. There was no way in the world he was going inside a church again, ever.

Karma came to meet Father Maloney on the stairwell of a tenement in Canterbury Street. It was late afternoon when Teddy made his move. The daylight was fading fast that December day and Father Maloney's dark overcoat and hat helped him to blend into the gloom of the stairwell. He had been ministering to an old man who was not expected to make it through the night, he certainly couldn't make the shelter in his consumptive state.

The shock of being pressed hard against the stairwell wall, as he turned on the halfway landing, made Father Maloney gasp for breath. The hand on his throat that pinned him to the bricks was vice tight. No air was getting passed the blocked trachea. As he fought for breath, that would not come, he was terrified he was going to die. If not from asphyxiation, then from the short clublike thing that was pressed against his face. The angry man that held him in the position of imminent death began to speak quietly.

"Listen to me you fucking piece of shit. Don't you touch my brother or any other little kid again from round here, or I will fucking kill you. Do yer hear me?"

The eyes were wildly looking round for help. None was available. He did not want to die. He nodded his head, only slight movement was possible due to the grip that held him, poised for dispatch to his own judgement day. The grip eased, slightly, carbon dioxide laden air came out and was replaced with fresh, life giving oxygen. He was alive, just, he thought. As his brain began to function better with the supply of oxygenated blood served upwards by his carotid arteries, he started to protest. His air supply was stopped again with just a slight movement of Teddy's fingers.

"Did you hear me?" asked Teddy. "No fucking ifs or buts about it!" he added. Death was waiting patiently in the stairwell ready to offer his services, despite being fully engaged across the world in this time of war, if Teddy went fully through with his plan. To kill the priest, if it came to that, and disguise his body so that he would appear to be just another victim of the bombing, caught before he could make the shelter. Father Maloney decided he was not ready to meet his maker and nodded agreement again, this time no protests came out when the air exchange took place.

"You are leaving this parish now yer fucker. I don't care where you go, but if I hear of any other little kids that get touched by you, I will come back for yer, and then you will find out about the fuckin' afterlife first hand!" To emphasise the warning Teddy gave the priest a short, sharp and very painful smack to his face with the headache stick.

"You decide how you fell over and got that. Any sign of the law or anything else and you will die. I promise yer that!"

Father Maloney stayed on the stairwell for several minutes, his hand pressed to his swelling cheek. The bone had been fractured he later learned. The casualty staff at the Royal Infirmary treated his fall injury. They were sympathetic when told the story of how he had fallen in the rubble of the holler in Canterbury Street, just after administering the last rites to one of his flock. He had been hurrying to get back to the rectory before the next air raid siren went off.

He asked Father Riley for a transfer back to Ireland blaming a bout of disbelief about his mission for the church. Father Riley was saddened to hear that he needed to leave. He would miss him dearly, as would the congregation and the choir. He was a good priest, and choir master, thought Father Riley.

Teddy insisted that Tommy stopped being an altar boy. The full story about why, only came out years later.

Chapter 22 The Big Key

Teddy was doing more rough joinery work due to the bomb
damage. He would shore up fragile walls with struts while
the clearance work went on. Collect any timber that was
deemed re-usable and keep it in his makeshift store, a
sectioned off area in a damaged warehouse protected by his
own sign warning of, 'falling debris'. He had seen these
signs around other damaged buildings and they were good
at keeping people away, so, he lifted one for his own use.
The timber was offered to any team of joiners he knew or
came across. This was useful income in the early part of
1941. Teddy was still using his barra to move stuff around,
vans and horses were expensive and in short supply, so
manpowered carts were common. Following the December
blitz large areas of Liverpool were devastated. Wide open
spaces appeared where previously had been rows of
buildings, junctions and markets. These were referred to in
the local vernacular as 'ollers, a bastardisation of hollows
that had been left from the explosions. These 'ollers were
impromptu playgrounds for children. There were life size
Lego bricks to build walls and dens with, sheets of ply
board for roofs and doors to lean up against existing walls
for tents. The smaller debris was a ready source of
ammunition for street gangs when it came to throwing

stones at rivals. These games often ended in tears, reprisals and occasionally lasting vendettas.

Lots of rubble was removed from the city and transported to nearby Freshfields' sand dunes and dumped. Years later this area was to be 'discovered' as a source of historic building materials that had once been used to construct magnificent buildings. The resulting emptiness where there were once fine edifices, transformed into 'ollers of open spaces.

Teddy needed help. He could manage quite well on his own for many tasks, but he needed more muscle power for the bigger timbers and rubble removal. He had the idea to give Georgie Poe a start. Georgie was a big lad, he had mental retardation. He was a quiet lad used to his own company, as most other boys had left him to his own devices while they were growing up. He was delighted with the job offer from Teddy. Georgie cracked his best grin, a face full of crooked teeth, at Teddy when he accepted the job. Together they dismantled various timbers, extricating good lengths from beneath roof materials or other demolition detritus. Georgie loved to show how strong he was. Whenever Teddy struggled to lift something, which in itself was a rare occurrence, he would offer his help. Invariably the wood would move under their combined efforts, visible by sweat dripping from their faces. When it was released from its death grip, the timber wood slide free like a Camel Laird launching, to grunts and shouts of 'there she goes, one of Georgie Poe's'. Teddy would use flattery to encourage Georgie. He had a flare for rhyming words to make his comments more memorable and influential. Georgie loved to hear that particular one. Hearing his name being aligned to the great ship builders across the Mersey for his strength made him feel good.

Wages were scant for Georgie from the timber reclamation side of things. Second hand wood was in demand but only raised a little actual cash, so Teddy supplemented Georgie's timber money from his night work.

Ground level entry was the only route Teddy could contemplate to enter a warehouse. Unlike Jimmy who could scale, monkey like, up any edifice to enter through the slightest crack of a window frame, he had to walk in. This called for a different mechanism of breaking and entering, as he later discovered it was referred to by Her Majesty's Constabulary and law courts. Small pocket-sized gems were not an option he thought, so he needed his barra to remove larger items.

It was an old device going back to Roman times, none the less it still worked very well in the 20th century. Rags wrapped round the wheels to muffle the noise as the metal trims went over the setts. Originally intended not to disturb residents while goods were transported over night to town and city markets. When most people were trying to shelter from the descending sticks of death that fell from the sky, Teddy would strike out into the night with his wheel cloaked barra. He would time the route to coincide with his knowledge of the shift patterns of the police and air raid wardens. It was a risky business. He would have sounded out potential buyers for the variety of items he had in mind, usually ones he had seen while making innocent enquiries, but really, he had been casing the places. He was confident that once he had the goods, he could shift them quickly and have money for all his needs, leaving no evidence behind to link the burglary to him.

That still required a means of entry, ideally one that would not be noticed by any passing constable that might catch him in the act. He called this device his big key. It was the biggest joiner's pinch bar he had, coupled with a length of steel piping over the end. This was a powerful lever strong enough to pull off any padlocked or externally hinged door set up. Once he was inside, he would close the damaged door behind him, wedging it place.

The May Blitz, as it was to be called, was aimed at the northern docks of Liverpool. It still sent all of the city into the shelters leaving just the emergency services, fire watchers, air raid wardens and the beat constables above ground. Teddy was on a revenge mission. He had been planning how to get back at the robbing Sol Greenberg for some time now. He felt this was the ideal moment, under cover of the May Blitz and long enough since their row over the missing ten bob he owed them.

The doors were impressive eight-foot-high and each one about four-foot wide. Secured with three padlocks across the join and secured top and bottom with inch thick bolts driven far into the timber crossbar and Yorkshire stone flagged base. Teddy parked the barra by lowering the legs. He took the pinch bar, positioned it under the first padlocked hinge pairing and extended its power with the steel pipe. Reaching upwards he brought all his strength and weight to bear downwards. Grunting a curse to add extra emotion to help the force.

"Greenberg yer fuckin' robbin' bastard yer!" The lock was torn from its timber home slowly at first and then as the screws lost purchase from their wooden home, they cascaded free one by one, to a humph of satisfaction from Teddy. The remaining two followed just as quickly. Teddy wheeled his barra inside, closing the door behind him and jamming it tight with a folded Liverpool Echo newspaper. He had another of his inventions, as he called them, to help him see in the pitch black. It was a paraffin lamp on a low light, shielded on all sides with cloth coverings. To light his way, he lifted one side of the covering so that it shone just ahead of him, and the low light setting stopped the whole building being lit up and seen from outside.

He knew where the best pieces were stored. He selected them and loaded his barra. This was a skill in itself. Putting the heaviest items over the axel and counter balancing, fore and aft with other items. Casually throwing the rope over the load he hobbled round the far side and quickly making a haulier's knot within the bight of the rope, looping round the cleat and pulling tightly he secured his load.

Just as he had secured his final hauliers knot on his ropes, he stopped dead. What was that? His breath came in slight wheezes, desperate not to make a sound, as his ears strained against the still night. Then it came again. The, tap and tap, tap and tap. He could see the sergeant clearly in his mind's eye. Swaggering along the deserted pavements, tapping his cane as he strode along.

"Shit, shit and fucking shit!" muttered Teddy. Beads of sweat had started to form on his brow. He heard the tapping get closer and closer. If he was discovered he would be in the black Maria, beaten for good measure, and after a night in the bridewell, be in Walton gaol before tea tomorrow evening.

The sergeant had two means of calling the other plod to his aid. He could rapidly tap his cane on the kerbside, a sound all the constables would recognise, and the other was the trusted policeman's whistle. Either way it would be the bridewell and a beating for Teddy and at least 6 months porridge. Teddy looked around for somewhere to hide. As he slid under his cart, he saw a light appear at the window. He was sweating profusely now, rivulets of moisture were coalescing and cascading down his nose and dripped onto the Yorkshire flagstones of the warehouse. Drip, drip, drip.

Coppers were tall, and sergeants were usually taller again. Teddy saw the face squash up against the grime coated pane, one hand shielding the moonlight from outside. Teddy felt he was bound to be caught red handed. He listened for the alarm whistle or the rapid tapping, he was feeling faint, he had stopped breathing in case the sergeant might hear him through the warehouse wall. He heard a different sound, it was a drum beat, very fast, getting faster.

The face was spectral in the gloom. It looked around the cavern of treasure. It was looking upwards at the stacks of furniture. Each side of the warehouse in turn was scoured by the ghostly countenance. He's not looking for me thought Teddy. Then what the fuck is he looking for? The moustache scrapped across the pane, distorting the face even more. It's the fuckin' devil himself thought Teddy, still sure he would be discovered.

Then the face disappeared. The tap and tap, began again. Teddy waited. It was getting fainter as the sergeant continued his rounds.

"Fucking hell" uttered Teddy as he wiped his brow with his shirt sleeve. The drum beat started to slow down too. It was only then that Teddy realised it was his heart beat resounding in his chest.

As he waited for the tap to completely disappear, the door caught a draft of wind and slowly swung open with a squeal of un-oiled hinges, free from the fourth estate manuscript that wedged it, now ready to shout out to the world and his wife of the crime it had been concealing.

"Fuck and fuck!" He quickly assumed the position at the handlebars, he lifted and pulled at the same time to make a racing start to his getaway. Leaving the door to swing, he made his way up the gentle slope and around the corner. His speed caused the cloaked wheels to make more noise than usual. He could not risk being caught, out in the dark night with a barra full of stolen goods, by slowing down so he put more effort into his wildly exaggerated gait. He could see in the moonlight the falling debris sign, could he make it to safety? His hearing was straining to listen for advancing size tens on the pavement. As he pulled down the tarpaulin behind him, safe in his own Ali Baba cave, he allowed himself to breathe more measuredly. The sweat was starting to make him cold while it evaporated off his body, sending a shiver down his back. As he waited for the dawn, only an hour or two away, he heard the all clear siren announce, to those that made it through the night, that all was well. People would soon be emerging from their shelters to the smoke of the still burning fires that raged over the northern docks and streets, relieved to see the sky clear of flying machines that allowed death to fall over their city.

Teddy walked slowly back to Bidder Street, mingling with the first of the night's survivors. He was looking forward to counting his chickens.

Chapter 23 The Fire Bomb

German propaganda was having a field day. It was the greatest conflagration seen so far during a night attack, reported *The Times* newspaper. The night of the 3rd and early hours of the 4th of May saw over 400 fires that had been started from a mixture of high explosive and incendiary bombs. The May Blitz on Liverpool resulted in over 6,500 homes destroyed, nearly 200,000 others damaged, and 70,000 people left homeless. The people of Bootle suffered the most. A wide area on both sides of the Mersey docks were hit by stray or deliberate attacks on civilian areas. Incendiary bombs were a cruel device aimed at reducing civilian moral from deaths, destruction and homelessness. Firefighting was being done by any able-bodied personnel that could be mustered.

In the days that followed the worst of the blitz Teddy was busy reclaiming timbers for selling on to any builder that needed them. Georgie was working diligently and was proud to have a job. He would present his wages to his Mum who took most of it.

"I will save this up. For when you will need it later son". In reality it was useful coppers to add to the family budget. Georgie would forget about his 'later fund' in the future.

The big clean up took some time. Sappers were called in to clear the city streets of rubble. Many hundreds of tons were removed. Temporary water pipes were laid over the streets to supply areas that had been cut off. People queued with all variety of containers to collect water from standpipes. Demolition crews pulled down grand facades that were deemed unsafe, to crash into the already big piles of rubble. Hoses were dampening down some buildings that were still catching fire from the residual heat.

Pub chat was all about the human side of the Blitz. How lots of people were homeless, with nothing but the clothes they stood up in to their name. Whole families were sitting on rubble that was once their homes, waiting for news of temporary accommodation in the spring sunshine, albeit the air was still heavy with the smell of smoke. This smell lasted for weeks.

Teddy was sounding out who might need some of his nocturnal goods while drinking in the pub, mainly the Monument, but he also went into the Prince of Wales higher up London Road and a few smaller establishments too. He had to be careful that whoever he sold to were sure to keep quiet on how they had come about to have their new furniture and other essentials. This was relatively easy as nearly everyone walked a grey line with the law in those times, but every once in a while, there would be a nark. The nark would snitch to a copper on who was selling stuff that the police were particularly interested in. On receipt of the information, the nark would get some sort of preferential treatment or allowance from the detective who had been asking about this or that.

It was while Teddy was chatting that he heard the story of a merchant seaman who was on leave. Jimmy said.

"His name was Geoff Maxwell." The story was just one of many that was going around, of how people were brave and lucky to escape with their lives, even after the planes had returned to Germany. Jimmy continued. "It turned out that this guy had just arrived back from a transatlantic convoy and had three days leave, before risking his life again with running the U-boat gauntlet. His parents terraced house had been next door but three or four to a fire bombed one. No one was injured, as they had all been in the shelters. It was on returning home again that the scream went up from the first-floor window. An unexploded incendiary bomb was hanging from the damaged ceiling, where it had dropped through but not gone off. As this feller went to take it off the broken slats, it went off with a huge bang!".

"Fucking hell!" said Teddy. "Is he dead?"

"No. He was flung out the first-floor box bedroom window. Landed on the coal shed and slid down, head first onto the yard."

"Well fuck me! Anyone else hurt?" asked Teddy.

"Would you believe it? No one else, the thing didn't even start a fire, it must have been a fucking dud, something wrong with the switching mechanism or something" offered Jimmy in explanation.

"Well he is a lucky fucker. I hope his luck last the rest of this fucking war" wished Teddy. "Hey! Does he need any gear?"

"I don't think so Teddy, as I said no fire. A hole in the ceiling and a new window is all".

"I should go and fix his window then." Offered Teddy still trying for a laugh.

"I don't know what street he lives in. I just heard the story before, off Wingy Billy", apologised Jimmy.

"Never mind there are loads of other little jobs to do. Are yer havin' another?"

"Yeah go 'head then" replied Jimmy.

Soon Teddy got to feel what it was like to be caught in a conflagration himself. He and Georgie were busy on a row of terraced houses that had been completely destroyed, about five or six all told. There were the usual street kids playing up and down what was left of the street, and on and off the rubble piles just like when he was young, before the lung. Every once in a while, they could hear kids playing with cap guns, he recalled his days as a Mexican bandit and then later as a Chicago gangster. He was amazed at how normal everything appeared to the kids. Bombs were falling almost every night, and they were just happy to play in the street dirt and have fun. Kids are great he thought to himself.

It was while they were having a brew, that Georgie had boiled up on a small primus stove, that the shout went up. Smoke was starting to billow out of a deserted warehouse building along the street, on the second floor. While they looked on, a kid shouted that his two mates were stuck inside the building. Teddy rushed down the street, hands in pockets to help with the purchase of his swaying walk. As he got to the doorway the kid who was crying said.

"They are on the second floor, it's all on fire! They can't get out."

Teddy rushed as quickly as he could up the steps, past the first-floor landing and into the billowing smoke that was now colouring black and poisonous in the stairwell. He heard one of the lads shouting. He pushed open a door that was slightly ajar and saw a boy kneeling and coughing, his arm over his face, trying to cover his mouth and eyes. Flames were reaching upwards in a deadly dance in front of the boy. Teddy looked around for something, he was not sure what would be of help. Then he saw what looked like a piece of tarpaulin on the floor. He grabbed it and wrapped it around himself, over his head, and lunged forward into the flames. He took small steps as he went on, shouting curses to hide the pain of the flames nipping a thousand bites at him. He grabbed the lad and wrapped him under the tough sheet.

"Right, let's get the fuck out now. Come on!" He had to pick up the lad, as he was frozen to the spot with fear and hypoxia. Teddy plunged back through the inferno, struggling for his own breath. The lad felt lifeless on his shoulder, a dead weight. He managed to get down the two sets of stairs and into the sunlight where he dropped him unceremoniously onto the pavement. He was alive, but unconscious. The kid that had called him to the scene said.

"What about Stevie?" Shit, thought Teddy, where was the other lad. He turned back to the stairwell, took a few deep breaths and carrying his piece of tarpaulin, set off up the stairs again. Now the smoke was terrible. It plucked the air out of his mouth and nose, leaving a tingling that started to burn inside his airways. He passed the landing and still went upwards. He was not thinking, moving on adrenaline. The door was wide open, taunting billows of smoke dared him to enter the room. He pushed on. He knew smoke rose upwards and often left a space at floor level, he recalled how one of his kerbside teachers had told him that most people don't die from flames in fires, but from being poisoned by smoke. So he reverted to his childhood way of getting about. Still covered in the tarpaulin over his shoulders, he pendulumed across the floor! Using his hands and arms as supports he flung his body forward to land on his buttocks, and with the aid of his good left leg he was off again, swinging and moving around like a chimp, eagerly searching as he went.

Stevie was not moving. He was lying crouched up in the foetal position. While he was still sitting on the floor, Teddy picked him up in his arms, shifted the boy's weight to hold him in just one arm like an infant, then heaving him over his shoulder in a semblance of a fireman's lift.

Wrapped the tarpaulin back and started off again the way he had come in. Pendulum swing by pendulum swing, taking much more effort than just propelling himself, Teddy made it to the doorway. Standing up once he was clear of the smoke and flames, he again picked up the boy. Over his left shoulder, to keep the weight on his good leg side, he started down the stairs.

Huge heaving breaths of fresh air were his reward as the sunlight hitting his face told Teddy he was out of the building. His head had started to spin as his lungs were failing to feed his blood with oxygen. The extra effort and adrenaline had sapped his muscles of strength and his brain had started the downward process of engaging with Death, who was again waiting in the wings. Teddy was not ready to speak with Death. He coughed and spluttered, spit and cursed, fought for air to get into his lungs. He was leaning his weight against the wall above where he had rested the two lads. Women were gathering around now and took charge of the two casualties. Shouts were filling the street. Ambulance! Ambulance!

Teddy became aware of a hand on his shoulder. It was gently rubbing him. His hearing started to function, a sign that his brain was once again being supplied with oxygenated arterial blood. She was saying,

"Are you alright love? You were marvellous. You got them out. The ambulance is on its way."

It was still some time before his eyes could focus, a mixture of clearing smoke and draining away of tears. The girl comforting Teddy was young, he did not recognise her, but she was being very tender with him.

"Are they alright?" asked Teddy through burnt blistered lips.

"I am sure they will. We have to wait for the ambulance men to make sure, and get them to hospital" she replied, still stroking his shoulder.

Teddy had recovered enough to accept a cup of tea that had appeared. He sipped it gratefully.

"What happened up there?", he asked the little kid that had called for help.

"We were playing caps when Stevie and Sean had the idea of making our own bomb. Sean said if we stamp on the whole sheet of caps it would be like a bomb going off. It was. We were having a good time at first, playing Air

Force bombers dropping sheets of caps and stamping on them. Then Stevie said what would happen if we did them all together? To make a two-thousand-pound bomb explosion like the ones that flattened the Customs House. So, we put them all in a pile and Stevie, because it was his idea, jumped off a pile of bricks onto them. They did explode just like a bomb, but they started a fire with all the stuff on the floor. I ran out the door first, but they didn't follow me. I think they tried to put it out."

The fire truck arrived before the ambulance. The crew put their ladder against the wall and a man ran up carrying a hose over his shoulder, his mate footed the ladder. The boss fire bobby asked no one in particular.

"Is there anyone else in the building?"

"No. I don't think so." Replied Teddy. "It was just three kids playing with cap sheets that started the fire by accident."

"John! See to the two casualties!" Called out the boss fire bobby, adjusting his helmet as he spoke.

Soon the ambulance arrived. The two men worked on the boys, inflating their lungs with a ball shaped bladder device. Shortly, the senior of the two men confirmed the sad truth. Both Stevie and Sean had died from smoke inhalation. Poisoned.

The crowd were hushed in their voices as they chatted. Teddy left the scene. Disheartened and covered in black soot. He did not want to be there when the law arrived, just in case they asked too many questions of him.

Chapter 24 The Fire Sale

VE Day celebrations had gone well that spring. A re-run of the street parties for the kids that heralded the Mersey Tunnel opening, but with much more emotion and sex for the adults. Teddy had turned twenty-one a couple of months earlier and was now a fully-grown experienced man, in every way. He had met Maggie Ferguson at a VE day party organised by a contact of his. She was adorable. Dark hair, worn up at the front and cascading down to her shoulders. She had blue eyes in contrast to the hair, and her character was strong, Irish genes breed straight and true down the female line. Maggie was two years older than him. Teddy was delighted to have such a good looker for a girlfriend. He had begun the habit of staying over with her, in the rented terraced house in Old Swan that she shared with her sister's family. The back bedroom, behind the closed door, was her domain. They spent many a night, afternoon and morning making love as she called it, Teddy had a different term for it.

Teddy had continued his work throughout the war years, it was easier for everyone once Her Hitler had shifted focus to the Russians. Reclamation work went slowly in Liverpool at first. As the end of the war came into sight more businessmen were looking for quick wins, peace dividend was a term often bandied about.

Maggie had told Teddy about the baby growing inside her. He was delighted and worried at the same time. Where to live as a family was one concern, how to ensure steady, straight money was coming in, was another. Luckily her uncle worked for the city council in the northern part of Liverpool. He was a wealth of information about getting council houses, even in the time of high demand when so many had been destroyed or damaged. He was well connected. It was through him that he had first met Maggie. Teddy had needed a permit to reclaim timber, once the practice had become common place. Ted had helped him to get started, for a small consideration of course, he now had the required paperwork should any copper or otherwise nosey person were to enquire what he and Georgie were doing on the condemned buildings.

Ted had got his relative the Old Swan council house with a little jiggery pokery. He had even ensured her husband got a prime job in Stanley Abattoir, processing cow hides, an essential job that exempted him from the draft, as it was a source of food and leather for the war effort. He knew people all over the city. He had a steady income in the form of backhanders. Anyone who was desperate and had the shillings, could get an angle and a leg up from Ted to help their application.

Ted had plans. He was going to be a chippy millionaire. His war chest was growing nicely. He was the sort of character that took everything steady. No ostentatious signs of sudden wealth, he knew how the Revenue worked. His 'Grand Plan War Chest', was a tin. It had been a pre-war biscuit tin of Scottish Shortbread. Decorated with the obligatory thistle and Saltire flag, with a magnificent antlered stag looking out for any threat to the valuable biscuits, now shillings, within. Ted diligently put every shilling he made on the side into the trove. No sign of illicit earnings at all, not even his wife knew of the tin. He had hidden it out of sight in the basement, under a large piece of Yorkshire flagstone. To guard against fire damage he had ensured that only silver coinage went into the tin. As the pile grew, he would exchange the sixpences, shillings and florins for half crowns. This was to maximise the value while minimising the volume. He was a bright button and secretive too.

The big chance came out of the blue for Teddy. He was sitting across the window ledge of the house they were stripping of timber. His weaker right leg, as usual resting on the ledge, the left leg and buttock supporting his balance on the inside. He was watching Georgie do his stuff. Effortlessly lifting timber and wrestling it free from any rubble grip, stacking it neatly on the barra. A black car pulled up. This was a rare occurrence, cars were not common at all in this part of town. Two men got out. They wore suits and ties, both fixing trilbies as they stood up.

"Who owns this building?" asked the taller of the two men.

"Why do you ask?" responded Teddy.

"I would like to buy it from the owner", replied the man.

"How much will you pay for it?" Teddy asked with his usual charming smile.

"That depends."

"On what?" He was all ears. He sensed a laugh at the very least, an opportunity for some extra cash as a backhander was a possible outcome.

"On how quick he can sell it to me. I want this one for my new plot. I am going to build a chippy and flat above it for the manager" offered the potential buyer. Teddy had a brainwave. He was going to be the owner.

"Well it turns out that I am the owner. Paddy Keely is the name", he offered his grubby hand to the man.

"Pleased to meet you Paddy. Nick Symonds. This is my brother, Michael."

"Hiya Nick, Michael, pleased to meet you both."

"How much will you take for it, Paddy?" asked the man.

"Well I was not going to sell it straight away, just tidy it up, make it safe like. I suppose I could sell it to you. What sort of money are these going for, at the moment?" asked Teddy.

"Well like this one, damaged, needing demolishing and the site completely clearing before rebuilding. Let me see. How does eighty pounds sound to you Paddy?"

"Well I was going to …", Teddy made a thoughtful face, the best one he could conjure up, full of hesitancy. Then easing the expression to one of resignation said, "Tell you what. Make it ninety, cash, and we have a deal. Today! That way once it's done, it's done, and off my hands for sure."

"Deal it is Paddy!" he offered his hand. Teddy shook it a bit too firmly, Nick winced at the grip.

"How shall we sort out the money?" asked Teddy.

"Well it will take me a couple of days to sort the paperwork out and draw the money from Martin's Bank, say we meet here on Tuesday next week and then we can get all the legal stuff done at our solicitors office in Renshaw Street. What do you say Paddy?"

"OK, yeah that will work for me" replied Teddy thoughtfully.

They shook again and agreed to meet at 9:30 on Tuesday morning.

Teddy was cock-a-hoop with himself. He danced, as far as his leg would let him, singing out loud his favourite song.

"Dum, dubba, dubba, dubba dum…" He had to have a plan for Tuesday. A good one. Where he can keep the money and escape any come backs from the deal. He had to speak with Ted. He would know the ropes about this one.

Teddy went to Ted's house. He had just got home from work and was having a brew before his evening meal. He still had his work clothes on, crisp white shirt with a tie, cufflinks and arm braces worn around the biceps to keep the cuffs from snagging on his desk. He had removed his suit jacket and still had on his fair isle tank top.

Ted was curious.

"Why are you asking how to sell a building, and all the paper and legal work that goes with it?"

"A couple of fellas wanted to buy the site I was working on this morning. So I thought OK then, I will sell it to them. Now I need your help Ted. I don't know what is involved in selling a building" replied Teddy.

"Well, have you got the deeds by any chance?"

"What deeds?"

"The deeds that give legal right to sell it. Previously without them it wasn't possible to sell a building, now though, with the war and all the fires, we can just about get away with it." Ted was deep in thought, he was in planning mode. Playing chess with himself in his mind, if this, then that, or possibly this other option. He fiddled with his cuff links as he thought, pausing only to fathom a complicated play he was thinking through at that time. Once he had a solution to that one, he would fiddle again, showing he was onto the next piece of the puzzle.

After two more bottles of stout and much cuff link twisting, Ted had the advice for Teddy.

"Tell you what Teddy you cannot be traced back at all with this, or you will go to gaol. You need a false address, one that has a Patrick Keely living there or better still once lived there. I can get that for you off the electoral register. You will have to tell them how the deeds were burnt in the fire that followed the bomb damage, gas pipe or whatever. You will have to apply for replacement deeds from the land registry, I will get you a phoney copy of that to show them that it will follow on shortly after the deal. They will want to credit your bank account with the money."

"I've insisted on cash. I will tell them I don't trust cheques or drafts as I have heard that lots of them bounce."

"That is a good one Teddy. Do that. Also tell them you don't need a solicitor, as it's a cash transaction you will have the money and no need for legal reassurance."

"OK. Anything else I need?"

"No you should be good with all this, if it works. If it doesn't, don't mention me."

"As if I would. If it goes tits up. I will carry the can."

"OK good. See me Monday evening and I will sort your gear and address out for your story. Then my fee for all of this is a tenner, cash of course." Smiled Ted.

Teddy gave Georgie the day off, promising to pay him for the day tomorrow. He waited in his best Sunday suit, big knotted tie and Fedora hat, tilted of course, in the Hollywood style. Nick and Michael arrived just before 9:30 and they went off in the Ford Poplar to Renshaw Street.

Teddy offered the paperwork from Ted and the fire damage story for good measure. His address was real, just not Teddy's, that Patrick Keely died in the December Blitz a few years earlier. It was to become a common way of acquiring an alias in the future, to get a copy of a dead person's birth certificate and adopt that name. If it was to be checked the registrar's records would show it as real.

Ted had read of this in a Graeme Greene novel. He was well-read for a Liverpool lad.

Teddy was sweating throughout the meeting. The day was warm but not enough to raise a bead on a clerk's head. His mind was racing. What if this, or that? What would he say. He could see a policeman handcuffing him in his imagination. Stop it Stop it! He admonished himself. It was going to be OK, he was going to get a load of money. Calm down Teddy he advised himself.

He had practiced signing Patrick Keely the previous evening. When the papers were offered for signature, he almost made a sweeping upwardly slanting T on the page, he recovered just in time to make it a fancy looking upright of a P. The growing bead of sweat streaming down his nose was caught just before it fell with a quick wipe and sniff.

"There you are sir" said Teddy with a flair as he passed the papers back to the solicitor. The solicitor separated the copies into three piles, before allocating them. Each said thank you in turn as they received their copy. Nick placed his in the brief case he carried. Teddy folded his lengthways and slid them into his inside pocket.

"Well we are all done Paddy. Can we give you a lift back?" offered Nick.

"No thanks Nick, I have some more business here in town. I will make my own way. Well it has been good doing business with you Nick, Michael, and I hope your chippy does well." He shook hands with them again and made his way down the flight of stairs and into the sunshine. He was trembling, he had ninety pounds in crisp white fivers in his pocket and was rich. The shout startled him.

"Paddy, Paddy!", called Michael.

"Oh shit!" Muttered Teddy he thought they had rumbled him. Teddy turned around to see Michael waving the Fedora.

"You left your hat Paddy."

"Oh that's me all over. Always rushing about. Thanks Michael" said Teddy. Grateful he hadn't been found out so quickly. He started to ease his breathing rate a little.

He continued down the hill towards the Adelphi. Why not he thought as he drew level with the grand stepped entrance.

"Why not?" he said out loud. He gave the barmaid sixpence tip when she served his pint of Higson's best bitter.

Chapter 25 The Lie

Building work continued in many areas of Liverpool in the post war years. New homes and business premises were key to the restoration of the city. Jobs for the poorly literate and unskilled were found in demolition gangs. These men would systematically demolish bomb damaged buildings and reclaim as much material for re-use as possible. The skilled men returning from war quickly found jobs. Electricians, plumbers, joiners and brick layers were all in demand as the city began to rise from the rubble of the war, albeit slowly at first. Young men, too young to enlist in the war, went into apprenticeships as they turned sixteen. The future was starting to look up for some in Liverpool.

Food rationing was still in operation and the supply of luxury goods were scarce. Spivs still operated at the margins of society. There was no shortage of poor people with aspirations of a better life and the desire for some trifle, they were not going to miss out on the promised post war economic boom. It was this, not quite so black, market that kept the skimmers, scammers and burglars in constant demand. Almost every corner pub had the man who knew where and from whom there were goods to be had.

In the Monument pub it was Teddy the Barra Boy. He could source for you or put you in touch with someone who could supply you with, the item or items you desired. There was as strict code of honour with these thieves. You never went into someone else's pub pitch, unless you had squared it first with the resident spiv or fence. Altercations were common. These were usually sorted with a raised voices argument, others spilt outside, drawing the customers along too, to see the fight.

Contrary to what might be thought Teddy had little challenge to his fencing operation. He was the undisputed king of the Monument's shadow business. Mainly due to his ferocious reputation for violent temper and revenge beatings of anyone that had crossed him.

Despite Teddy spending a lot of time now in the suburbs of Old Swan with Maggie and their daughter, he still used the Monument as his main place of parallel work. He and Maggie had not got married, Teddy was averse to lasting commitment, there was always something or someone better just over the horizon.

She wore stud earrings and had the widest smile and the most coquettish wink on all of London Road. She worked in the Monument.

Teddy had been cultivating his endearment to this girl for quite a while. She was a trophy girl. Everyman in the pub, regardless of age, would love to be with her. She had the quickest wit. Always ready with a humorous jibe and an unending array of wicked put downs for anyone that pushed it a little too far. She had a young family and a husband recently back from a prisoner of war camp. They needed the money, like most people at the time, so she worked five evenings a week and occasional Saturday nights too. It was one Saturday evening that Teddy had arranged to walk her home after work. He had been careful to say he was going to the Prince of Wales to sound out some business with Toffee Talbot their resident spiv. He was a keen Everton Supporter hence his moniker, he dressed the part too. Teddy had been seen drinking with Toffee and chatting with others in the Prince. At about ten thirty he had made tracks back to Old Swan, so it appeared.

He wended his way down London Road taking in the post war delight of street lights lit up and shining brightly now the blackouts were a thing of the past. This was great for morale but had the downside of being bad for nocturnal business escapades.

On Reaching the Monument, he didn't go in, but took up a sentry like position on the corner of the pub. He was waiting to meet her after work and take the short walk over to Crown Street where she lived. He didn't want anyone to report back that Teddy had been in that pub. At around eleven she came out and greeted him with her trademark smile and said.

"Well hello handsome, what the Devil are you waiting for?"

"Well I was thinking the most beautiful girl in all of Liverpool might like to accompany me on the short walk, and hopefully a detour, down to Crown Street on this fine evening", replied Teddy in his smoothest of flirting patter.

"Only if you can keep it totally secret? I can't have anyone let my fella know that a handsome rich young man had walked me home, down the scenic route" she replied in her throatiest of voices and confirmed with her twinkling eyes.

"Well if you insist on secrecy, I am your man, I know nothing about anything, ever!", reassured Teddy. She took the offered arm and they set off towards Crown Street. She leaned into Teddy's shoulder at every opportunity, he loved to feel the contact as confirmation she would not shy away when they reached the dark spot on the corner, near the

Crown Pub. He was relishing the thought of making it the first of many nights to remember when the shout cut through his reverie.

"Hey what da fuck are you doing?", she squirmed and snatched her arm from Teddy's.

"It's my John's mate, shit! I have to go, sorry Teddy." She ran passed the shouter in the direction of her place. Meanwhile the shouter stepped inside the Crown and called out for his mates. Teddy had nowhere to go, as usual he couldn't run. He was going to try and smooth talk his way out of this one.

"What's up with you mate? I was only escortin' her home. She's a friend of mine from the Monument. There's nothing going on here." He tried to re-assure the shouter. He was having none of it. Meanwhile his four friends had come out of the pub to form a menacing semi-circle in front of Teddy. He reached for his headache stick, shit he thought! It's still in me overalls.

"You are going to get a good fuckin' hidin' you. Yer fucker yer!" With that the five closed in on Teddy. The shouter was first to strike. He was taller than Teddy and had caught him with a sucker punch. Teddy quickly fell to the ground, part of his avoidance plan. He adopted the crouched cover position of the poor sod who was going to get a kicking come what may. Arms were used as guards against the flying fists that beat a tattoo on his curved back and reached up to his head. Then the fists were swapped for kicks. All five of them were squabbling among themselves to land kicks. Teddy was in full defensive mode on the ground, but he was clocking all five of them, in between and amongst the painful kicks. The tall thin faced shouter was burnt into his brain's eidetic memory. There were two short guys, could have been brothers, they both had eyes with pronounced turns. Another tall one had blond hair and blue eyes, his face was distorted in hate as he flung his leg forward time and time again. The fifth man looked for all the world like Weasel Wally, only younger.

The crowd that had spilled out onto the pavement from the pub were shouting for the gang to stop beating a defenceless man. Teddy vaguely heard a deep voice shouting something, the kicks stopped then. His ears were ringing loudly. His right eye was closed due to the swelling, his body ached all over.

"Hey that's Teddy Kelly, he's from Bidder Street. He was the one that went into that building fire to get the two boys out." The girl called to her three friends to help her with the injured man on the ground. "Are you alright Teddy?", she asked as the group picked him up off the pavement.

One of her friends shouted at the gang.

"Hey you bunch of fuckin' cowards, go on, fuck off!" The gang of five withdrew, not so much with the girl's words, but with their realisation that the law could appear anytime now.

"Come on let's get him back to Bidder Street", said the girl who recognised Teddy as the building fire hero. Teddy was in a bad way. Teeth were missing from his mouth, his tongue found spaces that were not there minutes before. He felt more teeth wobble in their gum's recesses. Spittle and blood were dripping from his mouth. He tried to speak,

"I'm ah right", he muttered.

"The hell you are. Those bastards really beat you up. What on earth for", she asked the semi-comatose Teddy.

"Ah nothin'." The usual story, jealous!"

"Well we are taking you home to Bidder Street." The girls half carried Teddy back across London Road, past TJ's store and over to Islington. They took him to the Kelly flat in the tenement and Auntie Nellie received him to a mixture of prayers and curses.

Teddy took some time to get over the beating. He didn't go out to work for five days while the bruising on his back stopped him from standing upright. He let Georgie know via a street kid that he would see him straight for his missing wages in a few days.

While recuperating his hot blood red rage, at being jumped by five fuckers, was replaced with a cold determination to get every one of those fuckers and sort them out. He replayed their faces in his mind. The little weasel faced one. The two brothers with north and south eyes, the blond one and the tall fucker. They all had their images burnt into Teddy's indelible revenge memory. It was only going to be a matter of time, that's all.

When Teddy told Maggie why he had not been around he had embellished the story of being jumped.

"A group of thugs, bent on doing some random person harm, had caught me while I was waiting at the tram stop. I had decided to take the tram as me leg was giving me jip, from all the work I had been doing lately", Maggie appeared to accept his side of things. It was becoming more and more common. The lies. She was seeing the real Teddy she thought, the longer this goes on the worse it seems to get. The money was useful. Recently there had been more than usual. She didn't know exactly how Teddy made money, she just knew some, or all, of it was dodgy. She decided for now to let sleeping dogs lie.

Nick and his brother Michael were busy supervising the crew on their recently acquired plot. A car drew up and a man wearing a suit went over to the pair.

"What's going on here?"

"We are clearing the site for re-building. Why do you ask?" replied Nick.

"How did you come to get the site?", asked the suited man.

"We bought it", offered Nick with a slight shrug and opened palm gesture, he thought, how else do you think we got it.

"Who did you buy it from?"

"Paddy Keely, the owner.", replied Nick, getting an uncomfortable feeling as the hair on his neck rose slightly.

"Who the fuck is Paddy Keely?", he demanded.

"The guy we bought the site off." Nick was very worried at this guy's demeanour, there was something very wrong here, but what he thought.

"Well you have been fucking had I'm afraid. Because this is my site."

"We have the documents and all…", Nick's words were drowned out as the suited man waved a bunch of papers in his face.

"Have you got these then? The fucking deeds to this site!"

 In the uncomfortable discussion that followed, and with the police later that day. Nick and Michael tried to see how they could have been suckered into such a scam. The detective wanted to know all they could recall of the seller. The detective was a tall man with a moustache and piercing eyes. He had been a detective a little while and was destined to go higher up the ranks. On recounting the information to his superior. He told of how the two brothers had been fraudulently sold the building and the description of the two men; the charming man with a limp, who wore a big hat with his suit and a hefty young lad that worked for him who had learning difficulties.

"Keep looking for these criminals Bert" the superior encouraged.

Chapter 26 The Proceeds

Posters like 'Turn Your Silver into Bullets' were common during the war. Teddy knew the value of saving for a rainy day. His Auntie Nellie was always scrimping pennies away for when the rain came. Now that Teddy had loads of money, he was careful with what he did with it. Ted had said 'watch out for any signs of people seeing that you have come into money', that was a dead give-away to the police. He had to stash it away somewhere safe.

Teddy thought about where to hide the huge pay out from the building sale. He kept back ten quid, after putting aside Ted's tenner, now he needed to hide away seventy pounds in whites. Maggie's place was out of the question, if he got lifted that was an obvious place to search. They would rip the floor boards up and pull the plaster of the walls he thought. Bidder Street was the same, they would turn the flat inside out. 'Where, oh where can I hide it' he mused to himself smiling his trademark grin at all his sudden wealth.

He had been to see Ted at his house. He was the same steady person he had always knew, no one would suspect that he had suddenly come into a nice windfall. The same sleeveless jumper and shirt braces. The same twiddle of cufflinks while he pondered an issue through to solution.

His voice never rising about the quiet tone as usual. Teddy admired Ted. He was measured, calm and never gave any indication of a hidden temper. The opposite of Teddy. He was the latest 'kerbside teacher' for Teddy, going back to his childhood analogy. Ted played a long game. He knew where he wanted to be and how he was going to get there. Little by little, save it by save it, tick off the milestones to his end destination.

"Tell me how it went Teddy" he asked.

"Just like you said. They were keen to get the documents signed. The solicitor was a bit concerned over the burnt deeds, but when I told them what I had done (you had done) with the replacement request, showed the fake form and he was happier with that. Then they were rushing to get done, so I said I had an appointment in town and had to get going. That's about it really Ted."

"Oh good, good. Now the fall-back position. You can't implicate me in any way if the police find you. OK?"

"Yeah, I know. It won't happen. I would never drop a friend in it." replied Teddy.

"You will have to say you paid some clerk in South Liverpool that you met in the pub, just to send them looking in the other direction from me."

"OK."

"Have you got a safe place to stash your proceeds?" asked Ted. "Don't give it to someone to hold for you, *it will* disappear!" advised Ted.

"I have an idea where I can hide it, in plain sight" said Teddy.

"OK, good. Now then all we need to do is to settle up."

"Here you are Ted, a pleasure doing business with you" said Teddy, handing over two crisp white five-pound notes to Ted.

"Thank you, Teddy. Anything else I can do for you in the future just ask, OK?"

Later that evening Ted went into his basement, closing the door behind him as usual. He lifted the heavy flagstone up with his claw hammer from the tool box. Inside the recess the Stag looked alarmed as ever, guarding Ted's secret dream for the future. He had decided, now that the war was well and truly over, that now he could safely keep folding money in his dream tin. He placed the two white notes in pride of place on top of the stacked half crowns. You will see more folding stuff soon he thought to himself. Replacing the tin's lid, the Stag's eyes seemed to say, 'it's safe with me Ted'.

Teddy called into his sister Annie's on the way home from Ted's place. She had recently had their first born, Jimmy, named after the father. Annie and Jimmy lived in a suburb on the eastern side of Liverpool in Dovecot. It was useful having friends in high places when it came to getting council houses, just five shillings for Ted's time had secured the prime real estate for his pregnant sister and her husband. Annie was grateful to her brother for his generosity and his network of friends.

"Hiya!" called Teddy as he went through the front door which was ajar, they still operated Islington customs, front door always open.

"Oh Hiya Teddy" called Annie, "we are in the kitchen".

Teddy walked along the short narrow hallway and into the kitchen. Anne was sat on a dining chair next to the space saving drop leaf table against the long wall of the narrow kitchen, holding the baby Jimmy. A clothes drier was suspended from the ceiling, secured with a cleat screwed to the wall behind Annie's head. The kitchen was quite dark as the only window, over the sink, was small and the drier occluded light too.

"There is tea in the pot Teddy".

"I am not staying, I want to get up to the Swan early. I have brought the little fella a pressy." He handed over a teddy bear with a vest on that said his name was Jimmy. "I want him to have this for ever. He is so cute!" Teddy stroked the boy under his chin. "He looks like you, yer know."

"Everyone says he's the image of Jimmy, but I can see me in him too" replied Annie.

"Listen I have to rush, it'll take me a while to get to the arches and the bus stop for the 10."

"OK, thanks for the toy, see ya!"

Teddy was back on his feet after the beating. He had set out to flash just a little of his cash with the barmaid, but that all went tits up he recalled. Now though his mind was not on sex – but revenge. The tall fella who started it was the top of his list. He went to the Crown, wearing one of his second-best suits, head ache stick secured in a sock with

plenty of leg length for an easy grip. He was calm for now.
He had his best nonchalant face on to fool anyone that
might be looking for signs of a fight. Teddy took up a place
in the parlour where he could see into the bar through the
etched window in the door. He was looking for a tall head
to pass through the clear top of the door window. He made
his bottle of brown ale last longer than normal, he did not
want to be drunk when he sorted this fucker out.

The head went passed as he had expected, a couple of
minutes earlier than he thought. He had enquired who the
tall man was previously. He was a post office worker at
Coppers Hill. He worked in the sorting office, started early
and would be in his local for about 2:30 each afternoon for
his daily pint before going home. Teddy waited till he was
served and had his first few gulps of Walkers best bitter.
Walking through the parlour door into the bar, unseen by
the tall man, Teddy grabbed him by the collar and dragged
him out into the sunshine on Crown Street. The movement
was so sudden the man was totally taken by surprise. His
breath was knocked out of his chest as he hit the wall of the
Crown Pub, pinned there by Teddy's strong left arm. The
headache stick at the ready.

"Now yer brave fucker yer, on yer own now aren't yer. Yer fucking cowardly twat, take this, and this and fucking this" each hit punctuated by the spittle of rage filled invective from Teddy's mouth. The man slid down the wall to a sitting position, head slumped forward, barely conscious. Blood flowing copiously down his face, left side.

Teddy turned away and with the body language of victory, walked steadily towards Islington. One down four to go he thought.

The Cheapside bridewell was the station investigating the fraudulent sale of the building by a conman. Detective Palmer decided he was going to catch this fucker who bare faced sold a building he didn't own, cheeky bastard he thought. He had quite a network now of petty thieves in his pocket or with a threat over them. He sent them to work finding out who worked demolition sites and walked with a limp or wore a big hat for Sundays and special occasions. Just a question of time he thought, before one of these slugs brings him a name. Then he would get another feather in his cap to help him on his way to the top.

Maggie had her doubts about Teddy. He was often staying in Islington, blaming too much to drink or late business he had to attend to. At first, she didn't mind too much it was nice to have her own space with her daughter. Then doubts were seeded, and they grew into monster weeds in her mind. She had visions of suddenly being left alone if he was killed in another brawl or sent to prison for stealing, or whatever it was that he made the real money with. What about the other women? These thoughts were always present. Teddy was an out and out flirt with women. It was as if he could not help himself but to flirt with anyone, regardless of looks or marital status. At first, she thought it charming that he was always pleasant and polite to women. Then the doubts had crept in, slowly at first then with increasing regularity.

They met in the Prince of Wales pub. Teddy had started going in there to stretch his fencing business, with the permission of the resident spiv on proviso he only shifted stuff that didn't clash with his own. She was Irish and had a lovely way of talking. Tallish with shoulder length hair, parted on one side, unusual for the time. She was the new barmaid and very popular with the punters in both the bar and the parlour. Her tips went into a half pint dimpled glass, usually well on the way to overflowing most Saturday nights, in recognition of her friendliness with customers.

"If I had a wife like you, I would stay up all night looking at her" said Teddy with his cheeky grin and smiling eyes, as she handed his change over.

"Hey! The state of you! You're a feckin' smooth one you, sure y' are" replied the barmaid. Her accent was slightly scouse thought Teddy. She must have been over here for some time.

"Did yer take yer own love?" asked Teddy.

"Too feckin' right I did. I didn't come all de way over here for feck all, did I?" replied the coquette.

The manager whispered to the locals that he was having a lock-in that evening and to be slow drinking up. Teddy was one of those notified, he said he would definitely have one, or several.

Mary sat next to Teddy whenever she was not serving. They kept a conversation going between pulled pints. She told him about going back to County Carlow at the start of the war to avoid the worst of the bombing. How she had worked in service to a bank manager and his wife in Dublin till after the war. Only leaving when he was moved to County Cork to take over the whole county business. Now she was back in Liverpool for good. They spent time laughing and leaning into each other till about twelve thirty. She said she would have to leave now.

"Then I will walk you home, to make sure no one gives you any trouble" reassured Teddy. Her smile hinted at his reward for his gallantry.

As they were let out of the locked door by the publican, they were unaware of the tall man standing in the door space of the Parlour, looking into the bar. Once the main door was safely secured again the very tall man with the moustache asked, of the man next to him.

"Who is that fella who just left with the barmaid, the one with the limp and the big hat?"

"That's Teddy Kelly Mr Palmer, he is a barra boy, well sort of", replied the snitch.

Chapter 27 The Bike

Teddy was seeing more of Mary, under the cover of more business in town he told Maggie. He bought a camera off Jimmy and was busy learning the basics of photography. He was spending more time in the Wavertree area, where Mary and her daughter, Maureen, were staying. He was all flattery with Mary and she enjoyed the attention and the small gifts that came with it. Mary was aware of Teddy's connection with Maggie and their daughter. Teddy had told her they do not get on and he was going to leave her soon, when the time was right. Mary was not going to push things this early on in their relationship, that would come later.

"Stand there, against the wall so I can photograph you in all your beauty", said Teddy. They were enjoying the early summer sunshine. Mary was dressed casually in a knee length floral print dress, no make-up and her hair just brushed back off her face. She was the standard thin frame of the post war years, rationing was still in operation.

"Oh you're a real charmer you Teddy Kelly. You could talk a wolf out of his lamb dinner!" replied Mary in answer to his flattery.

"Ahh, yer know yer like it, don't yer?" he responded. Her eyes gave the lie away by shining a brighter, glistening blue colour, caught in the sunlight cascading through the gaps where buildings should have been.

"Oh, OK then. How do you *want me*?", she replied with a wicked grin.

"I want you every way I can, but that's another matter. Now just stand there and smile before I come and get yer again" ordered Teddy in his matter of fact tone.

"Promises, promises…", she adopted a pose that she felt would flatter her figure and face.

"Perfect, perfect.", encouraged Teddy winding his black and white film reel forward as he took another shot.

"You will have to keep them hidden from you know who" suggested Mary with a tilt of her head. Just then Mary's attention was drawn to her child who was crying. Going over to pick her up she said, "There, there my princess. What's the matter with you?" She lifted the infant from her pram and cuddled her.

"She is a dark eyed beauty" stated Teddy.

"Yes she is. She is my very own real princess, full of wonder and promise" said Mary with conviction.

Teddy felt a pang of jealousy. He had to be the centre of attention, always. Changing the subject he said.

"I will have to get going, I have some business in town", he lied.

"Oh OK then. You get yerself off. I will feed her. When will you be back across here?", she asked.

"Tomorrow or the next day, it all depends on how things go in town. Meanwhile you take care round here! That gunman could still be in Wavertree and he might have a thing for beautiful women."

"He will be far gone. No one in their right mind would stay in the area where they have just shot dead two fellas. Besides that was months ago now, March wasn't it?"

"Yeah, well yer never know. Right I'm off, see yer soon." He gave her a pecked kiss onto closed lips and as she turned round a smack on her bum for good measure.

"Cheeky!" was all she said as he readied himself for the bike ride back to Islington. He slung the Leica over his shoulder and fitted bicycle clips to his trousers. He gripped the handlebars and shouted a farewell in Mary's direction. He scooted with his weaker right leg and then stepped through the bike's frame. It was a woman's designed bike.

He had raised the seat and handlebars almost to their full height, so he could peddle properly, the style of bike was chosen, not as it was the only one available, but so he could step through the frame and not have to lift his weaker right leg over the saddle.

He peddled confidently albeit slowly to allow his right leg to coast mostly, just adding a little weight to the peddle when required. He had a technique, like in most things he did, that compensated for the weakness, he pushed down with the heel of the right foot to add traction. His calf muscles were still wanting when it came to strength. He looked funny in his bike riding, just like when walking, but if was functional. He needed to get across several bus or tram routes to get to Wavertree from Islington, or Old Swan, to see his colleen with the flashing eyes and promise of wicked naughtiness.

As Teddy was heading over to Islington that afternoon, he saw a face from last year. It was one of the guys who had set about him outside the Crown Pub. He was the other tall one with the fair hair. The blond guy was leaning against the railings to Crown Street Park. Teddy had been using the inclines to make his journey easier, coasting downhill, no matter how slight the fall, was easier than peddling up one.

He saw his opportunity. Looking around for any sign of the law or busy bodies, seeing none he went into revenge mode.

Stepping through the frame, scooting to a halt, he flung the bike against the railings. Looking round to see what the noise was, the blond guy was taken by surprise. The lead pipe was out of the pocket and flying in the direction of his face. He could not say later what hurt first, the pipe or his head, as it was pushed by the hand on his throat against the railings. Teddy had done his trademark left arm lunge, his weight behind it, to pin the guy to the railings, trapping his head between the gap. The right arm bringing the lead pipe down and across the bridge of his nose, breaking it as it landed. Invective and spittle showered the offender. Punishment was being delivered by the judge, jury and victim of the earlier crime.

Teddy calmly got back on his bike, scooting a start along Crown Street, stepping through once again to continue his journey. Only wiping sweat and a few spots of the guys blood off his own face, which had been too close while shouting into the stricken one. Just one of those fuckers to go he mused. He had seen and sorted the two look a likes with the north and south eyes previously. He had stolen the

Nose Breakers technique to permanently mark his attackers. Both now sported crooked bridges to their noses, which added more character to their matching strabismus looks. Just the weasel faced fucker to go now, he thought, as he kept a mental track of his tormentors. Revenge was a long game.

Unknown to Teddy a detective had been asking about him around the pubs in town. He had been buying snitches drinks in exchange for any information on his whereabouts, usual drinking places, women he saw. The detective was building a case of how Teddy had managed to pull the wool over the Symonds brothers' eyes and their solicitor to sell them a building he didn't own. He knew enough to pull him in now, but he played a cautious game. He wanted to ensure that any criminal he landed was convicted and sent down, he had a reputation to think of. When he was satisfied that Teddy had two addresses; Bidder Street tenement and a floozie's place in Old Swan, he was ready to pounce. He arranged for two other detectives to accompany him to Bidder Street on the Sunday morning, before opening time. He had been assured that Teddy would be in that particular morning, by a snitch in exchange for two pints of Higson's.

They politely knocked on the door which was opened by his Auntie Nellie. She had seen the police here before, when someone had complained about Teddy fighting - as usual.

"How can I help you officers?" she asked.

"We want to have a word with Teddy please" said the overly polite senior detective.

"Well he's not here I'm afraid, he didn't stay over last night. Who shall I say wants to speak to him?"

"Tell him Inspector Palmer wants a word. He can come down to Cheapside when it suits him."

"Right yer are then. I'll tell him." She closed the door and said a prayer for her nephew. These coppers were not like the usual ones that came around. She felt trouble brewing, big trouble.

Teddy had gone to Old Swan that Saturday night to see Maggie. Mary had been working, and so he changed tack and went to the Cygnet in the Swan, and on to Maggie's for the night. The door went about ten that morning. Maggie said.

"Who on earth is that knocking at this time on a Sunday morning?" She opened the door to three men in overcoats and trilbies. "Yes?"

"Good morning, we are from Cheapside station and would like a word with Teddy Kelly thank you."

"Teddy!" she called into the body of the house, "It's the police, they want to speak to you."

"Ah fuckin' shit and shit" muttered Teddy as he grabbed his coat and hat after putting on his shoes. He knew he was going down town with whichever coppers they were. He didn't know for how long though. He began his mental preparation of his stories, depending on what they wanted.

The car was cramped with four men squeezed into it. Teddy was on the back seat with one of the detectives, the boss one was in the passenger seat, smoking in a relaxed manner, no rush or threats of violence, quite pleasant really.

"Teddy do you want a smoke?" offered the main man, reaching across with the opened pack to the back seat.

"Thanks" said teddy taking one. The detective next to him lit his lighter and Teddy took a deep drag on the Marlboro cigarette.

"We will have plenty of time at the bridewell to go over things that I need to know, meanwhile just take in the sights and sounds of this fine morning, on the outside." His words were delivered lightly but heavy with the promise of impending incarceration. Teddy was scared.

Inside the station the questioning continued in a matter of fact way. The detective was pleasant and calm. He just stated the facts, quietly and confidently.

"We know it was you Teddy. You have been clearly identified as the man who fraudulently sold a building, that you didn't own to Mr Symonds and his brother. We even know about your help, the retarded lad Georgie who was your accomplice in the scam." Teddy was horrified to think that Georgie could be caught up in this when it was nothing at all to do with him. Georgie was not suited to prison. He would get a hard time, be bullied and for nothing. What could he do or say to keep Georgie safe.

He was quiet for some time. Not confirming or denying the accusations levelled at him, and Georgie in his absence. He just nodded as sagely as he could muster to show he understood what the detective was saying.

"Now then Teddy I need a nice quick end to all of this. I am sure you know that we are all really busy chasing after the low life that shot the two men from the Cameo in March, he is still out there, and we need to be catching him, not dancing around an open and shut case like yours, young man. Now you just cough, and we can get on with it. No drama. The magistrate will be kind when he sends you both down for a shorter time than you deserve, but that's what we do here, we make deals that keep everyone happy.

There it was, the straw to clutch at, to keep Georgie out of trouble that he didn't deserve to be in.

"Well I can see what is important to you, catching the fuck…, erm I mean the man from the Cameo, and I can appreciate you want to see the culprit for the building scam sent down. If I can help, I need us to come to an understanding."

"I am interested." said the detective leaning forward resting his chin on one hand to indicate he was paying attention.

"Georgie was nothing to do with that business. He was just helping to pull out the timber as usual. If we go on, I need to know that Georgie will not be involved with this at all. How does that sound?"

"That is well within my remit to consider."

"Sorry, not consider. He must not be involved at all."

"OK then Georgie is off the hook, depending, on that I get a signed statement from you and a guilty plea to the magistrate in the morning. Do we have a deal Teddy?"

Teddy was ashen looking, the thought of prison was daunting to most people, even to petty thieves like him. He had heard stories of men in gaol: beatings, bullying and time in solitary as punishments. All these were weighing heavy for his own sake, yet there was no way he was going to let Georgie share his fate.

"Yes. We do."

Chapter 28 The Stir

Life behind bars soon settled into a routine for Teddy. Six thirty every morning was lights on and slop out. The bucket that was the only toilet facility for the four men that were crammed into a cell designed for two. They said the smell takes the longest to get used to, they were right. The pungent aroma of strong urine from the four men lingered passed the slop out procession, it clung to the walls of the cell, vapours of atomised urine were in the air. These entered the nostrils of the occupants and any prison officers, known as screws, that came into the space. In the rare event of faeces being placed into the bucket, peer pressure usually ensured that these movements were delayed till daylight, mostly, the molecules of shit thickened the air and they too lasted through most of the day.

The etiquette of prison society meant that all screws were referred to as Mr this or Mr that, never by the first name, if known, and never as anything derogatory, unless it was the flash for violence. All prison officers had a name that the prisoners knew them by in their own discussions. Sometimes these names would escape the sanctity of the cells and land on the ears of the screws, depending on how hurtful these names were deemed to be by the key holders, punitive beatings could take place. These were in the form of unprovoked attacks that had to be subdued. No inmates ever complained to the Governor, it was just the way it was.

The regime ensured that no man was idle for long. The workshops were used all day every day to make a variety of goods for the outside. Mailbags were produced from scratch. Sheets of material were woven on looms, cut and sewn into the bags to be used by the mail service. Shoe repairs and haircutting were special work details. Only trusted prisoners were allowed to get plumb jobs in these areas. Teddy was unable to work the loom, which needed leg power to be delivered in a steady continuous rhythm. He did learn to sew. He mastered the stitching required to join the sides of the mail bags together and the rim draw string hems. In fact he was rather good at it.

He didn't have to walk that far inside Walton Gaol. The wings were relatively small, stairs were few and the workshops all on the ground floor near the centre of the complex. He still had difficulty when exercising with the other men. They set a pace, on the walk a bouts, that he could manage for a time, but he needed to spread the weight better across his right and left legs. Prison uniform forbid pockets, presumably to reduce the sites for hidden contraband. This meant that Teddy could not use his hands in pockets technique to spread his walking weight. Necessity is the mother of invention, and so he set about altering his prison uniform trousers.

First, he had to make the two cuts, while he was wearing the trousers, using the counted out and counted back in scissors. He ensured the workshop watchers were looking at something or someone else.

"Hey Teddy! what are you doing?" asked the man next to him.

"Shush. It's OK I am not cutting my leg off or committing hari kari. I'm altering me kex." replied Teddy. The man continued watching him work the scissors, first on his right side then moving across to the left.

"Dixie! Screw loose." Warned his co-conspirator. Teddy moved the scissors bench side and busied himself with cutting a fresh length of bag material. The officer walked slowly along the line of men, idly watching out for anything that was out of sorts. The job was boring. Hardly ever was there any skull doggery afoot. Occasionally there would be a fight start in the lines of men at their work stations, these were a welcome change from the monotony of the slow walk. Officers would give out a call, and several others would join in, breaking up the scuffle. The men themselves enjoyed these distractions too. Cheering and shouting the combatants on, exclaiming 'nice one' when a particularly heavy punch landed, or blood was drawn. While shouting they were careful not to get up from their seats for fear of being embroiled in the melee and risking communal punishment.

Consequences always followed these interruptions to the work. Solitary confinement was the usual sanction after being presented to the Governor. He always ignored the cuts and bruises that were incurred in the scuffles. When in reality he knew that most were delivered by the officers as part of the informal keeping of order in the gaol.

Teddy had decided he was going to be a model prisoner. He soon figured out that the loud and violent ones got the worst deal. He learned to control his violent temper, to suck it up whenever the red rage flared inside his viscera. If he was put out by the wing bullies, he let it go, logging the insult in his memory for outside revenge, if he got the opportunity. He would let his imagination run wild in his bed. Seeing himself get even with anyone he would meet on the outside. It was not as satisfying as beating them with his headache stick, but it would do for the rest of his time inside.

Another source of consolation was that the law had not found his ill-gotten gains, as far as he could tell. Mr Palmer had asked what he had done with the money from the sale of the building.

"I had a great time", he answered. "Yes, the Adelphi took a lot of it, have you seen how much they charge for a drink?"

"Now come on Teddy, not even you could drink all that money away. You must have stashed some of it at least for a rainy day?"

"Honest! I did spend it all. I did get some new suits, all made to measure of course, and a couple of hats. I like hats."

"Yes we know about the hat fetish. What about the deed continuance, where did you get that?"

"What?", he had developed a time giving technique of getting the interrogator to repeat the question in order to think of a real sounding excuse.

"The paper you used to swindle them out of their ninety quid."

"Oh that. I got it from a fella in the Prince of Wales, on London Road" he added helpfully.

"I know where the Prince of Wales pub is. Which fellow was this exactly?"

"Just some fella Mr Palmer. He said he worked in a solicitor's office and could get me one. So I said great. Gave him half a dollar and then took it with me on the day."

The cat and mouse went on for some time. Politely offering lame responses that led nowhere. They had searched both addresses early on after he admitted the crime. Auntie Nellie was aghast at the intrusion into the family space, her sister took it better.

"It's alright Nellie, we will soon tidy this mess up and then I will give that lad such a hiding he won't do anything like this again, I can tell yer."

Maggie took it worse. She was fuming mad at the police for wrecking her neat and orderly house. Every drawer had been pulled out and contents unceremoniously dumped on the floor, beds stripped, and mattresses shoved aside looking for the money. She was going to give him a piece of her mind when she saw him.

Visiting Walton Gaol was a faff. You had to queue for ages and leave your bag behind. Nothing was allowed in while visiting prisoners. She was not going to let Maria see her father locked up or join the menagerie of kids, wives and girlfriends that queued up either. She hated the visits. She only went to see if she could find where he had hidden the missing money, as she was sure there would be some left over. She hadn't seen any of it she thought.

Maggie had news for Teddy. When they sat opposite each other in the visiting room, she waited to hear what he had to say, the usual stuff about what he had been doing, bragging about his pockets or whatever. The time was right she thought.

"I have some news for you."

"Oh yeah, what?"

"I am pregnant again."

"Oh great!"

"It's not great. I will have had the baby before you get out and then I'll have two to feed besides myself. I just don't know what I'll do to make ends meet." She let the words land in his head. She could see him formulating his lie as she watched his face.

"I will sort out any loans you have to make when I get out. I will do a couple of little jobs and that will be that."

"Oh no you won't!" She almost shouted back at him, raising a look from the nearest officer. "You are not doing anything else that gets you locked up or even slightly illegal, ever! Do you hear me Teddy Kelly?"

"Yeah, yeah. I hear you. OK. I will still sort your loans out though, just have to get a proper job that's all."

"What about this missing money? You have got some stashed away. That's what they say."

"Who says that?"

"The police for a start!"

"Take no notice. I had to pay off the loans I had with Sharky Shaw, he knows how to charge interest that fucker does. Also I had to give me fair share into Auntie Nellie, she had been borrowing too. Then I had a couple of suits made, to look nice for yer. And we went to the Adelphi a few times, didn't we? So it all added up and now I'm skint again and locked up, so I have no money." He almost believed himself on that one, he lived the lie to make it convincing, just like he did with the original police interrogations. He had plans for when he got out. Mary had even been in to see him, just to keep in touch she said. It was because he was charming, and had a few bob, he thought.

Try as she might Maggie got nowhere near to finding out where, if any, his money might be.

The money was itching at someone else. Despite being extremely busy chasing ghosts in the Cameo case, he couldn't get the image of the smiling, polite Teddy Kelly out of his head. He knew Teddy was lying about spending it all. 'I will get that cocky fucker' thought Mr Palmer.

A breakthrough had happened in the Cameo case. Despite all the time spent, and thousands of interviews that had taken place, the police had nothing at all to go on in the double murder Wavertree cinema case, known as the Cameo Murders in the papers. An anonymous letter had been sent implicating a petty criminal type. The evidence was thin, and from his time in the law courts as a constable to the magistrates, he knew that more rope was required to secure a conviction. He had built a strong case, in his mind, against a guy called George Kelly as a result of the letter. The conviction would need more than just this though. He played a long game and despite his superior's concerns kept fleshing out the details. He needed an ace. He needed the accomplice, by all accounts there had been a second man at the cinema that Saturday night, to cough that it was George Kelly that did the killing. When he had someone in the frame, he would make the offer. He would be safe from the gallows if, and only if, he swore that it was Kelly. Yes, he would go to gaol but that was what scum deserved.

A possible patsy came into his mind when he discovered that Teddy Kelly had another girlfriend that lived in Wavertree. Yes, that would be a nice coincidence, wouldn't it? Both just happened to be called Kelly.

He asked his junior to dig out the usual about Teddy Kelly and his whereabouts on the night of the Cameo job.

Chapter 29 The Frame

Mr Palmer was disappointed when his junior returned with the copious amount of people who had definitely seen Teddy in the Monument that March Saturday night. He had had a win on the horses they said. He was quite tipsy and showing off his lady friend, a Mary Byrne of Wavertree. Apparently, she is a looker added the junior.

Never mind thought Palmer, it happens. Shame I can't teach that smarmy fucker a lesson for not telling me where his money was. 'All in good time. All in good time' he repeated to himself.

"Now this Connolly guy. Where are we up to with him?" he asked.

Teddy had acquired a new skill in Walton Gaol, he was now trusted to cut prisoner's hair. He learned from an old prisoner who had been a barber on the outside. Harry was in for something or other, serving 10 years. Teddy never asked him what for as was usual with fellow inmates. Harry had two more to go. He was proud to be a barber. He had kept up to date with styles by watching the visitors that came to Walton, and also the screws. The officers were usually conservative in their hairstyles. Some of the younger ones, who had migrated into the same line of work as their fathers or, as freemasons were gifted a steady job for life, had more adventurous cuts. Still short at the back and sides but longer on the top, this was kept in place with a pomade such as Brylcream. The more fastidious wearer always kept the ear margin clear and extra short, the side part was razor sharp, indicating that he took great care with his appearance.

No electric clippers were available inside, although they were now normal on the outside, possibly due to safety concerns, but probably due to budget restrictions. The regime was old school in Walton Gaol. Teddy learned to grip the hand operated clippers, moving them smoothly up the back and sides of the head while squeezing the wide grips to make the cross-scissor action at the cutting edge. The hand-held scissor and comb technique to blend in the sides and top of the head took some time to perfect, but perfect it he did. Teddy enjoyed the factory type setting of the gaol barber shop. Men would sit on the bench seats chatting to each other in a welcome break from the workshop monotony. The duty screw would stand or pace slowly up and down the line of men, ensuring the chat was quiet and no skull duggery was afoot.

Court appearance haircuts were always given extra time and care to ensure the best possible impression was given from the dock. Remand prisoners usually only had one or two days in court before their incarceration was confirmed and the next few years were destined to be of the same boring routine. Very few escaped the *trappings and the riggings* of the law, to walk out of the court as free men. Charlie was an exception. He had been to court previously and was returned to Walton after a mistrial was declared. He was to get another court haircut soon.

His story was one that inmates talked openly about. He had been lifted out of the blue by the detectives investigating the Cameo murders. He had definitely nothing to do with the horrid affair, but the case against him was built to order and designed to stick. He was trapped in a frame so tightly that there was never going to be any chance of escape.

Teddy had done his hair previously and Charlie asked for him again. He had been sent for re-trial to face charges alone. His alleged co-conspirator was also to be alone facing the murder charges, after the first session was declared a mistrial.

Charlie was not a talkative type. He kept himself to himself inside. As he was involved with murder, so the story went, no inmates gave him a hard time. If any were to, they would have soon found that Charlie was very handy in a fight, as he was an ex-navy boxer. Teddy used his cheeky humour to get Charlie to open up a little while doing his hair.

"Tell me Charlie, how did you manage to get caught up in all this shit, when you have a good reason to be seen as having nothing at all to do with it?"

Charlie looked at Teddy in the mirror for a while before deciding to trust him and share his fears and frustrations.

"I swear it was co-incidence. I had been out of work and wondered what the courts were like. There was all this stuff in the papers about the Cameo and I thought why not go in the public gallery and have a look see what goes on in a court? No harm can come from it can it? Or, so I thought. There was me in the public gallery watching some poor sod get three years. It was all done in a rush, it seemed to me. The coppers on the witness stand all said the same thing, exactly the same thing, as they read from their notebooks. The magistrates all sat Stoney faced listening to the crap the coppers came out with, and then before you could say anything, they announced him guilty and sent him down. Just like that. It was dead quick."

"Well I thought that was rough at the time. How little did I know that I would be seen in the gallery by the magistrate's copper and recognised by him later when he said it was me in there again to see Kelly get remanded in Walton? A clear case of vested interest or some such shit."

Teddy said little, fearing he might break the spell he had cast to get Charlie to talk at all, never mind about the case. He hummed sagely a few times and nodded slightly in the mirror with an accompanying tight-lipped expression.

"So this big shot detective said it straight out to me. That if I didn't admit to being the accomplice, I would get the death penalty, as Kelly was definitely going to swing, and I would too if I didn't cop a plea and get a sentence of eight or ten years. Eight or ten years!" his voice had increased at this outrage.

Teddy put his hand on Charlie's shoulder, looked him in the mirror.

"I am sorry Charlie." The look lasted, to emphasise the empathy, before patting his shoulder a few times to encourage a lighter mood in him.

"Now don't tell me, or any other fucker in here what you are going to do Charlie, keep your powder dry as they say.

But do not allow yerself to go into that I-wing. Do yer hear me?" Teddy inclined his head for gravitas and steadily stared at Charlie's reflection, getting him to agree, with the slightest of eye movements that he would stay out of I-wing, the execution holding cell and gallows built to house and dispatch condemned men.

The clippers made the only sound for some time after this exchange, followed by the scissor and comb combination nibbling away at Charlies shorter sides and neck.

Teddy was superstitious strangely enough. If he didn't believe in all the religious crap, as he called it, why then, should he believe in some other sort of crap? He was convinced that Charlie's appearance in the court, out of curiosity, was behind his framing as part of the Cameo atrocity. Stay out of court was his take away message from that haircut. He was unaware of just how close a shave he had had, nearly becoming fitted into that frame himself.

Teddy was out before the Cameo conspiracy and miscarriage of justice played out its fateful dance. The only good thing that was to come of it was that just one man would be wrongfully hanged. Charlie went on to stay in Walton after finally deciding what he would do in his separate trial. He never spoke to any other inmate about anything of merit, after his last court appearance haircut.

After being locked away for so long Teddy was really looking forward to seeing Maggie and Mary, in that order. He arrived in Old Swan after getting a combination of three tram and bus journeys across Liverpool. Maggie was home with their young son Edward, that Teddy had only met previously at visiting. Edward was asleep in his pram in the hallway. Teddy embraced Maggie, she responded less avidly.

"Now, before we go upstairs", she said "I want you to promise me that you will not get into any more trouble again. Do you hear me?"

"Yeah, yeah. I won't be bad ever again. Now come on get yerself up the stairs I have a present for yer" he held the bulge in his pants to show he was bursting with anticipation of their first sex in ages, and ages.

She resigned to his overwhelming urge and went up to the bedroom. It was very quick. All the pent-up anticipation of sex had exploded within seconds of the start of their resumption of marital relations. They did it again a little later. It was more like the old times then. He waited long enough for her to reach her climax before resuming his animalistic urge to a more satisfying orgasm of his own.

Maggie was mad at him just hours later.

"You are not going to town tonight. You have only just got out for God's sake!"

"I have to see how everyone is down the Monument. I have not seen anyone for ages, have I? Beside you have to mind the kids, I won't be that long, just a few swift halves that's all."

"Oh go on then! I don't care what you get up to, you haven't been here for so long, you may as well not be here at all! But mind my words, if you bring any more trouble here, you are out do you hear me? Out!"

Teddy put his best suit on. He felt normal again. He put his hands in his pockets, that felt good he thought. Picking up his hat he shouted goodbye to Maggie, who was feeding little Edward.

He was warmly welcomed in the Monument by the locals. His friend Jimmy was eager to see how his mate had been getting on while inside. They had had a few pints when Teddy started telling of how life had been inside. He kept it light, reflected on how many times he got one over on the screws. Each tale was finished off with a belly laugh and self-congratulations.

"I was the only prisoner in all of Walton Gaol to have pockets in me trousers. I sewed them up with hidden stitching, so they couldn't be seen. I could walk about easier with me hands in me pockets. If a screw was about, I would snatch them out of me pockets like this." He made few steps and quickly pulled his hands out of his trouser pockets, feigning a normal demeaner. "None of them ever fuckin' knew I had sewn them!" He and Jimmy laughed and laughed.

Teddy was not keen to go back inside. He hated the thought of being locked up. Trapped. It was somehow like when he was young and locked inside the iron lung. He did not want to re-live that horror again. He would change the way he went about things in future. He would get a steady job, joinery or something, and not do any more break ins of his own. He would still fence off stolen goods that came his way, but he would be the middle man, not the thief. That way there was always the get out of gaol card of, 'I didn't know they were stolen, honest'. The money he had hidden away would come in really handy, he thought, but he couldn't rush to reclaim it. He felt sure that the detective would be watching him, and now that he had served his time, he would want to steal his hard-gotten gains for himself. Leave it for another few weeks he thought.

Chapter 30 The Stash

Teddy kept an eye on the trials of Kelly and Connolly in the two Liverpool papers, the Daily Post of a morning and the Echo in the evening. He was not going to go into the public gallery that was for sure. He hadn't met Kelly, but he took a shine to Connolly. He was a poor sod trapped in a no-win situation through no fault of his own. It was that bastard Palmer that was behind him being framed. He was truly a devil walking among men thought Teddy.

The papers had all sorts of details about the tragic night of the previous year. How the manager along with the deputy manager was counting the night's takings and the ice cream sales money, in the office of the Cameo cinema. They had all the change out on the manager's desk arranged in piles, when the door had burst open and a man in a mask, of some sort, had pointed a hand gun at them and demanded the takings. The manager had tried to reason with the robber when suddenly he was shot at point blank range by the masked man. He fell down, fatally wounded. The deputy manager rushed to the door to get help for the dying man, when he too was shot, in the back. While on his hands and knees, the killer then shot him again.

Conversations around the topic were had in every pub in the land not just in Liverpool. This sort of murder was unheard of at the time. Even robbers themselves thought the Cameo murders were beyond the pale. You didn't hurt people if you could avoid it, and you never ever shot them for no reason. Public opinion, revved up by the press, was angry at the accused men. The case against them was revealed one morsel at a time in the next day's newsprint. Each revelation brought more cries for the death penalty for the evil that the accused had brought to Liverpool.

The trial was going well in the eyes of Palmer. His meticulous ground work was paying off with the court and public opinion. He was going to enhance his reputation as a hard-line policeman as a result of this case. It was going to help his ambitions of promotion and who knows how far I can go on the back of this, he thought.

Gaiety was back on the agenda for people in Liverpool. Trips out of the city to the countryside of North Wales or the attractions of Southport and Blackpool took place on a regular basis. It was one of these that Mary was asked to join by her friend from Wavertree. Celia was a single mother too. She needed some time away from the hardships of raising a child without a steady man around to help, and the Blackpool trip was just the tonic she told Mary. There would be drinking, singing and dancing to be had.

"Oh Mary go on! Come with me. We will have great fun. It starts out from the Wellington pub at the corner of Picton Road and Rathbone Road at 4:00pm on Friday. It's only half a dollar and you get a fish supper on the pier for that too. The charra is brand new they said, and it has all plush seats and everything. Go on Mary come with me and we can have some fun."

"I will have to see" replied Mary. She was thinking who would mind Maureen while she was out all afternoon and evening.

"Your Annie will watch out for Maureen, she will love it" suggested Celia. Mary's face showed she was more than just open to the idea she was actively trying to think it through. She wondered what Teddy would say, then she dismissed that thought as she hadn't seen that much of him for the last week or so, he was keeping away for some reason.

"Oh frig it!" I will feckin' go. We will have a good time Cely" said Mary using her friendly handle.

The coach was new. It had been chartered by the organiser of the trip, a local furniture shop owner, he wanted to get his girlfriend away, so they could spend quality time together out of sight of his wife, who would have to stay home to look after their three kids. The two friends joined the queue to get on the charra, as they were called in Liverpool at the time.

"Let's see if we can get on the backseat Mary?" urged Celia pushing her friend forward up the coach steps.

"Steady on Cely, I nearly went on me arse then" cautioned Mary.

"And what a fine arse it is too." The man was tall with light brown hair, bushed back off his forehead and kept in place with Brylcream. He had shining blue eyes, and a cheeky smile that softened any insult he cast out, searching for kindred spirits.

"Hey, easy tiger. The night is young, and we are out for a good time, not for any smooth-talking fella to insult my mate" said Celia.

"Me! Smooth talking? I haven't said anything yet. How do you know what I'm like if you don't sit with me and Archie?"

"Hey! Who the friggin' hell is Archie?" asked Celia.

"That's me." He was also tall, he had black hair and his brown eyes promised excitement.

The backseat was full of trippers already as the two girls negotiated the aisle, so they picked a double seat on the kerbside of the coach. The two men sat behind them.

"Hey now don't be thinking you are with us." Celia was in a flirty mood. She flashed her eyes at them both, they found Archie's to be the most hypnotic.

"Hey Mary mine's alright, yours is OK too!" they laughed and feigned disinterest in the men behind them. Every time they pretended to watch the scenery as it went passed their window, they would catch the eyes of the two possible dates. Soon there were offers of bottles of pale ale being held over the seat for the two girls. Once they accepted, the foursome was sealed.

Shrieks of laughter were emanating from the backseat. Loud hurrahs and shouts of 'do it again' went up. Two floozies were flashing their breasts out of the rear window at following car drivers. This had an electrifying effect on the men with them. The adventurous mood tumbled forward bewitching every double seat of occupants, with a naughty spell of ribald adventure.

The August sun finally gave up the ghost as it slid below the western horizon, leaving a short-lived orange glow to vie with the bright lights of the Blackpool illuminations and its attractions. The four had all gone around together since leaving the coach at the central bus station in Blackpool. There was an agreed time for the fish supper at the end of Central Pier, followed by a last toilet break then back on the coach to Liverpool. The foursome had split into couples to walk arm in arm along the promenades. Chatter, smiles and laughter were the sounds of people enjoying the evening. It was a time out event. It gave respite from the daily hardships they faced, juggling childcare, lodgings, family expectations around marriage and morality. What was a modern woman to do. Just conform to the old ways of doing things, the old school way of keeping women down where they belong. No!

Before the rendezvous time and supper, cuddling was on the cards. Archie and Celia were first to pick a doorway, just off the promenade for their spot. Taking his friend Archie's lead, George led Mary to the next doorway. They embraced into a natural kiss hold. Heads tilted to one side

295

to make the meeting of their lips easier. Each taking turn
with their tongues to probe the other's mouth and gauge the
extent of the growing bond between them. Bellies were
pushed together by both parties. George explored further
with his hands, each one taking a buttock and with a
combined squeezing and lifting motion, placed Mary into
position. They both pushed harder. Once the silent signals
were sent and received George sent his exploratory hands
further afield. He took it in turns to touch then to squeeze
each breast, over the dress at first, then down into her
cleavage to connect with the skin. The skin couldn't lie. It
wanted more. It said so in its reciprocating warmth on the
finger tips that traversed the contours. It shouted out 'yes',
as the fingers engaged the nipples, these could not lie any
more than the skin itself. So it was agreed, without
anything being said, that now, here in this doorway in
Blackpool, they were to enjoy each other further. His leg
was inside hers providing a muscle hard surface to press
against. She took the opportunity to rub hard on it,
amplifying the desire.

As the four walked back to the Central Pier and the chippy
they were quieter. Still arm in arm, still cuddling up to each
other. The only light was the alternating colours from the
fly catching glowing bulbs of Blackpool. The supper was

eagerly eaten. They were all ravenous after their entre of sexual encounters in their respective temporary recesses of privacy. The return trip saw the four sit together as couples. Eventually all four fell asleep as the brand-new coach made its way back down to Liverpool. Everyone had had a good time, from the organiser and his girlfriend to the driver. He usually got lucky on these trips too.

Teddy was completely unaware of Mary's Blackpool excursion. He had been trying hard, in his eyes, to make things work with Maggie. Since his release his mood was increasingly resentful. He had missed so much while inside he felt. Maggie had changed. She was more confident in her decisions, she appeared not to need Teddy's advice, or even to seek it. As for his company she let him know that she could take him or leave him. He wanted a break from the atmosphere at Maggie's in Old Swan and decided that a trip to Wavertree would be the answer. Mary would be more understanding. He thought that a smart night out would be the medicine he needed and that would impress Mary too.

They went to the Adelphi. Mary loved it. She was enchanted with the affluence that seeped out of the very fabric of the building. Teddy had picked his spot well.

Deciding to spurn the bar, where some less than nice people were known to frequent, he chose the lounge and waiter service. Mary ordered a Snowball. She had no idea what it was, she just liked the name on the drinks menu that the tailcoat waiter had given her first, before handing an identical one to Teddy, along with a 'Madam, Sir' to accompany the impression of being of the Adelphi set.

The waiter appeared out of nowhere to offer Teddy a light, as he had been patting his suit pockets to locate his Ronson with the cigarette in his mouth.

"Thanks mate" said Teddy returning the book of matches to the waiter.

"Please sir, keep them as a memento of your visit to the Adelphi" replied the waiter obsequiously, working his tip in the proven fashion of the lounge. Teddy slipped them into his jacket pocket where the Ronson should have been, he must have left it in one of his other suits he thought.

The magic of the high ceiling, tall windows, extravagant chandeliers and the fellow lounge clientele worked just as Teddy had hoped for. They had a great time and went back to Mary's that evening.

When Teddy did return to Maggie's at Old Swan, she kept it short but clear. He was out.

"I want nothing more to do with you!" she said with finality. He was arguing against her decision to throw him out in vain. Once he realised that was the end of their relationship, he roared back at her. "Well if that's how you feel you can fuckin' go and fuck yerself! I will take me and me fuckin' money, fuckin' elsewhere!" He slammed the door behind him as he left. Anger at not being the instigator of the row scratching at his sense of self.

He decided that enough time had lapsed and that he could now safely retrieve his stash left over from the building sale. He went to Dovecot to see his sister Annie. She was pleased to see Teddy when he arrived, it didn't last.

"Where is little Jimmy's teddy bear? The one he wouldn't go anywhere without. The one I bought him ages ago?"

"Oh that got thrown out after he had a paddy and threw the bear onto the fire in his temper. It got all burnt black down one side, so I taught him a lesson and made him watch me throw it in the bin."

"When was that? Is it still in the bin?"

"Oh no, that was ages ago. You were still being entertained by her majesty then."

After a temper tirade and much swearing Teddy left his sister's house. He was Skint.

PART 3

Chapter 31 The Angry Man

Teddy was reading the Daily Post and saw that his friend had been sentenced to eight years in prison. Connolly was done and dusted as part of the framing. Teddy was aghast at the news. He still found it hard to believe that a policeman could manufacture such a case and follow it through with the courts to this. He was to be even more shocked shortly.

Mary had been delighted when Teddy told her he had left Maggie, blaming her variable moods and unreasonable behaviour, he lied. They set up house in Earl Road in the house that her mother, Kitty had. It was a terraced house that they shared with three of her sisters, Kathleen, Margaret and Theresa. Her sister Annie had recently set up home with her first husband and their first born, Alan. In the main these early months went OK as they all learned to get along with each other. A few niggles had happened due to the crowded space. It was during this period that Margaret learned that Teddy was not a good person. She watched him and listened to the way he spoke about things. She soon realised that he lied a lot and tried to manipulate their surroundings and behaviour. From this point on, she took whatever he said with a pinch of salt, and always sought the motive behind his suggestions.

Mary was pregnant again. The time of conception was close to Teddy's release. The doubt seed had found fertile ground in his imagination and sent shoots into his viscera colouring his spleen a deeper red. How to be sure he thought? Mary was popular, that was for sure, she had always had a line of admiring men along the bar when she worked in the pub, looking at her with desire. At the time he took pride in their jealousy, that he had netted the catch of the season, but now those faces and muttered comments about her taunted him. Anger was omnipresent in Teddy's head. Mostly it was controlled, but the slightest stimulus would trigger at least a vehement outburst or occasionally a violent episode. The subjects of the violence were often anyone close enough to strike out at. Teddy had not struck Mary directly, he thought that men didn't hit women, but hurting them was allowed in his warped mind. And warped it was by this time. The pressures of the challenges he had faced as a small boy, illness, incarceration in the iron lung, his mother leaving them, and the bullying had all shaped the man he was now. There was little chance of a rewind and softening of his temperament by this stage. He was now a very angry man.

He had scared Mary half to death, as she would later share with her sister Margret, when he voiced his fears of Mary's pregnancy and if he really was the father of the unborn child.

"If I find out that this baby is not mine, I will fuckin' bash you to a fucking pulp and kill the fucker who's it is!" Mary was fearful for the rest of that year till respite came out of the blue.

Money was tight. Teddy had a job shoring up buildings, due for demolition, till the crews could arrive to take them down. It was not well paid.

The horror of being incarcerated was waning in his memory as he sought ways to do a little thieving without getting caught. He was walking down a street in his old neighbourhood when the smell of cigar smoke triggered a memory of priests in the garden.

A couple of nights later without his barra, that had gone while he was away previously, he took his makeshift big key to the back of the tobacconist's shop. He easily broke through the locks, slid inside the doorway, and just like before, jammed the door shut behind him. This shop was in a residential area, unlike the warehouse jobs he favoured previously. Any noise was less obvious, and most people had been sheltering away from the airborne death too. This neighbourhood was now in full light, the blackout a long-gone thing of the past, and the houses all had occupants. The crash of the door locks had not gone un-noticed.

Teddy was inside the shop. He quickly scooped up packs of cigarettes into his shoulder bag and his eye caught the Cuban cigars on the top shelf.

"Why not?" he said out loud "Those fuckers can wait for the next banana boat for their cigars." As he put two boxes into the bag, he stopped dead. Straining his ears he heard voices. Shit! He thought. He waited motionless in the gloom of the shop to see if the voices went by, heart beat racing like a motorbike engine. Then the realisation came to him that he had been caught! The back door had opened, and torchlight started to sweep in a crisscross pattern back and forth. A deep voice called out.

"Anyone there?" no answer. "This is the police! If you are in there make yourself known now." Teddy had dropped to the floor as soon as he saw the torchlight. He silently scooted under the counter and balled himself as small as he could. Arms wrapped tightly round his knees and head pressed forward. His swag bag in his lap. A second voice announced.

"He must have heard us coming and scarpered. Its empty in here." A switch was flicked, and the shop was brightly illuminated. Teddy was still balled up, not moving, trying to keep his breath from being heard.

"Here you are Brian, have some Woodbines, there what you smoke aren't they?"

"Oh yes. I will have some of those. Here give me another couple of packs." He had to wait while his fellow police officer stacked his own pockets with Capstan Full Strength, patted them down so as not to be too obvious, then he tossed two packs of Woodbines in quick succession to his colleague. He caught the first one neatly but dropped the second one. It hit the floor with a gentle whack sound.

"Oh bugger. Me and me butter fingers." As the officer bent down to retrieve the fallen loot, he saw Teddy hiding under the counter.

"Well, well, well. What have we got here?" He made eye contact with Teddy. All He could think of was to give a small smile and shrug his shoulders.

"OK my lad out you come." Teddy swung his legs out from under the counter, shuffled over on his bum a bit and managed to stand up without too much effort.

"And what is your name?" asked the cigarette slinger.

"Teddy Kelly"

"OK Teddy Kelly, you have been caught having broken your way into a locked premises with the intention of stealing goods. That will be these goods in your bag. I am arresting you for breaking and entering." Teddy didn't listen to the rest of what he said. He was mad at himself for rushing into a job too quickly in his desperation to get more money. The other policeman called the station on the shop phone and requested a van to collect the prisoner. It arrived after about five minutes and another two officers came into the shop. After a brief look around to see that their colleague had the prisoner secured, they began to help themselves to cigarettes too. Teddy looked on silently. There was no point in saying anything, it was no use. The missing goods would be put down to him, and the store owner advised to claim accordingly for his losses on his insurance policy.

The officers were nice to Teddy in that they didn't beat him. They saw he had a form of disability and allowed him to walk at his pace into the van and then into the bridewell in Cheapside. The night was long for Teddy, he kept replaying the stupid decisions he had made in doing a job on a whim and not planning it properly.

After a meagre breakfast in the holding cell and a quick wash of his face, he was back in the van on his way to the magistrate's court. The three sombre faced men looked impassively at Teddy while the two policemen described how they had caught him in the act, with a bag of cigarettes and cigars, and his pinch bar entry tool. The centre magistrate asked.

"How do you plead?"

"Guilty Sir"

"Very well, I sentence you to eighteen months in prison. Take him down."

It was as quick as that. One minute he was living in Earl Road with Mary, a poor decision made the previous night and now, the following morning, he was in the van on his way back into gaol. He was dreading the return of the closed in feelings, being trapped again.

When Mary got the news she was horrified and relieved at the same time. Her man was in gaol, again. But he wasn't going to frighten her now, not till after the child was born. If he was still going to be around that is. Mary set about sorting things out for the new arrival who was due in a few weeks' time. She gathered a variety of second-hand furniture for the baby, a cot, a nursing chair and some hand me down baby clothes too. She loved being pregnant, she blossomed with health and vitality, her hair shone, and her eyes were brighter. When she walked, she held her shoulders high and back for all the world to see her bump.

Michael was born in April, on the Queen's birthday. Mary had registered his birth at St Georges Hall and given him James as a middle name. She liked the sound of Michael James Kelly. She had decided to stay with Teddy. Even though he was in prison for now, he would soon be out, and he would get a proper job. Then they would be a proper family, all four of them. Maureen, Michael, Mary and Teddy.

Charlie Connolly was still in Walton. Teddy spoke with him a few times more during exercise breaks, and the odd time they were seated together at meals. Teddy recalled how Charlie didn't like talking with other cons, so he kept the initial encounters very light, often just saying hello and remaining quiet to see if he would speak first. This proved to be the right approach.

Kelly, the completely innocent man, had been hung some time ago. He had gone to London for his appeal hearing, but that also was a waste of time. The case made against him, and that the public and establishment needed a culprit, for the heinous crimes at the Cameo cinema the previous year meant he had no escape from I-wing.

I-wing had had many prisoners before Kelly and he was just the latest in a long line of executed men. The hangman was Albert Pierrepoint. He had been the Queen's executioner for some time and knew his job well. The report in the Liverpool Echo stated that Kelly had been executed for the double murder at the Cameo cinema in Wavertree. It had been the result of the longest murder trial in UK history, and justice had been done.

Teddy consoled Charlie when he realised that he was upset that some prisoners had inferred that he had sent him to the gallows by pleading guilty to an accessory.

"Listen Charlie, if you hadn't you would have been in I-wing with him, and then two innocent men would have died. It was that bastard Palmer who is to blame for all of this. Heaven knows why he did it. Framing two innocent men and seeing one of them swing in full knowledge of that. It beats me. But you stay calm, do you here?" The slight nod confirmed that he would try. "You just keep yer nose clean and do the time. When you get out, don't let any of these fuckers get anywhere near yer again, Right?"

Teddy never knew how close he came to being in that position. As that frame process went well, there was another one while Teddy was inside. After that two more innocent men met Mr Pierrepoint.

Chapter 32 The Right Path

Teddy was back in the old routine of slops and stinks. His days went like clockwork, slops, breakfast, workshops, meals and exercise breaks, locked back up. It was the evenings and nights that haunted him. After the usual and often repeated chats in the four-man cell built for two, the silence descended, and the fears grew in Teddy's mind. The feelings of being constrained within the iron lung came back every night, they signalled the hour at least, that he would lie awake with his fearful thoughts. He recalled seeing the world upside down in the mirror above his head. How the coffin like lung made him feel as if he was going to die, had died, and was now waiting to be buried. The thought of being conscious when buried terrified him. He played this scenario out many times in his imagination. The worst was to wake up in his coffin and realise he was not dead. To scratch and bang the lid in terror. Not knowing if the coffin had been buried yet. Yelling at the wood inches away from his face. Strangely he never felt as if he should reflect on his life when in these fits of terror. It was always too emotional for rational thought. His chest went through the same changes every time. Heart rate increased instantly, contracting with more force on every beat, expelling more blood than usual from each chamber. The blood was sent rushing through his arteries at great speed and under unusually high pressure. His heart beat was pounding in his ears as well as his chest. He would become light headed, and if he was blessed that night, fall off to sleep, if not then the horror would play out for longer, leaving him exhausted and sweating in his prison bed. He woke every morning to a sense of relief that he was still here and spared the torture of being buried alive.

He had reverted to his best behaviour to ensure he would come out unscathed, in body at least. The plumb job of shoe repairs was up, and he asked very politely if he could be put forward to learn it adding.

"You never know I could become a cobbler when I get out?"

Teddy was given the chance to learn another skill. He started in the boot repair shop. He was introduced to the workspace of the cobbler, a shoe makers last, as it was called. He had lightweight hammers and tack-like pins for attaching new heels to prison boots. He learned about various glues for fixing replaced soles and how to trim any excess off with a curved sharp knife. All of these tools were again all counted out and back in again every day. He fancied himself as a cobbler at times after finishing a pair of boots off. Then on reflection he dismissed that thought and had to remind himself he was going back to joinery, of some sort, when he got out.

Visiting time came around and the day that Mary brought Michael in to see him was a day of delight, and later doubt.

"Look at him Teddy. Isn't he lovely. He has my eyes and your hair, although it's a bit lighter at the moment, it will get darker as he gets older." Teddy was allowed to hold the infant in his arms. As with most people his heart softened when the child was helpless in his strong arms. Michael looked up at the man staring down on him, he didn't know who it was. Not one of the usual faces or smells. His fragile consciousness always trying to make sense of his surroundings and events. Building one layer at a time into the model of the world that he would soon be an active part of.

"Yes he is lovely Mary" said Teddy, a hint of a tear in his eye.

"When you get out, we are going to be a family together, and soon after that we will have our own place and more children. How does that sound Teddy?"

"Yes that's what I want too. I am sick of being in here. It's horrible really." He started to choke on his words. He quickly regained his composure. He did not want to be seen as one of those cry baby cons at visiting time. He was a man. "My nose is itching something wicked today, it's all the dust in the workshop" he lied rubbing it and his eyes at the same time. Mary saw the ruse for what it was and said nothing, she was keen not to rile him.

"You will be out soon enough. You can go back on the demo if you like. There are still loads of sites that need clearing."

"No I am going to work on building my joinery skills and then get a proper job."

"And stay out of trouble, yes?" She encouraged, her eyes holding his gaze waiting for the answer.

"Yes. I am never coming back in here, ever again!" He meant it. He had had enough of the life behind bars in Walton prison. The mind dulling daily routine, inane chat of illiterate convicts, little laughter. He feared the nights the most. "I have a meeting before I get out with the probation service man. This time I am going to listen and get him to help me get sorted with a job. I am going to be the model ex-convict when I get out."

"Yes that will be good. Then we can get on being a family all together." Teddy nodded agreement while his mind was still playing out a nightmare vision. He pushed it far into the recess of his head. "Is everything OK Teddy?" asked Mary. She had seen the change of expression that had come over Teddy's face and was concerned.

"Oh yeah, yeah. I was just thinking about when I get out and all the good times we are going to have." He made a lewd expression and it made her laugh.

"You and your cock. Is that all you ever think about Teddy Kelly?"

"No sometimes I think about me belly too. I don't want to go hungry, do I?"

The officers signalled that visiting time was coming to an end. Mary gathered the baby's clothes together and took the child back from his Dad. They exchanged the regulatory pecked kiss and Teddy went back to his side of the Walton line, and Mary made her way out into the daylight. Her bus ride across Liverpool back to Wavertree was uneventful. Michael had fallen asleep, mesmerised by the heavy idling of the diesel engine and the swaying as the bus went round corners. Mary had time to reflect on her decision. She knew it was the right one, for all concerned.

Mr Roberts was an ex-policeman. He had retired from the force in his early fifties and now worked in the probation service. The combination of police pension and probation salary meant he was comfortable when it came to money. Yet despite his relative wealth he saw the world for what it was, a hard place for working class people to make good if they didn't have a trade. His one-man crusade was to help any convict that he felt was truly repentant and wanted to stay out of prison. Not every man that came across his desk was of this ilk. He had seen every form of deceit as he interviewed people in his prison office and then afterwards in his outside office. He could smell a rat even when the words were given in earnest and accompanied by tears for effect. He liked the young man with the limp. He had taken a shine to the man that brought good humour to their discussions. "Ok then Teddy, tell me what your plans are for when you are released?"

"Well Mr Robinson I was thinking of building on my joinery skills and then getting a job as a joiner proper."

"I see that you are not a time served joiner Teddy."

"Yes that's true Mr Robinson, but I have picked up loads of stuff over the years. I worked with a guy called Johnny in

Islington for about two years when I was younger, during the war. He taught me lots of things."

"OK. What about a preference in joinery? Do you have any idea what sort of work you might be good at? To help you get started outside."

"Not really. I think I can learn anything quickly and all I need is the chance to show I can do it and stay out of trouble."

"That goes without saying Teddy. Any more trouble that gets you back in here and we are going to fall out." Mr Robinson set his gaze on Teddy. The policeman was still in there, when required.

"You can rest assured on that. There is no way in the world that I am coming back in here, that is for sure." Mr Robinson heard and saw the truth in Teddy's face. He was going to win with this one he knew.

"OK then, I have an idea that you will like. What do you know about ships joiners?"

"Ships joiners?" repeated Teddy, thinking.

"Yes. Have you not heard of them?"

"Sorry Mr Robinson, I haven't."

"Well these are joiners that work on ships when they are in dry dock. They could be in for a few repairs or even a full refit. The work will expand your knowledge of joinery and you will be working with time-served joiners. They will help you get to grips with the new skills to add to your repertoire." Teddy didn't know what that was, but he figured he would, sooner or later. He was watching the approach that Mr Robinson took with him. Patience, collaboration and listening were clocked and stored away in Teddy's mind. He still collected anything he felt might come in handy in the future. "OK then Teddy ships joinery it is when you get out." He offered Teddy his hand and they shook on the deal.

It was still a few months till Teddy was due for release. He spent the time in the same routine. His mood was slightly better, he now had an advocate for when he got out, and Mr Robinson was going to see him straight for a job in the docks. Happy days were on the way.

Margaret answered the knock on the door. She was home alone with her mother, her sisters were all out and about. The man was tall and well dressed. His hair was short at the sides and longer on the top held very neatly in place with Brylcream. Margaret was the second youngest of the Byrne girls. She was courting at this time. Her beau was a guy called George. They had met when he had knocked on the door to chat about the contents of the magazine he was giving away, the Watchtower. They got chatting about the world, in the manner that these conversations usually went, and they had agreed to meet again at the Jehovah's Witness meeting rooms on Lodge Lane. They were soon going to be married and bring the family up as Jehovah's Witnesses.

"Hello" said the tall man. "I am looking for Mary Byrne. I was told that she lives here, is she in?"

"Not at the moment. She is out with … with her friends. Why do you want to see her?" asked Margaret politely.

"We met a while ago and I wondered if she wanted to meet up again? When do you think she will be back?" Margaret thought for a moment before answering. She didn't like Teddy Kelly at all. She didn't trust the man, he was a liar and had a roving eye. Should she upset her sister's plans by telling her of this man's visit or not. She had to think about Mary and her children. Mary had said she was going to make a go of it with Teddy. What should she do? Then in a moment of decision she said, "She is not here all the time. She stays with her boyfriend some nights, to give us a break from her two kids", that should do it thought Margaret. "Who should I say called when next I see her?"

"Tell her it was George. George from Blackpool, she will know who I am."

"OK I will. Bye"

"Bye." The man walked off down Earl Road. He never came back to call again.

Chapter 33 The Second Chance

The early fifties were a time of promise. The war had been over for some time and the economy was starting to take off. The NHS had been formed and the Empire was starting to fragment after the partition and independence of India. A new era had begun. The docks that were devastated during the blitz were being refurbished along with the dry dock facilities for ship repairs and refurbishment.

Teddy had got his start as a ship's joiner thanks to Mr Robinson, he was doing well. Learning new skills and refining his existing ones. He found he had a new audience for his recognition need, his fellow workers at the dry dock. He could get a laugh out of most everyday things, news articles, the way other men worked or even ate their sandwiches were all fodder for his humour. Most of the time everyone joined in with the laughter, but there was one exception. Teddy. If the men who had just been parodied laughed and then returned the compliment by aiming some funny jibe at Teddy, then the temper rose up with Vesuvian force. A standoff would ensue, where the canny man would back down, and the fool would get hurt. The awkward silence that followed these episodes were soon forgotten by Teddy and another wisecrack would appear to clear the air, as his co-workers feigned a laugh.

Money was still tight at this time. Mary did wonders with the weekly hand over of housekeeping. Like many women of the time she didn't know how much her husband was paid, she was just grateful there was money coming in every week. Mary had learned to make ends meet when she worked in Dublin as the house maid for the banker and his family. She was given an allowance for the food and incidental expenses and had to make sure they lasted the full week. Even though the banker was reasonably well paid he still followed an austere approach to money. The lessons learned here were to follow Mary all her life. Like many she had a tin for 'must pay' bills and rent. Money went in and out within the week mostly, leaving a pittance to accrue over time.

It was over a money conversation that Mary had extracted the promise from Teddy that he would not go back to prison again.

"See, you are earning money every week now, aren't yer?" she asked of him.

"Yeah, yeah I am now. Soon I will get a rise and then we can spend a bit on some nice things."

"Oh never mind the nice things, we need to save for a place of our own. There are some maisonettes going up in West Derby I heard. It would be nice to get one of those."

"Well I think that is a long way off. I will have to do a little skull duggery to make it happen quicker."

"Oh no you don't Teddy Kelly! You must promise me that you will never go back to prison. You inside are no use to me, or beast." The Irish expression settled on Teddy's ears. He recalled how beasts fared better than inmates in many ways. The horror of the coffin, iron lung and claustrophobic cell made the fear come back to him.

"I won't go back inside that's for sure! I have had it up to here with all that." The hand hovered about his eyebrows to emphasise his sincerity. Mary looked at him with a steady gaze, searching for any sign of his trademark grin when he was only slightly lying, she saw none and was reassured.

"Good that is that settled then. We don't have to worry about you disappearing overnight again, leaving us in the lurch."

"I said I won't go back inside, didn't I?" temper had let a threat tone enter his voice.

"Oh I was just confirming what we agreed." Recovered Mary. She had soon learned that the funny Teddy Kelly was also a bad tempered get, again the socially acceptable Irish term for bastard was substituted in her mind. Actual swearing was kept for absolutely essential occasions.

They had settled into an amicable routine after his release earlier that year. It was just before Easter when he got out and returned to the shared dwelling in Earl Road, to resume his relationship with Mary, her daughter and his son Michael. The doubts had been growing while he was in Walton. He had no way of knowing for sure. Now he was going to be certain the next child would definitely be his. He waited till he knew Mary was not pregnant then made his move. Mary announced she was pregnant again around the Whitsun holiday in May. Teddy was delighted. This child was going to be his, no question about it. The doubt over Michael persisted. He looked for any sign of a characteristic that might not be in line with his paternity. Was his hair just a little too light, not the Celtic black that his own had been. He had blue eyes, but so did Mary. Some of his sisters had blue eyes too, so that could be OK.

The factors that moulded Teddy never went away. He was set in his ways. He showed any one of several faces to the

world, depending on the situation. At work he was the
funny guy and the union advocate. In the pub a wise
cracking Philadelphia lawyer type with lots of experience
to call upon. At home he was a fiend on occasions, yet a
loving father too – depending. He had an overwhelming
desire to control his environment and all those within it. At
work he managed this to some extent, but it was in the
home that his need was mostly felt. He soon learned that a
mother will do anything to protect her children, this was in
contrast to his experiences with his own mother. Where she
had not taken care of him, after his discharge from Alder
Hey, mainly by not taking him to physiotherapy to build up
his muscle strength and range of movements, then to leave
the five of them motherless while she went off to form
another life with *him*. Mary however was altogether
different. She loved her children and suffered every hurt
they felt.

It was this love that Teddy saw he could use to control
Mary in everything she did. He would punish the children
for the slightest misdemeanour, removing privileges at first
then with beatings for more severe discretions. Both Mary
and Teddy were brought up in the time of corporal
punishment. Spare the rod and spoil the child was an adage
often used to justify beating one's children. The birch had

only just been outlawed in England a few years before. If Maureen was deemed to be naughty, she would miss out on a halfpenny ice cream block. Michael would similarly be chosen for sanctions along similar lines. What Teddy said was to be the punishment, it was. There was no going back on a proclamation.

It was a cold December night that Leo was born. The longest night of the year. Teddy was delighted that he now had a definite bond with Mary and family, no doubt about it. He made every effort to please Mary while she juggled the three children and the household. They were still living at Kitty's terraced house in Earl Road. Space was eased as Margaret had married George and moved out, Kathleen had moved away too with her man John, leaving just Teresa the youngest at home. Kitty had lived apart from her husband, Paddy Byrne, almost since he returned from the POW camp after the war. Her eldest child, Paddy had moved to London to better his prospects, he never visited.

Teddy brought little Leo a variety of gifts on a regular basis. These varied from cuddly animals to toy bucket and spades and such like. On the surface this was admirable behaviour for a father to display. In reality it was another facet to his coercive control. Visibly favouring Leo over

Maureen and Michael to niggle and hurt Mary, to assuage his fear of not being in control.

The promise of not to go inside again was being kept. Teddy met regularly with Mr Robinson, his parole officer, and he reported that Teddy was doing well in his reformed behaviour and was holding down his ship's joinery job. Mr Robinson had told Teddy that any trouble he got himself into could get him back inside Walton to serve the remainder of his sentence. So the watchword was to stay safe and well away from trouble of any kind. Teddy had been focussed on being in control, especially of his temper. He knew that he could be up before a magistrate again if he was caught in any sort of fracas. He wanted to stay out of trouble at all costs. He wanted to please Mary by being a good father, in his mind at least.

Teddy had been seeing his friend Jimmy regularly at the weekends, usually Sundays, at a variety of pubs in town. Jimmy had changed his ways when Teddy had gone inside the first time. He had been to see him at Walton and was horrified to see the austere building, all the barred windows and locked doorways. Teddy had told him a little of the life behind bars while visiting, and Jimmy had decided then and there that he was not going to follow Teddy inside. He was going to focus instead on making a go of his small business and cutting his cloth to suit the income it generated.

It was while they were walking through the concourse of Lime Street Station that a blast from their past came walking towards them. They were idly chatting when Teddy suddenly said.

"There's that weasel faced fucker!"

"What fucker?" asked Jimmy.

"One of them that jumped me outside the Crown" replied Teddy. His hand automatically went to his pocket reaching for the headache stick, then he remembered that he no longer had it. He had not had it for some time, since he went down the first time actually. The weasel faced attacker was lost in his paper as he scoured the back pages while idly walking through the concourse. Teddy looked around, no sign of any transport police nearby. He adjusted his direction slightly, Jimmy followed suit. As they came alongside the man looking down at his sports news, walking slower than normal in order to read, Teddy slapped the page downwards and when the man looked up with the beginnings of a curse on his slips.

"Hey! Yer remember me don't yer?" before the man could reply Teddy swung his right fist directly into the man's face, just once. As the man fell, in what looked like slow motion, he commented, "Take that yer fucker and go for a bobby!" It was a silly thing to say but it made Teddy feel good. The weasel faced man crumpled to the floor. The two friends continued their traverse across the concourse, walking slightly faster than before. They had hardly stopped at all to administer the vengeance, it was so fast.

A few people went to the aid of the fallen man, questions flew in quick succession asking was he OK? What had happened? Had he fainted? It soon became visible that he had been struck very hard in the face. He couldn't speak due to his jawbone being smashed and was hanging strangely, loosely on the left side of his face. No one could see anything untoward as they looked around. Just a variety of people, mostly in Sunday best, walking or standing waiting for their trains. The two slightly shorter men in suits were just turning into the side exit of Lord Nelson Street, towards the Lord Nelson pub, one had a limp and wore a big hat. They were sharing a joke about something.

Chapter 34 The Chippy

Almost two years after Leo was born Teddy and Mary had another child. He was named after Mary's favourite saint, Anthony. Yet he was never called Anthony, always Tony. Mary had put her foot down after the naming of Leo. Teddy had gone to the registrar to record the birth while Mary was at home in Earl Road nursing the baby. He had decided that he could be called Terence, but as his middle name. He was going to call his boy Leo. When Mary saw the certificate, she was angry with Teddy. She felt that Leo was a strange name for a Liverpool baby at the time. She only knew of one other person with that name and that was Teddy's youngest sister's husband. He was a third generation Italian by the name of Tremarco. He had his own furniture removal van business. Teddy was taken by the Italian sounding name, an echo of his childhood as the Bidder Street Chicago gangsters at play.

Leo's middle name, Terrence, was what Mary called him when Teddy was not around. All her family called him Terry. So when Tony was born it was a catchy duplet for the two similar aged boys to be called Terry and Tony the little terrors. They were far from terrors when young, but they were boisterous.

At the registration of the new baby, Mary was insistent on Anthony. So she went along too, to ensure no further gangster names were afoot. As the occasion was a little fraught, they had been exchanging words again at the treachery of the earlier registration of Terry, Anthony was the only name given. A little unusual for then as most kids had a middle name of some sought. It was a little later that Anthony was christened, Teddy didn't go of course. Tony then he got, what he thought was his middle name, Edward. It would be years later that Tony discovered the rationale behind the Edward name, and also that it was not legally recognised as it was not on his birth certificate.

A strange thing happened the year Tony was born. The great news that an American doctor had developed an injectable vaccine for poliomyelitis. The clinical trial used was one of the first to employ new statistical methodology, that the vaccine was the only intervention that could be responsible for any change in outcome in its design. In the fifties a common statistical negative comment was that, association was not causation. So Jonas Salk set out to show, using rigorous statistical methodology, that there could be no doubt that it was the vaccine that reduced the number of children affected, and was not caused just by some random association. He had demonstrated that the vaccine did work. That it was going to drastically cut the number of people affected by this crippling disease all over the world, and in turn reduce deaths and disabilities in young children. One would think that this news was received by all and sundry as the great break through that it was.

Teddy was angry. It was another blow to his psyche. Why had he missed out on such a breakthrough? It was only a few years difference really, in the greater scheme of things, that he could have benefitted from this vaccine. Poor me.

Mary had been going on about a place of their own for some time now. Ted had come in handy again. Teddy had made the journey north to see him. He was still working for Liverpool Corporation even though he now had two chip shops, the first of his empire as he liked to think of it. The Stag had indeed watched over the tin of dreams, keeping it safe from fire or scrutiny. Now the money that Ted made on the side was hidden in plain sight in the takings of the two shops as cash transactions. He still did favours, as he referred to them, for people and friends. He classed Teddy as friend. The friendship was sorely tested some years earlier when Teddy had been arrested over the building sale. Ted had heard about the arrest and spent several weeks waiting for the knock on the door. He recalled how Teddy had said that he would carry the can if he got caught. Carry the can he did. It was months later that Ted realised that Teddy was as good as his word. The dreaded knock never came. It allowed Ted to breathe easy again and to focus on the fast food dream of his.

In Ted's parlour he looked exactly the same thought Teddy, he still had the same sleeveless jumper and the shirt cuffs were safely kept up out of harm's way by the expandable bicep bands. Ted had the same measured pace of speech as before, the same cufflink twiddle when thinking.

"I will keep my eye out for you Teddy" said Ted when he knew what Teddy had asked about.

"I have been going down that way a few times Ted and there are some empty ones by the look of the windows" offered Teddy.

"Yes there may well be. But they will have been allocated to people on the waiting list in the housing office. It will take a me while to bump you and Mary up the list, maybe even a couple of months" added Ted.

He had done this many times before, in fact it was a major earner for Ted. Lots of people wanted to get out of the still damaged city centre and the housing near the docks that had been struck during the war. He had to pay a minion in the housing office when he bumped someone. This was a small amount to pay, he never told anyone what he made from the scam. Once the minion had got his money the list was altered without any sign of wrong doing being evident. Ted would announce to his client that he had made an extra effort, and at his own expense, to make the allocation quicker than he had expected, as the client had said how desperate they were to move into quality accommodation. This always worked and if they could afford it a little extra went through the chippy till.

They were still in Earl Road in Kitty's house, when Teddy rushed into their room. Shouting and rummaging around the corner where he kept his toolbox. Michael was playing with Leo, who was about four at the time.

"What on earth is the matter Teddy?" asked Mary. She knew that face and what it meant. Someone had slighted him in some way and he was going to scare them, or worse seriously hurt them. "Now don't you be going and getting yerself arrested again. Yer no good to me in friggin' jail!" warned Mary.

Picking up his claw hammer from the box behind the sofa said,

"I am just going to fix something at the chippy." With that comment he slammed the door behind him.

"Jesus, Mary and Joseph!" uttered Mary. She could only sit and wait anxiously for the outcome.

Teddy rushed along the road to the corner chippy. He had been in there for his payday treat when four men had started to call names and threaten Li the owner. Teddy liked Li. He was always happy and gave everyone a warm welcome in his shop. Teddy loved his accent and the way he spoke in typical second language English. The four had been calling him all sorts of horrible racist names and were threatening to put his window through and to beat him all the way back to China. As there were four of them and one of Teddy, who no longer had his headache stick, Teddy had rushed home for an equaliser.

On reaching Li's shop Teddy called out to the four yobs.

"Come on now! Yer fuckin' shower of shit house bullies yers! Go on hit him now will yers? And I'll smash yer fuckin' heads in one by fuckin' one!" The four saw the face on Teddy. A brief risk assessment was carried out simultaneously by the four antagonists, and the price for continuing with their bullying of the Chinese owner was too much. They backed out of the shop, none of them wanted to feel the hammer coming down on the back of their head. Once outside they moved quickly to put distance between them and the hammer man who stood outside the shop yelling threats of violence in the direction of their retreat.

On returning inside the chippy, Li was grateful to Teddy,

"Thank you. They were going to hurt me."

"They won't be back Li. If they do, you send me word and I'll come and smash the lot of them!" replied Teddy.

Li forced extra portions of chips onto Teddy's order of pie and chips, he accepted them reluctantly. As Teddy walked the short distance back to the house, he started to compose himself, slow his breathing down, let his pounding heart rate ease. Growing up in Islington Teddy had lived in a white monoculture. People usually kept to the neighbourhood they lived in. It was only when he moved to Wavertree that he met people from other cultures. He readily accepted everyone at face value, if they were OK with him, he was OK with them. The first time Teddy had encountered curry was at the docks. A guy from the West

Indies had been eating his lunch and the aroma coming from the cold dish in the tin was evocative.

"What's that ye've got there Billy?" asked Teddy. With a mouthful of food Billy responded with "Curry and rice." He inadvertently spitted several rice pellets from his lips.

"That smells great. Gizza bite?" asked Teddy. Billy offered him some from the same spoon he was eating with.

"No thanks, I will use me chisel as a spoon, no offense I am just dead fussy." Taking a makeshift spoonful Teddy put the new food in his mouth.

"Hmm, that tastes really good." Seconds later Teddy started to turn red in the face, not with anger this time but with the chemical heat generated from the Scotch bonnet chillies that Billy used in his curry. "Fuckin' hell Billy what's in that, fucking' fire or something?" Billy spattered a few more rice pellets in the direction of Teddy and laughing said

"What's up man? Don't yer like hot curry?" It took Teddy a moment to find his tea mug and taking a big swig of the hot tea. Then he continued with his exclamations.

"Fuckin' hell Billy how do yer eat that? Yer not even sweating! Look at me face its dripping!" Billy had played that trick before, he always found it a good laugh.

"Here Teddy have a swig of milk, that'll take the edge of it."

"Hey Billy! Yer have to give me that recipe. Even though it's burnt me gob off I want more, just not as hot as that though."

"Yeah man! I'll do that. I'll get the missus to make yer a baby one." All the men laughed at this including Teddy.

True to his word Billy's wife had made a 'baby curry' for Teddy. He took it home and gave his kids a taste. Even though it was aimed at babies, albeit West Indian babies taste buds, it still had the same effect as Teddy had felt, just not quite so painful, or was it. Taking his clue from Billy he told Michael and Leo to have a drink of milk to stop the burning sensation on their lips. The two boys drowned a full pint between them to ease the fire like tingling on their tongues. Teddy was delighted in his mischief. Mary accused him of cruelty after she had tasted a tiny spoonful herself. The two boys, now recovered from their ordeal, laughed along with their Dad as their Mother cried out in pain.

To ease the tension that his mischief had caused Teddy announced that he had seen the man from the housing and they were moving out in a week, to a new estate in West Derby where there were fields and wide-open spaces. Mary went from hurt to ecstasy in a moment.

Chapter 35 The Flamingo

Mary and family now had their home in the quiet district of
West Derby bordering the fields of Lord Sefton's estate.
There was green space all around and the feeling was
peaceful away from the hustle and bustle of Wavertree and
the packed together, back to back, terraced houses. Money
was coming in on a regular basis and she was happy. Her
youngest, Tony was a quiet child and easy to raise. His big
brother Leo was more boisterous and got up to the usual
boy stuff. Michael and Leo played well together, and
Maureen was the boss of the kids, as expected of an older
sister. The household was settled. An ideal time for another
child.

Mary was pregnant in the spring of 1958. As usual her
pregnancies were uneventful. She carried the child well, as
before with all the others. Her focus was on family. She
was still making do with money. A large family took a lot
of book balancing, not that she had a book, it was a tin as
usual. Teddy duly turned the weekly housekeeping over
every Friday evening, retaining what he needed for his
enjoyment down town. Teddy had new haunts to frequent.
As they lived in Wavertree for a while, he found that some
places were more exotic than the usual pubs of town and

Islington. The mixed culture component of the area near parliament Street was a draw for thrill seekers and spivs.

You could get anything in the pubs and drinking clubs in the area. Teddy had started his foray into purely fencing at this time. He had left the breaking and entering behind him and that was now history. These days he was a budding entrepreneur. Buying and selling stuff for profit, regardless of its origins. He observed fashions and trends. What were the young people wearing or wanted to complete their image. He sent out feelers for how much was being spent on various items. His education with Old Man Shanley of making a third profit, or what the market will bear, was at the forefront of his mind. If he could sell desirable stuff for a lot less than the high street, then he had a good thing going.

A popular haunt in the Toxteth area that bordered Wavertree was a drinking club known as the Pink Flamingo on Princess Road. It was just one of many that were in the area and Teddy made this his favourite, as his business had started there and was flourishing. The locals were a diverse crowd from all facets of the community. People of colour and every creed were to be found in the Pink Flamingo. Some kept themselves to themselves while others intermingled with everyone to increase their exposure to opportunities. Teddy was of the latter variety. He was known to many as the man who can supply you with almost anything, apart from drugs, he never went down that road. If you wanted the latest clothes then see Teddy, he had a network of Pearlers, shop lifters, that would sell their gear on to him quickly. It was then off their hands and if anyone came calling there were no goods to be found. Teddy for his part quickly shifted the gear on to willing fashionistas. Sometimes Teddy would strike up a relationship with one of the Pearlers. These women were often married and were supplementing family income with their shoplifting forays. They had discretion high on their agenda and were relatively safe for Teddy to get involved with, confident that they would not lead trouble to his door in the east of the city. These relationships followed a similar pattern. He would call to their house to collect the goods and pay them, often staying for a brew and to discuss the next sought-after items to be collected, and the shops that were likely to have them. As he was naturally charming with women, especially when he wanted something, they were often flattered by the attention. If he found a kindred spirit of the carnal kind he would call by more often and they would have sex, in the lounge, bedroom, kitchen or on the stairs.

The risk of being caught, in more ways than one, made the adventures more exciting.

When Mary was pregnant, which was frequent during that time, Teddy had groomed a succession of women eager to have a piece of the action with the funny, charming and well-dressed man, with a few bob. Mary was unaware of most of them in person. However she could tell when he had been with another woman. He would come home in a frivolous frame of mind and play silly games with her, smooth talking to make her feel good. He never thought about her sense of smell. For often a perfume would follow him home to shout out the lie he was having with one of these floozies.

Mary for the most part took these tell-tale signs quietly. She had once called him out over a blatant indiscretion. That backfired on her with a violent outburst from Teddy. An almighty row, as she told her sister Annie later, broke out. Annie offered the advice to leave him and his philandering ways, but the economic reality of being a single mother, and soon to have five kids, was not something she could countenance.

In the late summer she gave birth to Carl. He was to be known from then on as Carlo by Teddy and Carl by Mary.

Teddy still had his Latino based sense of humour. He had a
Leo, Antonio and now a Carlo. Mary hated the name,
again. Carlo was the straw that broke the camel's back
when it came to space in the West Derby maisonette.
Teddy had seen his contact in the council again and Ted
had made the arrangements as usual, through a minion, to
get Teddy his first proper house. It was requested to order
by Teddy. It had to be near his sister's house in Dovecot, so
he could visit his Father and Auntie Nellie who had moved
in with Annie and her family. Ted had played a blinder. He
secured a house in the same road, just a little way down and
across from Annie's. Teddy was delighted and paid his fee,
which silently went through one of Ted's growing empire
of chippy shop profits.

Teddy was again a jobbing joiner at this time. He lost his
dry dock ship's joiner job after he and another communist
sympathiser painted a slogan on the wall of an old
warehouse that read, 'Buy your Daily Worker'. The
foreman discovered who it was an they were both sacked
on the spot. It was lucky for Teddy that his parole had
finished some time earlier, or Mr Robinson would have
been on his case too. The day job was good for most
outgoings and he still made forays into Toxteth

occasionally, but less frequently due to travel being awkward.

As was usual with Teddy if he could make a statement to show off his recognition need, he would. So he soon replaced his bicycle with a very desirable form of transport: a Lambretta scooter. This was not of the mod's variety, all mirrors and gleaming chrome work that were just emerging, it was purely functional. He had a windshield with a small slit cut out to see through it when rain accumulated on it and large over mitts to keep his hands warm in winter. He was now fully mobile and could get across town or any area he needed to be in for work or his selling business. He went to the local pub on his scooter.

His youngest kids were fascinated with the scooter. They would watch him put his crash helmet on, which he called his skid lid, and start the engine with a unique style. He kick-started the scooter with his left leg in order to generate the required power to crank the engine, while twisting the throttle to encourage the burst of revs, signalling the scooter was now operational. He would then step through the gap and only then would he fasten his helmet under his chin while the engine idled before riding off. His youngest boys would pretend to start their own scooter engines in the same way, kicking down with their left legs and twisting their imaginary throttles with their right hands. Teddy advised them that he only did it because his right leg was shorter and weaker. When asked why that was, he kidded them that he was shot in the war by a Japanese soldier while he was trying to escape a prisoner of war camp. He had to be in a good mood to lie in a humorous way.

It was while the boys were growing up that they got their first exposure to Teddy's selling business. He had started to sell on items that he felt there was a market for. He had been talking with a guy in the Boundary pub, his new local, about chickens. They were the new Sunday roast item as they were selling for less than the usual lamb joints. All he needed was to buy his chickens readily dressed, after slaughter, plucked and de-headed if possible, then sell them door to door in his street.

Teddy found an outlet in Derby Lane that he could source his chickens from. He started small and stayed small. He would sell the chickens to his neighbours. Making what he described as a small profit and a quick return. He would employ the family in his selling business. Maureen would be sent to Tuebrook via two buses to get a dozen dressed chickens, which she had to carry back to Dovecot. The three young boys, Michael, Leo and Tony would then be sent to various houses in the street with a shopping bag with a chicken inside. They were schooled in what to say. They had always to use the polite terms of address as Mrs or Miss. The usual opening line went.

"Hello Mrs Gornall, my Dad said do you want to buy a fresh chicken for one and six pence." While opening the bag to show the contents. This worked reasonably well.

As ever Teddy was looking to minimise his outlay and had the brainwave of breeding his own chickens and getting eggs into the bargain. So he built a chicken coop in the back garden, complete with egg access doorways and chicken wire enclosed run area. This worked well for some time but the supply of chickens for meat was not to be had from this approach, he soon discovered. He needed a different 'must have' item for re-sale.

There were two men he knew from the Boundary who worked at Stanley Abattoir and meat market. One in particular was really useful to Teddy. He went by the handle of Little Billy. He was all of five foot one and had red hair. He lived in the Dovecot estate too. It was Little Billy that put Teddy onto meat for sale as a change from the chickens. He could source him with a few joints to see if there was a market in his street for fresh lamb. Most lamb was still frozen as it came from New Zealand. The boys were again sent out to the neighbours to see if they wanted any fresh lamb for Sunday, shoulders, loins and legs. There was a system of wealth applied by Teddy in his selection of which neighbour might spend ten shillings on a shoulder and those that might stretch to the nineteen and six pence for the leg, if they could afford neither they were offered the loin for their roast.

The meat sales went on for a while and soon the stock had to be bought legitimately, Little Billy could not supply more than the odd joint at a time. So Teddy went into the meat market directly to buy his stock. It was always a Friday morning, ready for the coming weekend and to coincide with weekly pay packets. The boys learned a little about joints of meat and that the material used to wrap it was called loincloth. It soaked up bits of blood and helped to keep the meat from going off too quickly when stored in a larder, few people had fridges in those days.

One day Teddy arrived home from the meat market with a large bull's horn for Leo and Tony to play with. They had been watching Robin Hood on TV. There was always a horn call blown by someone or other in the TV show and the boys were often seen playing with imaginary horns in the garden. Teddy told them to bury it for a while in the back garden, then they could dig it up and it would be ready to use as a horn. The boys eagerly awaited the exhumation of the horn. When it was dug up it looked the same. It still had a filling of some sort inside it. Teddy had previously asked someone in the abattoir how to make a horn, and to impress his boys he took hold of it in one hand and tapped the wide end down on a piece of wood. The inner material slid out smoothly, he discarded it. After removing a small section from the end with a saw, he had a bull's horn just like on Robin Hood. He wiped the end clean of soil with a rag and gave it to the boys to blow. Neither boy could make a sound from it, so Teddy had a go and a loud farting sound came out. The boys laughed and wanted to make farting noises too.

Tony recalled this occasion and later remarked, that it had been one of the very few good times they had spent with their Dad.

Chapter 36 The Shame

Over time the money-making schemes varied somewhat. The chicken coop had gone, all the birds had been slaughtered one afternoon by Teddy. He told the boys they all had some disease and had to go. The structure was dismantled, and the wood stored against the garden fence for re-use later.

A new idea had come to Teddy when he was in the pub. A sort of unofficial lottery was popular at the time. It was a sealed game of numbers. Tickets were sold for a shilling and there were prizes for the winning tickets. All the tickets would be sold in the pub by Teddy, or one or two helpers. Cash prizes were the most popular, but Teddy also gave a couple of consolation ones too. These were often Pearler items that he found difficult to shift, but they added an extra surprise element to the draw. Tickets were sealed at the printers by sewing up the folded paper with a semi-circular band of stitching. The integrity of the ticket was guaranteed by the stitching being intact.

Again the family were involved in this scheme. Maureen was employed to stitch up the folded papers with their random generated number printed on the inside cover. She would be given a selection of papers to sew. It was important that she sewed them in exactly the same needle holes as the originals to make the stitch seals appear as new. Cotton of the same colour was sourced by Teddy. Maureen had to learn how to tie off the cotton when she got to the end of the curved line. These doctored tickets were for occasional use. A very trusted few would buy the winning ticket. When a random person, usually a woman, was picked to open the sealed prize ticket number, the owner of the winning ticket winner would appear to be ecstatic with their win. The other participants would be consoled with how close they were to the winning number. Better luck next time.

The window altering business was just about ticking over. Maureen would be used to sound out neighbours who might be in the market to have their small Georgian type windows replaced with large 'picture' windows. Teddy told her to use the phrase, 'do you really want to keep these old-fashioned windows that look like a galleon in full sail, or do you want nice bright modern picture windows?' When a neighbour did decide to have their galleon sails replaced Teddy would take along his two lads, Leo and Tony, and set them to work alongside him. They had to carefully break the glass out and bag the shards and splintered wood. Teddy would show them how to place linseed oil putty into the cleaned-out troughs ready for the new large pieces of glass. He would show them how to hold a large piece of putty in one hand and feed it through the fingers into the trough, pressing it down as the line of sealant went into the recess. This was a real skill and Leo was the better of the two boys at it. Soon Tony was only allowed to brush up and leave the skilled bits to Leo and Teddy.

Recognition was always on Teddy's radar. He would look for ways to have people recognise him as a source of service. The telephone was a dual feature. The Kelly's house was the first in the road to get a telephone. It acted as an essential communication tool, but also as a sign that Teddy Kelly was a man of means and moved with the times. The GPO engineer came and fitted the phone in the small hallway of Aldwark Road. The telephone cable from the post just up the road was a clear sign of connectivity. Maureen was particularly keen to tell her friends about the new phone. She wanted the other street kids to see her on the phone and would stand with the front door open and chat away to imaginary friends to impress onlooking street kids.

She also had to do other messages as they were referred to. Teddy was keen to be known as a union man. Part of his communist sympathiser thinking. He disliked the 'haves' and saw the 'have nots' as the oppressed. His solution was to distribute the wealth evenly. He never saw the irony of his own money-making schemes to get wealthy as being out of kilter with this philosophy. So every month for some time Maureen would get two buses across the city to pay Teddy's union dues. As he was not employed in a firm, his dues were not collected directly and so he made this arrangement. Maureen would go to the house and wait while the union man entered the weekly amounts in Teddy's book and stamped them as paid. Maureen later told of how she felt really uncomfortable being placed in this position. Having to wait in a man's house alone with him while he busied himself with the union book. Nothing ever happened she said, but she did feel vulnerable at the time, especially in winter and the dark afternoons and early evenings. Teddy never thought anything about it.

Maureen had met John at a local disco. He lived in a neighbouring road in Dovecot. He sported the Beatles look hairstyle and she thought he was gorgeous. They started courting. She was just sixteen. Teddy was suspicious of any boys calling to the house and soon banned John from calling. If she wanted to see him, she did so away from the house.

"I don't want any scandal coming to my door" he told her. So Maureen duly met John away from the house to save any more friction. She could still feel the indignation and hurt after he had banished her upstairs, when she flirted with a man who had called to price a job for Teddy. She had been in the garden when big John was discussing the job Teddy wanted doing. She was showing off in front of the handsome man by answering her father back. Teddy moved quickly and roughly shoved her out of the garden and warned her to behave. She ran away sobbing hurting more inside due to loss of face.

This was just one of the many attacks made towards her by Teddy. Maureen had had a hard time from Teddy since as far back as she could remember. Starting with being left out of treats as a punishment, progressing to more stringent controls of her *errant* behaviour. Her crime, as behaviour went, was nothing more than her love of reading. She would read in bed for hours. The first time Teddy was aware of this was on his return from the Boundary pub one night to see her light still on. He could be a skinflint at home and saw the light burning as a waste of electricity. He shouted at her when he found her awake and reading. Mary was helpless in pleading a case for her as he ignored any counter arguments to his own position. He was the master of his house.

Mary was in cahoots with Maureen after that. She would call up the stairs for her to turn the light off as he was due back from the pub about then. Maureen would pull the switch and settle down to sleep. This system worked well for some time. It failed when Teddy acted out of character one night. He came home earlier via a different route and could see a light burning upstairs. He was immediately angry. When Mary heard the sound of his scooter, she called up for her to turn the light out quickly as he was home early. On stopping his scooter he raced upstairs to her room and balled at her, sticking his own face right up to her face while admonishing her for disobedience. She was an unhappy person living in that house.

Maureen made her own decision to go to secretarial school, in Quarry Bank College, on leaving Grant Road Secondary at age fifteen. She was keen to make her own way in the world and to escape the yoke of fear that Teddy had wrapped around her neck. She later told of how her childhood had been punctuated by his punitive actions, mostly she thought, directed at hurting Mary more so than her, as part of his coercive control.

Maureen was becoming more independent in her thinking and plans for her future. These future plans were niggling at Teddy's sense of control, 'how would he get her to do what he wanted, if she was off doing her own thing?'. The solution to this lack of control came out of the blue. A neighbour mentioned to Teddy while he was drinking at the Boundary that two lads had been shouting up to the front bedroom to get Maureen's attention the other night. It was John and his friend Norman who wanted to take Maureen out somewhere. Teddy was furious. He finished that pint and raced home on his Lambretta. He dragged Maureen out of bed instructing her to get dressed. Mary was distraught 'what was going to happen?' Teddy was shouting about her bringing shame and scandal to the house and so she was going off to Kirkby to live with her Grandmother. Before Maureen knew what was happening, she was on the back of the Lambretta being transported to her Grandmother's flat in Kirkby, some twenty-five or so minutes away. She was dumped there where she wouldn't be any more trouble.

This cemented her resolve to make her own way in the world and to have nothing more to do with him. She had to time visits back home when she knew he would be out.

It was a few weeks after the forced expulsion from the family home that the reason how Teddy had caught her with the light on that night became clear. He was not at the Boundary as he had claimed, but he had been seeing a woman, while her man was in the pub. The affair had been going on for a while and mostly their trysts were of the daylight variety. That night the opportunity to spend more time together came when the darts match was on. Her man was keen on darts. On leaving her house, after their prolonged time together, to make a token appearance in the Boundary his route took him near the back of his own road where he could see the upstairs light was on. The affair became common knowledge after the driveway fight.

The younger kids were asleep when a commotion erupted outside the house, it was late. A group of men had banged on the door looking for that 'bastard Kelly'. It was the husband and his two eldest lads of the affair woman, who had come to teach him a lesson. His Dad had found out about her and Teddy and he was mad with her.

"Where does this fucker live?" he demanded of his wife. "If you don't tell me I will bash you up so badly you will need to go to casualty to save yer fuckin' life!" She was fearful he would hurt her, she thought frantically of what to say.

"Aldwark Road Dovecot" replied the terrified woman. Still fearful of her husband's wrath she added for good measure that "Teddy made me do it. He said he would tell everyone I was shoplifting if I didn't do it."

"The fuckin' shithouse!" exclaimed the man. Leaving her to recover he called for his two eldest sons in their late teens. "Hey, you two. We are going to teach this fucker a lesson, get yer coats."

They brought a pick axe handle to bash him with and it was this banging on the door and breaking of the car windows, along with the shouts that disturbed the sleeping kids.

"Jesus, Mary and Joseph!" cried Mary, "What on earth is going on Teddy?" Teddy didn't answer, he was frantically looking for a weapon to equalise the odds with. His tool box was still stored in the under-stair cupboard, rooting in the dark he found a hand saw, that would have to do.

Opening the front door Teddy charged out.

"Hey yer fuckers yer! Fuck off or I'll fuckin kill the lot of yer!" he was wielding the saw like a sword. It may have been this that startled them long enough for Teddy to grab the husband by the collar, lean him over the car bonnet and bring the saw up to his neck. "Now you tell them to fuck off or I will cut yer fuckin head off right now!" The man was completely startled by the turn of events. He had assumed they would be able to beat the daylights out of the crippled guy, now it was him that was in dire need of a reprieve.

"Its OK lads leave it, leave it. Go on I will catch up with you in a bit." The man was scared, but as time went on and he didn't feel as if his throat was being severed, he grew calmer. Teddy still had him in a death hold, saw at the ready.

"Now what the fuck is all this about?" he demanded.

"You and my missus. That's what! You have been forcing her to have sex with yer, yer dirty fucker yer!" This was news to Teddy. What could have made her say that, he thought. Then the penny dropped. He had found out and it was to save her face, literally from a beating, that she had made up the story. He thought fast, still holding the saw to the man's neck. He left it there while he delivered his line.

"Well it was fuck all, she was just there that's all. Now I will make you a deal. You leave it where it is now, don't blame her, do yer hear me?" there was as light nod, constrained by the saw teeth against his skin. "Good. Now I will never see her again. And if I see you or any of your lads ever again, I will come back for yer and I will cut yer fuckin' head right off. Do yer hear?"

The man managed to say "OK, I will stay away and leave it at that."

"Good now you fuck off before I change my fuckin' mind." The man gathered his clothes together and walked away down the path over the broken car window glass. He didn't look back or ever call again.

"What on earth was all that about, who is the woman they were talking about?" Mary wanted to know. Taking his lead from what her husband had said he embellished his response.

"Ah it was some Pearl diver I was using, she is a bit mad and she complained about me not taking stuff off her, it was the wrong type of stuff she lifted, so she made up a cock and bull story about me and they were coming to fill me in. I have sorted it with her husband now and he won't be back here, and I won't be using her again either."

"Too right yer won't!" added Mary.

The road's curtains were twitching 'ten to the dozen' as Mary later described in her account of the evening.

Chapter 37 The Acceptance

The Spanish Galleon window conversion had dried up on the Dovecot estate and so Teddy decided to go back to a previous idea, the fruit barra. He sourced a barra from JWs in Queen's Square market that needed a little work doing on it. He easily made the few woodwork amendments and replaced a couple of rusted bolts. He decided that it would not require painting as he would cover it with the new false grass sheeting that was popular in the down town barras. As he had no one at home at this time old enough or big enough to move the barra he started a young lad he had met, Georgie from the Edge Hill area of Liverpool. Georgie was one of the sons of a Pearl diver he knew. Teddy had picked his spot at the end of the Dovecot shops, next door to the Post Office at the start of the service road to the back of the arches' shops, as they were known. It had lots of passing pedestrian traffic from the main section of the Dovecot estate and being just a few doors down from the first of the two greengrocers in the arches shops it was great for comparing prices.

The regular shop owners were aghast at the brazen encroachment on their legitimate businesses. The local people thought the discounted prices were a real bargain and as more of the shop's business went to Teddy and his fruit barra, resentment grew. The two small boys Leo and Tony were regularly sent on spying missions to see how much the local greengrocers were selling their potatoes, tomatoes and other items for. The prices were all written on the windows in a white solution to draw shoppers in for a bargain. Leo and Tony would report back on the listed prices per pound or five pound for tomatoes and spuds respectively. They enjoyed being spies and were told not to be seen while doing the reconnoitre walk byes. So they had a variety of methods to employ. These went from idle walks past to play fighting to ensure they had all the information. While in a headlock one of the boys would say the prices out loud to ensure they were remembered, once clocked they would break off their play fight and report back to their Dad. Teddy would then alter his prices accordingly on his small black board of special deals. His calling out of the specials ensured that women would stop to listen on their way to the shops or coming back having paid more than his specials prices. He used the comments of the women to entice those on the outward journey not to make the same mistake and to buy their spuds off him instead. Old Man Shanley's lessons coming back from the early days in Islington. Sell for a small profit and quick return.

Needless to say that the owners of the shops affected by the brazen trespass on their business, of Teddy the Barra Boy on their patch, were annoyed. The police often arrived with anonymous complaints of obstruction and that Teddy had to move his barra. Teddy would argue the legality of the complaint with the lack of yellow lines on the kerbsides. Mostly this worked, and the constables would report back to the shop owners that there was nothing they could do about it. On the odd occasion that a young officer would push the 'crime of obstruction' it would result in raised voices, mostly on Teddy's part. The inevitable van or car would arrive, called for by the constable on his newly issued walkie talkie radio kit. Teddy would get arrested and when he explained to the duty sergeant of the lack of yellow lines would be released without any further charge.

Georgie would arrive at the Kelly's house in Aldwark Road early in the morning to collect the barra and wheel it down to the arches' shops. He would start the display off with the small amount of residual stock from the previous day, waiting for Teddy to go to the market for the rest of the goods. Teddy paid Georgie at the end of the week when the shopper's pay packets had been collected and supplies secured for the weekend. The system was working well. Money was coming in regularly and Teddy splashed out on a car. He had decided he could save on delivery costs if he had his own wheels. The black Ford Poplar with its three forward and one reverse gear was a hit with all the boys.

The early days of the fruit barra went well. The two young lads enjoyed going to the new fruit market on Saturdays and school holidays, just down and across from the Stanley abattoir, in their new black car. They loved to see the wagons loaded with large bags and trays of goods and the variety of people that worked in the market. They heard strange accents that were really exotic to their ears. They normally only ever heard local Liverpool accents, but the market voices were from Lancashire, Cheshire and even North Wales.

The Ford would be loaded to the gunnels with a few bags of spuds and trays of fruit and tomatoes. Teddy's aim was to shift as much of the stock on a daily basis, leaving very little to carry over to the next day. This was especially important on Saturdays. The barra was always quiet sales wise on Mondays and Tuesdays and Teddy only bought essentials on those days. Any fruit that was 'bruised' as he called it was sold off really cheaply or he encouraged the boys to eat it. The two lads grew well and developed bigger arms and stronger backs than their age compared counterparts due to the heavy weights they were used to lifting. They spent every Saturday and school holiday working at the family barra. Tidying up, filling the display trays with more fruit and tomatoes. Carrying the half hundred weight bags of spuds out of the car, then spilling them onto the sloped section of the barra for scooping up into the usual five-pound amounts, as measured on the weighing scales.

One day as Tony was leaving primary school his Dad arrived to pick him up. This in itself was really unusual for two reasons, one his Dad never picked him up as the school was just around the corner from Aldwark Road and secondly, he was driving a bright yellow Ford Anglia estate car. It was Teddy's way of impressing anyone that saw him in the neighbourhood that he was doing well. He never lost his impulse to impress as part of his recognition needs.

Michael had been exiled, in a constructive way, to live with his Grandmother in Kirkby in order to help her out. He enjoyed the freedom from Teddy's tyranny and he felt he could develop in his own way, far from any overt scrutiny. Michael was gay. He always knew so from an early age. He also knew that Teddy was a typical homophobe, like most people. It was illegal. Michael learned to keep his lighter personality hidden. It suited Teddy not to have Michael around in the early days. He was often reminded about his doubt when he saw the boy who didn't look like Leo or Tony at all. So when Mary's mother moved to a brand-new pensioners flat in Kirkby Teddy suggested that Michael would be ideal to live there to look after her. Mary read between the lines and agreed, mainly to remove Michael from the constant picking at him by Teddy. She hated the way Teddy would use any reason to beat Michael with his bamboo cane, that was kept ready at the side of the fire place. Spare the rod and spoil the child. Spare the child and avoid the rod she thought.

Michael was a big lad, when he and Maureen changed places at his Grand ma's. Teddy needed bigger help than the two younger boys could deliver in order to keep his barra business a going concern, after losing the services of Georgie. So Michael was returned to the family house in Aldwark Road. As he was now bigger and needed by Teddy, he was spared beatings. The beatings had been transferred to the two growing boisterous boys. Teddy needed Michael to be able to drive the car, so he encouraged him to apply for his license. At age seventeen he was one of the youngest with a license in Dovecot. Teddy could now carry on his business as before but with added flexibility of sending Michael to the market. Also he had another plan in mind for the lad.

Michael had left school and he needed money for his own lifestyle, Teddy didn't pay him for working on the barra. He said that he was fed and sheltered in return for what he did. So Michael decided to get a job of his own, one that *had* to fit in with Teddy's regime. Michael became a window cleaner on the Dovecot estate. He built up a small round of customers and he enjoyed the freedom to chat to a variety of people while working. He had his own money, after turning over an agreed amount with Teddy for the housekeeping notwithstanding the unpaid work he did on the barra too. Michael was the same age as his cousin Francis. Francis was from his mother's side of the family and was one of Annie's. He was used to living on the wrong side of the law. He dabbled with various illicit activities and was a regular suspect hauled in by the local police for questioning. Teddy needed transport for his latest Pearl divers, two girls he had been developing, and so it was Michael that was the most obvious driver, Francis only had a provisional license. When Teddy explained what was required both Michael and Francis were delighted with the glamorous opportunity. It started out as transporting the girls, then they progressed to accompanying the two girls into the shops and eventually all four were accomplished Pearl divers. They picked items to order as was Teddy's preferred way of doing business.

The two youngest still went around the road to a select few customers with a new line of patter, still of the polite variety but this time it was coats, dresses and trousers that were the sale items. Leo and Tony had no idea they were involved with selling on shoplifted goods. This aspect only came to light years later, when they actually met some of the Pearl divers. A succession of young women would call at the house to see their Dad. They would talk for a while and soon they would leave after Teddy had given them some money. They always left a carrier shopping bag. It was Leo that sussed out what was happening when one of his friend's sisters arrived one day. Leo then sought more information from him. When he had the full picture, he in turn told Tony.

Michael was in his element. He had money for his new clothes which were essential for any gay man to show off when going down town. The work itself was glamorous he could brag about it to impress potential lovers. The clothes he wore he picked himself off the racks while working, leaving more money for splashing around as the epitome of the gay man with means. Many years later he would tell his brother Tony that they were the happiest days of his life. How he loved being a simple Pearl diver and man about town.

Teddy had managed to drive the doubts of Michael's paternity out of his mind while the side business was doing well. He never raised the topic of his fear again with Mary or threatened her with violence either. He was never to know the real story. He had finally accepted Michael into his family.

Chapter 38 The NSPCC

Teddy was displeased with all of his kids at one time or another. Mostly this would result in a beating with his bamboo cane that stood against the side of the fireplace, on the righthand side of his armchair for easy reach. Often the two boys, Leo and Tony, would get simultaneous beatings for some misdemeanour or other. As the two were typical boys, they got into squabbles and low-level fights over trivia. If Teddy was out of sorts, with a hangover or worry about something, usually money, then the cane would appear in his hand and a bellowed warning if they were lucky, a flurry of whip-like strokes if they weren't would rain down on them as they scrambled towards the door to escape. A rage of shouts would chase them up the stairs where they sought sanctuary from the anger.

Migraine was a common excuse for rage. If Teddy was feeling a little relaxed, he would describe his prodrome symptoms.

"It's like flashing lights going on and off in your eyes" he would say. One or other of the boys would be sent to the corner shops for Beecham's Powders. Teddy had a strange way of taking his pain killing medicine. They were designed for dissolving in water then to be drank. He would carefully open the folded paper and then pour the dry powder into his mouth, swilling it down with anything from a drink of water to cold tea. The boys thought this was a gross thing to do as they knew just how bitter the powder tasted. This was just one more idiosyncratic behaviour of Teddy's, of which he had many. Mostly his quirks were superstition based, of his own creation. When he was putting on his shoes, he would always put the left one on first, then the right. Then he would return to tie the left shoe up first. When Michael was working with ladders, he always advised him not to walk under them, as it would bring him bad luck – Michael was a window cleaner at the time!

Teddy never took any notice of what the boys learned in school, only a passing interest if a bad report came home, usually dealt with by the flailing bamboo cane. One day Leo brought home his brand-new exercise book where he had written his homework in. It was almost a full page. He was proud of the work. His class teacher was Mr Dutton and he was an old-style school teacher. He liberally used the cane, almost every day with his B class group of kids. Leo was caned by Mr Dutton regularly. Leo didn't know why most of the time, he would be just joking about something or other with his friends and the call would go up for them to come to the front of the class. Mr Dutton would then administer two to six strikes of his bamboo cane to the outstretched hands of the boys who had dared to be disrespectful of his teachings.

Leo just happened to say to his brother.

"I have done my homework, it's about my Dad and its quite good." Tony just acknowledged this with a typical non-verbal expression. On this occasion Teddy was listening, he must have been bored.

"Let me see your homework then" he demanded. When he read the first line of the twenty-five or so lines, he raised his voice to the usual bellow. "What the fuck is this? 'My Father doesn't understand me.' What the fuckin' hell do you mean by that? Of course I fuckin' understand yer!" The class homework was to write about one's relationship with one's father. Leo had been truthful in his piece. He never got to fully explain what he meant by the opening line. Teddy had flung the book away, causing Leo to cry out that he would get into trouble and get the cane off Daddy Dutton (his nickname as the kid's called him). "I'll give yer what for, 'my father doesn't understand me', he quoted from the homework. Leo was crying over the reaction to his piece and the tear in his exercise book. Mary felt she just had to intervene.

"Now *you* leave him alone, he was only writing about what he thinks for the teacher."

"I'll not have my kids saying anything about what goes on at home to anyone, or a fuckin' teacher" spat back Teddy.

"Leo go upstairs son. I will write you a note about how the book got torn so you don't get into trouble." Leo went off to the sanctity of the bedroom, away from danger. Tony sat very quiet. Looking, but not looking, in case he was the next subject of Teddy's rage. He escaped any fallout on that occasion, spending the rest of the evening not saying a word, hoping to be invisible.

Teddy was an enigma when it came to his kids. He would be a tyrant one day and a funny man bearer of wonderful gifts the next. There was no way of predicting what any day was to be, they were so changeable. Teddy's recognition need was sated with the smallest of signs on occasion. He would feel very good if he brought home an unusual toy that the two younger boys would enjoy, especially if no other kid in the neighbourhood had one. A wooden puzzle that required great skill to complete, by freeing a large piece out of a set of various sized pieces through an exit slot, by moving one piece at a time, was such an item. As the boys couldn't figure it out by themselves, he felt superior by instructing them how to do it. Taking great satisfaction when they failed to follow his instructions exactly, then he would use the replay demonstration to underline his superior knowledge of the game. In reality he was shown how to do it by the man who sold him the puzzle, as he couldn't solve it on his own either.

Teddy wanted to be the boy's kerbside teacher like the ones he had when he was young. The boys listened to his cautionary tales illustrating this or that when they were young. Teddy had to be the top dog in everything when it came to being street savvy. He used his powers of observation to illustrate some lessons. He could see into the minds of the two boys they thought. He could often tell what they had been doing while he was out by examining the house or garden for tell-tale signs, like a detective at a crime scene. So the boys were more circumspect when playing as they got older to avoid being found out and the ritual caning and early to bed that followed. They loved to play fight. This started with watching the wrestling on TV. Their dad was amused by the wrestling, he knew it was all fake, usually. He only took an interest if he thought there was a real grudge match on.

Bear hugs were a popular imitation move the boys employed on each other, as were the headlock and getting a submission out of a particular hold. Leo was the better fighter. He was almost two years older than Tony, but Tony was bigger. Most bouts went Leo's way. His wiry frame was amplified by his great mental ability to be stronger, he feared nothing, apart from his Dad's rage. Occasionally the play fights would get out of hand and one would get hurt. This resulted in a real scuffle and usually tears of rage on one part or the other. Teddy would advise against too rough play with his usual prediction.

"It'll end in tears! Then I will make you cry for real." indicating the corner of the fireplace. This usually did the trick and stopped the fracas dead.

One day Teddy had brought home the latest gadget, a Grundig reel to reel tape recorder. He had got it cheap of course from a guy at the pub. He entertained the boys with recording their voices and playing them back. He recorded farting noises to make the boys scream with laughter. This was a time of great fun they were to remember. The Grundig was to be put to another use a while later.

As the boys got really good at replacing the dislodged furniture after their play fighting, Teddy could not find signs of their fights. He knew they had been fighting by the red marks of headlocks and stuff. The boys had said they had been playing races in explanation for the facial and neck redness.

The day they were found out to be fighting again, despite Teddy's warnings not to, was a bright sunny afternoon after they had returned home from school to an empty house. The fight started slowly with a curse.

"Shut the door. Shut the fuckin' door!" from Leo to Tony who had left the living room door ajar. "Shut it yerself" was the response from the kitchen. Psychologists say children imitate their parents and learned behaviour can be transmitted across the generations. In the case of aggression this appeared to be the case. The boys had learned that in order to get your own way you had to threaten or carryout violence. The inevitable fight that ensued was a particularly violent one by the boy's standards. Much grappling and bear hugging ensued along with a great variety of swearing, mostly what they had heard their Father utter.

This fracas ended abruptly when the yellow car drew up outside. The two boys quickly set about tidying up, re-arranging the coffee table to exactly the right angle that Teddy had always left it in. The hushed but urgent conversation was peppered with cursing for emphasis. They were happy the room was as it should be and they both flumped into the couch as the door opened. Mary went into the kitchen as usual and Teddy walked straight over to the corner table. He never spoke, which was really unusual, he should have remarked about the redness on the boys faces by now. A puzzled look was exchanged by the boys. Then disaster struck. Teddy was fiddling with the Grundig when a louder than normal voice was heard via the loudspeakers, 'Shut the door, Shut the fuckin' door!'

Leo's heart sank. He knew straight away what had happened, Tony was slower on the uptake. Teddy never said a word as the recording of the fight was relived in louder than normal volume. Mary came in from the kitchen.

"What's going on?"

Teddy silenced her with a gesture then added,

"This is what these two get up to when we are not here!" The two boys offered their own versions of what happened, each blaming the other for starting it. He ignored them both as he listened to the full exchange captured in every detail and swearword. On completion he timed the fracas by looking at the mantlepiece clock, then declared.

"The neighbours must have thought you were killing each other. I'll give yers what for."

He was particularly cruel in his punishment. He deferred it till after the evening meal was had. This amplified the sense of foreboding in the boy's minds. Then with ritual deliberation he called for each in turn, starting with Tony.

"You didn't start it, but you did leave the door open, so you are getting off lighter." He beat Tony across the buttocks as he bent him over the couch by the scruff of his neck, a few strokes hitting his back as he squirmed and screamed out in horror as much as pain. Then it was Leo's turn to walk up to the punishment couch. He strode up bravely, however soon he too was dancing away from the bamboo cane that was delivering its admonishment to the usual staccato dialogue.

"Don't let me catch you two fuckin' swearing and fuckin' fightin' again." Sweat was breaking on his brow with the exertion of delivering the beatings. Mary was screaming for him to,

"Go easy on them. They are only kids, they didn't know they were being recorded!"

"That's beside the fuckin' point!" Whack, whack, echoed the bamboo stick in emphasis as it landed on the victim.

"I am going to get the NSPCC on to you. Yer fuckin' bully yer!"

Chapter 39 The First One

Teddy had lots of money-making ideas over the years. One that nearly went severely wrong was a saving club he ran for local residents in Dovecot. Known locally as the Ton tyne, people would pay into a fund usually for Christmas savings. They could if required cash in part or all of the fund for un-foreseen events. The 'banker' would pay a little extra into the fund as an interest payment on completion of the agreed term. Teddy was acting as the banker, using the extra money for his cash flow, and he should have been saving most of the money in a separate tin. Like many people who need money and they have some in a fund, temptation and best intentions to re-pay, mean the stash gets raided. It was just such a situation that put Teddy in a bind. The fruit barra was doing reasonably well and profits were coming in, albeit on the small side. What Teddy had spent the money on he never revealed, just that he didn't have the money when one of his customers announced that she had to cash in her Ton tyne early.

"How much money have you got in the housekeeping?" Teddy asked Mary.

"Not much, maybe Ten pounds. Why do you ask?"

"I need about forty-five pounds now."

"What for?"

"One of the Ton tyne women want's her money and I haven't got it."

"What! What have you done with it?" demanded Mary. She was showing anxiety all over her face. It was a common sight with her when around Teddy.

"I have been using the money to buy stock for the barra. Things have been a bit slow and I don't have the money." Teddy replied with a resigned look on his face.

"What are you going to do to get the money?"

"I'll have to think of something" replied Teddy, his expression lost in thought. He was relieved that Mary had not pressed him harder on the missing money. What he had done was spend a little more than usual over the last few weeks as part of his showing off to his latest lady friend.

Elsie was a woman who lived locally. She was a frequent visitor to the fruit barra to chat with Teddy. Mary often thought that there might be something going on with her. She could tell by the flirting manner she showed whenever she was chatting with Teddy. Teddy loved attention, especially from women. He gave her lots of time to chat. He listened and laughed when appropriate, only breaking his attention away from her to bark out an order to the kids servicing the barra.

Mary found she could almost set her watch by Elsie's arrival mid-morning. Elsie had stopped actually buying anything most mornings, she was just stopping to chat on her way home from the arches' shops. Teddy had moved the barra pitch from the service road because of the hassle with the police and the yellow lines that had appeared on the corner one morning. The nearest greengrocer had friends in high places in the council. He was tired of seeing his customers get bargains from the barra on the corner while he had to pay rates and rent on his shop.

The new pitch was just across the road from the arches. This was not ideal as most of the shoppers came from the heart of the Dovecot estate behind and around the arches, relatively few came from across the main road. The new pitch took some time to establish. Profits were being generated, enough to keep the barra as a going concern, just.

As the pitch was not obstructing any roadway the police visits became less frequent. Chalk boards were deployed to attract potential shoppers to cross the road to seek a bargain. Prices being set by the same ruse of spying by the lads, who were now a lot bigger and made their forays openly to gaze at the window displayed prices. Slowly the sales picked up and the barra became established.

As the two lads were getting bigger trouble began following them home. Leo had friends from a relatively rough side of the estate. They were typical boys. Stealing apples from gardens in the late summer and autumn was a great way to get some excitement and a chase by the owner. The boys would regroup after the hue and cry and eat their bounty. Retelling any funny bits that happened. If any boy showed any fear of being caught, they were vicious in their ridicule. One lad known as Gibbo, an adaptation of his surname, was a common naysayer. One evening he warned.

"Hey that wall is too high to climb. We won't get back over it in time if we are seen."

"Oh fuck off Gibbo! What's goin' to happen? He'll just smack yer head and that'll be that!"

"What if he gets the police? My Dad will kill me if I get into trouble with them."

"Yer big girl's blouse!" called one lad

"Yer! Yer hom!" joined in another.

"Well I am not going over the wall" said Gibbo resolutely.

"Suit yerself then" said the leader of the gang.

One lad was brave beyond reason, he was not the brightest, in fact he was not bright at all, his name was Froggy. Average height for his age but stockier and strong. He led the scramble over the six-foot sandstone block garden wall. The others, bar Gibbo, followed him. The boys were eagerly picking up apples off the ground and from the trees, stuffing them in pockets and the fronts of their shirts as makeshift pouches. A shout from the house went up and the boys scattered in all directions yet managed to find the garden wall OK. Froggy started throwing apples at the man who had caught them in the act. Froggy put a lot of effort into his throwing, aiming at the man's head. The man kept back long enough for the boys to scale the wall and help Froggy make his exit too.

As they ran away, they were shouting in exhilaration of their near capture and escape. Some names were shouted in their excitement, Froggy, Gibbo, Leo. They hadn't realised that their names were dead giveaways to anyone that heard them.

The community constable strolled up to the barra a few mornings later. Teddy was flirting with Elsie. The two lads,

Leo and Tony were stacking the goods up as they were sold to keep the display looking attractive. On sight of the policeman, Leo busied himself in the tailgate of the yellow car as if he was earnestly searching for some missing item. Tony stood his ground, his usual curious expression showing no sign of concern. Peter was the typical community bobby. Older and portly, no use in a chase or climbing over walls.

Teddy called out to him.

"Hi Peter, how are you?" he enquired.

"Oh, I am OK thanks Teddy. Can I have a word?"

Teddy indicated to Elsie that their morning chat was over with just a look, she saw and understood.

"I have to go now Teddy, see you tomorrow no doubt, Bye"

"Yeah, see yer." Answered Teddy.

Making himself more comfortable on his makeshift seat, an upturned empty cauliflower crate, he waited for the constable to start.

"Teddy your lad Leo has been naughty" began Peter with a grave look. What has Leo done thought Teddy as he saw the look on the copper's face, robbed a bloody bank or killed someone?

"Oh yeah" acknowledged Teddy "What has he done?"

"Him and the Longreach Road gang were scrumping the other night when the owner was pelted with a load of apples. He was injured when one of the apples hit him in the face, he was really upset and hurt. He heard your Leo's name being called along with Froggy's and a few others as they were running away" told the constable. 'Well fuck me!' thought Teddy 'is that it?'

"Yeah?" questioned Teddy.

"Well I just wanted to let you know that your lad is knocking around with a bad lot. He will get into serious trouble one of these days and I won't be able to stop it at my end." Peter had been telling Teddy of the things he could do for him, in return for small considerations on Teddy's part. Teddy had taken the nod and had been dropping the copper a few bob over the last few months, to keep him sweet, was the expression.

"OK Peter I will give a him a good talking to when I get him home tonight" reassured Teddy. Taking the serious look as the message was received, he lightened his expression and looked at the display of tomatoes.

"They look nice" commented the policeman. Grabbing a brown paper bag used to sell the delicate goods in, Teddy began to fill it with the Guernsey tomatoes, leaving just enough space to twist the bag tightly shut with a flourished rotational movement leaving two small ears of twisted bag at each end.

Teddy gave the bag to Peter who slickly place it into his voluminous tunic pocket and fastened it with the shining button.

"Thanks Teddy" as he was turning to leave the copper spotted someone of interest cross the main road towards the Finch Hall estate. "I have to get going now Teddy, sorry." The radio on his epaulette was pressed into transmit mode and the squelching sound indicated the line was live. "Four nine to control" he waited for the acknowledgement. It came within seconds.

"Four nine to control. I have just seen the Saint crossing East Prescot Road heading down Finch Lane, over." The look on Peter's face was of excitement and urgency. Tony looked on, impassive as ever, as the officer continued his urgent dialogue with the unseen lady in control. Tony was amused at the display of urgency. He knew the Saint. He was a few years older than Leo and was a harmless bragger. He was not in a gang or, as far as Tony knew not a criminal type at all. His only notoriety was his home-made tattoo, on the left forearm of the TV series logo, a matchstick man with halo that he had needled himself. Simon Templar was as far away from this lad as could possibly be.

After the constable crossed the road Teddy called to Leo.

"What's all this then? What have I told you about bringing trouble to the door?"

"It's not like that at all. We were just getting' apples and it was Froggy that threw them at the fella, not me or any of the others, honest!" pleaded Leo. Teddy weighed up the excuse while Leo kept his distance away from any sudden swipes of those powerful arms.

"Well we'll see about that when I get you home" threatened Teddy. Leo remained a safe distance away for the duration of that afternoon. Tony for prudence also ensured that he was out of Teddy's immediate reach and field of vision as much as possible, just in case he was to be sucked into the anger zone. Teddy's mood softened as the sun shone on the barra and brought with it more shoppers spending money.

That evening Leo ate his meal and went straight out to play to avoid the delayed punishment that he was almost certain to get. Teddy appeared to have forgotten about the community policeman and the news that Leo had been involved with a fracas. Teddy didn't finish his own meal that evening complaining to Mary about indigestion. He still went to the Boundary pub though at about nine that evening, returning as normal just gone eleven. All was well until about five the following morning when Teddy was woken by severe indigestion, he thought. He was restless and couldn't settle back to sleep. Mary woke up and asked.

"What's wrong?"

"I have really bad indigestion after that meal you gave me!"

"Everyone else is OK. Are you sure it's indigestion?"

"Of course I am!" shouted Teddy in his pain.

"OK, steady on then."

"It's like I have my chest in a vice and it's getting tighter and tighter" gasped Teddy.

"Do you think it could be your heart?" asked Mary.

"Shit. Yeah, it probably is. Best call an ambulance" advised Teddy.

They waited for the sound of the ambulance in an awkward silence, broken only by Teddy making gasping sounds as he sat uncomfortably on the edge of the bed, his arms wrapped around his chest trying to stop his heart from bursting.

The boys woke up to the news that their Dad had been taken to hospital with a suspected heart attack. This was received with mixed feelings by the two of them.

Chapter 40 The Letter

Teddy survived his first heart attack. In order to keep money flowing Mary had taken over the barra operation with the boys and help from Michael, he drove the car to the market for stock and set up the barra in the morning, and helped the boys break it down again in the evening. Mary did a good job in Teddy's absence. Her boys worked well with her and no arguments or upsets occurred. Elsie passed often and enquired of Teddy from Michael, she never stopped when Mary was manning the barra.

After several days in Broadgreen hospital Teddy returned home.

He was pleased that Mary had taken the initiative and kept the barra business going, although he never actually praised her for the efforts she made. He couldn't help himself but to comment that she had paid too much for the King Edward potatoes from a supplier he didn't usually use. On hearing this Mary had cried out.

"Oh friggin hell Teddy! I was trying my bloody best to keep everyone friggin' fed and worrying about what was going to happen to us if you friggin' well died!" responded his exasperated wife. As usual Teddy never apologised. He knew he was out of order but the word sorry never, ever passed his lips. Mary went into the kitchen to escape making him angrier. The doctor had said that Teddy had something called a 'type A personality' and he needed to avoid becoming excited or angry. She had held her tongue when the registrar at Broadgreen told her this, as Teddy was sitting on the bedside chair. She had visions of him falling down dead if she said anything negative about her husband in front of someone else. He would have a massive heart attack right there and then she thought. So Mary just nodded and looked sadly at Teddy.

Teddy had taken up permanent residence in his usual armchair by the fireplace. His requirements were met by the family who had been press ganged into his service. When he wanted a cup of tea, he would instruct the boys,

"Wash your hands and make me a cup of tea!" was a common instruction given to Leo, Tony or Michael. Carlo was too young, and Sharon was still a toddler. Mary had been programmed previously to always wash her hands when providing for Teddy. The obsession with cleanliness had arisen in Teddy's youth. After he was afflicted with polio one of the doctors had told him that it was transmitted through poor hygiene. As kids were known to be dirty by nature, he was not taking any chances with grubby kid's hands or habits.

If he was given a cup with a crack in, the offering was rejected with.

"Make me another one and don't put it in a cup with a crack in it!" The anger never went away even though the doctors had said it could kill him.

Teddy was used to bringing home unusual items and gadgets. He had procured a large radiogram as they were known, to replace the original record player. He bought a box set of relaxing music LPs based on South Sea melodies. These all had colourful pictures of flowers and ukuleles, pretty girls with far a-way looks on their faces told of wistful tales. He would play these records when he felt like relaxing. His efforts to relax were often short lived, children like to play and make a noise.

"Shut the fuckin' hell up!" was the signal to get out of the house and make yourself scarce, before the lumbering ogre could catch you and slap your head for disturbing his relaxation.

Things went back to normal quite quickly.

The Ton tyne issue was sorted by Teddy with a loan from a pub friend. He would have to pay the friend interest but that should be OK with the increase in Christmas shopping at the barra. One line of worry was removed from Teddy's plate. There were still plenty more to annoy and make him angry with.

Mary and the boys serviced the barra. The boys would walk the barra down to the pitch and leave it there on their way to school. Teddy would go to the market, mid-morning, for stock and then return home to his armchair for rest. Mary would serve the customers and stock up on her own when the boys were in school. She would have to wait for Teddy to return when she needed to use the toilet. He would come back at the same sort of times each morning to relieve Mary for a while. The afternoons he would leave the boys on their return from school to help their mother out. Only driving the stock back at the end of the day while the boys pushed the barra back home to Aldwark Road.

It was a dispute with a nosey neighbour that convinced Teddy it was time to make the next house move. A lady who lived across from them had been overheard gossiping to another neighbour about the Kelly's and the carry on at their house. The carry on could have been one of many events that created juicy gossip. Teddy had declared that the nosey neighbour was to be called 'Yap-Yap'. This delighted the boys as they could go around the road shouting Yap-yap whenever they saw her, with their Dad's approval. This was a puerile tactic on Teddy's behalf. Mary had not wanted to disturb the neighbours any more than they had been, especially after the car smashing and saw fight.

She decided that the time was right for a change.

Mary couldn't say outright what she wanted as that would just generate a straight forward refusal by Teddy, so she had to seed the idea and feed it once she had seen it take root. She had to make it appear that Teddy had the idea and that he wanted to do something about it, whatever the issue was. So Mary had decided they were to move away from Aldwark Road. She started to remark on just how nice the corporation parlour houses were on the main road, and that some had double fronted outlooks too. She made the remarks when he was quiet and resting in his armchair, then she would give him space to machinate on how he was going to make it happen.

Her plan went like clockwork. He started to drive slowly passed the section of road she had highlighted looking for possible candidate houses. He found the one he wanted. A double fronted affair, just down from the swimming baths. He put the usual actions into motion. He went to see Ted again. Ted had been busy building his empire up and now had around five shops and a legitimate extra income, albeit there were some skeletons in his cupboards too. He no longer had the need for small backhanders to do favours for, but he still liked the challenge of sorting out things for friends. After some plotting and preparation on his part Ted announced that there was a house for Teddy to transfer his council residency to. Teddy gave Ted the usual fee for his help and went home to announce the triumph to Mary.

He had the idea to announce the coup while driving passed the house. He got Mary into his car on an excuse of going up to Old Swan. While slowing down on the main road he asked what she thought of the double fronted parlour house on the left. Despite the speed limit being forty he had slowed almost to a stop while approaching the house. He did pull up outside.

"Oh that is a lovely house" remarked Mary, stifling her hopes that it would be that one. "I would love one like that" she added for good measure. She looked at his face for a clue. It could just be a cruel joke he was going to pull.

When she saw the smile, she thought damn! He was winding her up.

"Well if you like that one, we will have to move in there in a couple of weeks' time, then won't we?"

"Oh Teddy that is lovely. How on earth did you manage to get such a lovely house?" her reaction was mostly joy, but she had peppered it with enough cogent flattery to make him happy with himself.

"Well I just have friends in high places, don't I?"

The Old Swan trip was aborted, and they travelled back to Aldwark Road to discuss the move in more detail and what they would require once they moved in to 382. Mary was delighted with her long game plan. It had worked out even better than she had hoped for. She was soon to be the occupier of a double fronted parlour house, she was really pleased. For now.

The move to the main road went as planned that summer. There was plenty of work that needed doing. Teddy did none of it, because of his condition, this was done by the boys and Mary herself. Teddy occasionally lifted himself from his window on the world, a hardbacked dining room chair set in the bay window, to illustrate how to use a particular tool if the boys were not making the best use of it. He would then sit back down again and watch to see if the lesson had been assimilated. The decoration was done by Michael, he had a flair for it. His suggestions of colours that would go together was challenged at first by Teddy, then when he realised that his son had better taste in colours than he did he accepted it, without acknowledgment of course.

The barra was doing well, the new pitch had settled in and shoppers were savvy about investing in crossing the small road to get bargains. Elsie still stopped by asking about Teddy when Mary was not serving. A blow came to Teddy's business when the bus stop was moved across the far side of the traffic lights at Finch Lane, making the stop off at the barra awkward for some. Teddy was annoyed with the council. He discovered that Ted couldn't help him as it was too far away from his control or stretch of minions. So Teddy decided to try something himself. He was going to write to the council and request the bus stop be moved back to its former site.

He enquired about who had control of bus stops and was planning his letter of complaint and suggestion to return the bus stop to its former position. He needed someone to type the letter to make it appear more officious. Teddy couldn't type, he didn't even have a typewriter. It was Elsie who suggested her daughter might be able to help him with the letter, she was a pool typist in a local office.

Elsie's daughter was also called Elsie. She was a quiet girl, wore glasses and had a nervous laugh. She arrived at 382 one day and sat next to Teddy while he thought up his draft letter. Tony was sent to make tea for them both. He duly did what was required, checking Teddy's cup for hairline cracks. Once he had distributed the tea, he took up his own seat and started reading again, he was always reading something. He was idly listening to the draft as it took shape. Young Elsie would read out what she had noted down so far, and Teddy would change the odd word or even the full line on hearing it read out aloud. Tony heard nothing out of the ordinary while they were plotting. His book was pulling his attention inside the pages.

A day later the finished letter was available. Teddy was pleased with his ingenuity and the printed page before him.

"Tony, read this and see what you think about it" Ordered Teddy. Tony took the page and read it. Giving it back to his Dad he said.

"Not bad. It should say 'attracts rats, not causes rats' though." Teddy snatched the page from Tony to read it again.

"Oh shit!" He started to put his shoes on quickly. He was annoyed. Tony stood back in case he was going to get the blame for the poor construction of the wording.

"Where are you goin?" asked Tony.

"I have to get this changed before it gets posted." He grabbed his car keys and left the house.

Chapter 41 The Tree

Teddy's anger at not being able to get the bus stop moved back to the other side of the traffic lights was excitable but short lived. He had managed to intercept the posting of the 'causes rats' version of the letter before young Elsie posted it. He stayed in her house while she amended the wording and typed it out again on her own Olivetti. It wasn't long before his next caper started to take form. Often women would get a piece of fruit on their way to work in the factories off Edge Lane for the afternoon shift. Teddy liked chatting with women. So his idea of getting a minibus to run the women to work and save them a few coppers on their fare seemed a reasonable enough project. He could do this while the barra was all set and Mary or the boys were looking after things there, 'time and motion' he thought.

He invested in a used Bedford van that had been converted into a minibus by the addition of bench seats down each side and windows cut into the sides of the van. It could hold about twelve passengers in the back, six on each side at a push and two in the cab with him if needs be. He started the factory bus runs from the barra pitch opposite the church of the Holy Spirit in Dovecot, where a curved residential road ran parallel to the main road and had ample parking and waiting space. His fares would be seated while waiting for the full load to arrive and they would chat away with each other. Teddy stood guard like at the back door looking up to where the late comers would be likely to emerge from. He enjoyed the life of the entrepreneur and had lots of women to chat with too. His only problem was how to keep the van safe while parked on the main road. It was a forty road and any parking required side lights to be shown during the hours of darkness. He had a solution.

One day he said to Leo and Tony.

"See that tree? The one outside here"

"Yeah" replied Leo.

"Well get the spades out of the shed and dig it up."

"What? What for?" asked Tony.

"I need to make a runway for the minibus and I can't have a straight run in if that stays there."

"What if we get caught?" asked Tony cautiously.

"I'll say it was blown over in the wind and was unsafe."

"OK then. But it's not our fault if it goes wrong" warned Tony, trying to avoid any angry outburst if it went awry.

Leo encouraged Tony with.

"C'mon we'll get this out dead quick. It won't have deep roots, it's only a sapling." How Leo knew about roots was news to Tony. He went with Leo for the spades as directed.

The tree was a small trunked affair, about four inches in diameter and about ten foot tall all told. The two lads set about digging it out under the watchful eye of Teddy in his window seat. If anyone looked at them, they would offer the wind-blown reason and the obvious danger to passing traffic for uprooting it. Leo was right, it only took a short while to get it out and lay it down on the ground. Just as the tree was lain to rest on the verge a panda car pulled up and a tall young policeman got out and asked them.

"What are you doing?"

Tony practiced in the lines about the wind offered the lie first. The policeman looked at him. Tony kept his best angelic expression while he answered.

"It was all leaning over this morning when we got up. You should have seen it, it was like that." He indicated with his arm at roughly a thirty-degree angle off the horizontal plane. Our Dad said we had better go out and see if we can straighten it, but all the roots, here, were sticking out too so he said you better take it out then." The officer was uncertain with the boy's explanation, he looked around for other signs of mischief, seeing none and possibly being presented with Tony's best impassive expression he said.

"I'll have to take your names down then while I make further enquiries." He took his notebook out of his top pocket. Just then Teddy called from the doorstep.

"I can help" he offered. The young man walked over to the helpful man on the step, indicating to the boys to wait there.

"What's going on here sir?" asked the constable.

"Do come in officer" invited Teddy. He led the way into the lounge making sure he could see his limping waddle. Offering the armchair seat next to his own window seat. As he sat down Teddy lifted his right leg up in his hands and secured it in a semi squat position, resting his heel on the seat of his chair. The policeman literally had an eyelevel view of the shrunken right limb. A deliberate action on behalf of Teddy, seeking the sympathy vote. Teddy repeated the wind story and the dangerous angle the tree had found itself in after the previous night's gusts. After the details were recorded in the notebook, Teddy made light conversation about the policeman's lot. He asked about Peter, the community officer, and made sure he knew he was an acquaintance of his. Soon the young copper was satisfied.

Teddy suggested "You might like to let the council know on Monday about the tree and see if they wanted to collect it. Or would you like me to let them know?"

"It would be easier if you can give them a call on Monday, I am on a rest day then."

"No problem I will let them know and see what they want to do about it" offered Teddy generously. The policeman returned to his car and just waved at the boys to carry on. Leo was beaming a wide grin as the panda car accelerated up to speed in the direction of Eaton Road police station. Tony returned the smile. They brushed up the soil spills and tidied up the square patch of green that was the trees home. The once upward facing tree now lay dead on the ground. Teddy appeared at the door again.

"Now take it over there and dump it with the other trees and stuff." Teddy was indicating the derelict area that was once a prefabricated estate across the dual carriageway, it was waiting final demolition and clearing. The two lads heaved the tree up to shoulder height. The weight was nothing in comparison to what they were used to carrying from their work on the barra and fifty-six-pound bags of spuds. The weekend traffic was lighter than usual and so they traversed the road easily and went through a break in the estate wall to toss the tree down into a green area.

Crossing back to the other side they were quite pleased with their skills of digging, heaving and lying.

After a couple of weeks and as the obstruction was now removed part two of Teddy's plan was started. He directed the boys to dig up the hedge marking the edge of the front garden and the rotted fence panels behind it. Soon the only thing that was left of the front margin was the gate and its posts. The hedge and puny fence panel pieces were sent across the road to join the tree after it went dark. Soon the truck arrived with the paving flags for the drive way and the landscaped front garden.

Teddy only got up from his perch to show how the two boys how to do things. The flags were awkward to pick up and carry to where they were to be placed. Teddy said.

"You have to walk them."

"What?"

"Walk them not pick them up. Like this" he lifted a flagstone up on to its edge then using a hand on each side of the stone tilted it up to pivot on one corner, then moved it forward then down. He repeated this with the other side. Immediately the two boys picked up the tip. They were moving flag stones about like professionals, helped by their well-developed barra muscles. Once the driveway was completed the boys moved to the smaller decorative flagstones, they were easy to handle in comparison than the three by twos they had started with. The front wall was built by a local brickie in the same decorative stone colours and finish as the flag stones, shades of pink and white. The final look was impressive. The main entrance gate was replaced to match the drive way gates, and the trophy house was there for all the world to see, that Teddy Kelly the barra boy had done good.

Tony was always in awe of his Dad. He was never stuck for something to say, even if it was unfair or later proved to be untrue, but he still was first out of the blocks with comments and ideas. That was until he was sent to tax the minivan at the Liver Buildings at the Pier Head. The main road tax station was there, and if the fourteen-day grace period had expired, the only place you could get your vehicle taxed at. Tony was sent with the various documents required and the correct amount of money to pay for six months road tax.

After queuing for a while the man behind the post office like counter said the documents were incomplete, or some other form was required for the payment to be made and the tax disc issued. Tony phoned the house and recounted what the teller had said. Teddy was struggling to find the next appropriate course of action, he made air sucking sounds down the phone and uttered lots of 'Errs and Ums'. Finally Tony confirmed that he couldn't get the minibus taxed unless the paperwork was complete. Teddy agreed that he should return home on the bus. On the journey back Tony reflected that that was the first time he had ever heard his Dad struggle for words or what to do.

Soon after the tax disc failure Teddy was admitted to hospital again with his heart. He spent a week or so at Broadgreen again. Mary once again orchestrated the barra with her boys and Michael drove the untaxed minibus to the market for stock, hoping he wouldn't get stopped on route.

Teddy was discharged and warned again about his temper and how important it was to take things easy. The minibus was beyond economical repair, even for the short term. A new strategy was required for the barra to keep going. Teddy tried taking taxis to the market and getting a minicab driver to allow him to put a couple of bags of spuds in the boot and trays of tomatoes or apples and oranges in the back seat. If additional stock was required, he would send Michael on the bus to carry trays or boxes back. It was not going to last without a car of some sort. A holding plan was needed. Mary had a friend who worked as a cleaner across the main road in a pensioners supported living home. She broached the idea with Teddy of her going out to work to bring in steady wages and not be reliant on the barra work. Reluctantly at first, Teddy agreed for her to go to work to supplement the family income. He didn't like it for several reasons. He had always been the main provider since he was a child growing up in Bidder Street. Now he was becoming even more of a disabled man, having to let his wife go out to work to keep him. Also there was the fear that she would talk to other men. Despite his many indiscretions over the years, he was against any idea that his wife could follow him down the infidelity route. Especially now. Now, that his problem was becoming more frequent.

Chapter 42 The Outing

Teddy had a message for Tony to go on. He was to go to the chemist shop in Kensington, for the new medicine he was taking. The name was written out exactly as it appeared on the empty packet. Tony was peeved, he was to meet his school friends that afternoon. Despite Teddy not beating him for the last few years, he had still scared him plenty of times with his haymaker fist under his chin at the first sign of resistance to one of Teddy's suggestions. He knew his friends would have to have fun without him that day, there was no getting out of the errand. Tony still complained to his Mum.

"Why can't he just get these from Clitheroe's chemist shop in Dovecot?" asked Tony.

"They are special tablets" she replied and added "they are only available in that chemists in Kensington."

"What's so special about these tablets?" asked Tony. His mother smiled, it was only a hint of a smile, but she did smile, her eyes confirmed it.

"He thinks they will keep him young" she replied, still smiling. Tony accepted her account and harrumphed his irritation as he went for the bus.

Teddy's prowess was failing. He was on a variety of drugs for his heart. He had changed to drinking shots of whiskey instead of pints as a doctor had once said whiskey was better than beer for hearts. He failed to get the money together for more wheels, his wife had to work to keep things going. Hardly anyone asked him to source knock off gear anymore either. He even thought that the boys were not as afraid of him as they were before all this.

It was very reluctantly that Teddy agreed to Mary's day out with the staff at Morley, where she worked. He was sorted for the day, sandwiches made for lunch in the fridge, she had assured him she would be home by about tea time and would make his meal when she got in. As it happened the day out was a great success and the train, they got back from Southport didn't leave till nearly seven that evening. So he was in a foul mood when she walked in. All the fun and laughs she had had with the women from work was shattered in an instant.

"What fuckin' time do yer call this?" spat Teddy as Mary went through the lounge door. She was expecting words of some sort from him, but his manner took her by surprise.

"I have only just got through the feckin' door! Give me a feckin' chance will yer!" she had not decided to make a stand till the words came out of her mouth. Once she started speaking, she had to maintain her position.

"Don't fuckin' answer me back or I'll give yer a fuckin' belt!" he raised his clenched fist in warning for her audacious behaviour.

"Yeah that's you all feckin' over isn't it, yer just a feckin' big feckin' bully yer are!" she stormed off into the kitchen with the obligatory door slamming for emphasis. Teddy had been taken unaware by the ferocity of her counter argument. Her words had a strange effect on him. He hated the bullies that hounded his early years and the latter ones that wanted some of his wealth or women. He had been stopped dead in his own realisation that he was a bully. How he had not faced this particular truth earlier was a mystery.

He never apologised or thought that he was in the wrong, about anything. He was not going to start now. He pushed the thought of being labelled a bully deep into his mind. He decided that he would leave Mary to her own devices in the kitchen. He was off to the Boundary pub. His shoes went on and he got his coat from the stair post, closing the door behind him. He hailed a passing taxi for the short trip to the pub.

The atmosphere was frosty in the house for some time afterwards. Young Carlo and Sharon were unaware of any discord, but Leo and Tony could see it and feel it. It was a time to keep out of his way. When he was really peeved about something, he was dangerously unpredictable.

Michael had left home a little while earlier. He did so voluntarily after a blazing row with Teddy. It was sparked by a comment made in the pub by the friend of Teddy's nephew while they were drinking one night. Teddy had mentioned that Michael wanted to go to live in London and added the comment for god knows why. The guy responded.

"Oh common Teddy it's obvious why he wants to go there, he's gay, that's where they all want to live."

Teddy was instantly angry.

"What the fuck are you saying, he's gay, no he isn't!" The lad persisted with his standpoint.

"Teddy everyone knows, you only have to look at him to know, and once he opens his mouth it's even more obvious, he's gay. Full stop." Teddy was furious, he was going to take the lad outside for a fight, but his nephew held him back with measured reason.

"Uncle Teddy don't be silly. You can't fight him, he'll flatten yer with one punch. Look at the size of him. Anyway what he says is true. Your Michael is gay, just ask him." The moment had passed for violence. Teddy knew he was not in any state to fight anymore, not without major equaliser power in his hands anyway. The atmosphere cooled down and all three resumed an uneasy peace for the rest of the evening.

The next day Teddy went looking for evidence of Michael's gay lifestyle. He rooted through his stuff in his room and found a magazine in his leather jacket pocket. Opening it out he saw the title, *CHE Campaign for Homosexual Equality*. He was annoyed that people knew about his gay son before he did. He would have it out with him.

Michael had been to town that Sunday afternoon and returned home more than a little tipsy, he too liked whiskey. Teddy challenged him by waving the magazine in his face as he entered the lounge, before he had even shut the door behind him.

"Why the fuck? What have you got the likes of this magazine in your pocket? Fuckin' queer stuff!"

"Because I am queer." Responded Michael in his best affronted queer voice.

"Well if that's the way you are you can fuckin' be it somewhere fuckin' else then!"

"That is exactly what I am going to do. Why are you such a fucking idiot anyway? You are just a fucking old cunt!" He was knocked against the wall with the blow that caught him unawares. If he wasn't drunk, he would have certainly felt it more than he did. He went up to his room without saying another word. Drunk as he was, he knew he could be really hurt if he persisted with his irritation of the beast.

Michael was the second of his children to be driven out of the family home. He was not to be the last.

Mary was upset that Michael was off to London with his cousin Francis. He was to stay there off and on for many years. She consoled herself that her son was safe away from Teddy while he was living down there.

Money was always tight in the Kelly house. Teddy had a plan for increasing the income, he encouraged the boys, Leo and Tony to leave school at the earliest opportunity, to get jobs and to 'bring some money into the house'. This was around the start of the 1970's and Tony was quite taken with the thought of leaving school and so agreed to leave early. It was the last year that O level study was still optional. He had a difficult time with teachers, he had done since his first school days. He didn't know that it was not normal to be aggressive if someone annoyed you. Aggression was normal to Tony, he saw it at home almost every day. He had a simple way of seeing things. If he was put out by some kid or other, he rightly responded in the way he had seen his father doing, with aggression. Despite being a sweet kid at heart with curly blond hair, blue eyes and cute looks, he was chunky and fearless of other kids in his class. The school kept records of the altercations that followed him through school. Often other kids would egg him on over something, so they could see a fight in the playground. Tony fought in play-fights with his older brother almost every day at home, and school kids were no match for him.

Mary was called in to talk about Tony, and his fighting temper that came out of the blue, when interacting with other kids. She couldn't account for it. He was very quiet at home and a dream to be with. Tony learned eventually that violence was not the answer to everything, but he kept his distrust of teachers for their note taking and re-telling of things long after they were relevant. So, when the option came sanctioned by his Dad, not to stay on at school he went for it. Using it as a bragging device in his last few months at Yew Tree. He did regret this action, not too long after that.

The barra was proving to be impossible to maintain. Mary's earnings and Teddy's disability allowance made enough income, along with the boys' housekeeping turned over each week. Teddy reluctantly made the decision that he could no longer keep it as a going concern. Especially after he sent the next child of his packing.

Their argument was over a messed-up sun lounger that had sunscreen lotion spilled on it. Teddy was furious and wanted to know who had done it. Mary had no idea how the chair had been left like that. Carlo suggested that Tony had been on it, and maybe he did it. Seeing as no one else was around to offer any possible solution, it was left that Tony would explain when he got in. Teddy had been stewing in his anger all afternoon. Mary had stood her ground against him again, she had no idea what had happened to the chair. She knew that if Tony had done it, he would own up to it and get told off and that would be that. She rejected any temptation to get embroiled in his petty issue.

Tony arrived home about four thirty that afternoon. He had been with his girlfriend all day at a martial arts competition. He was not due to fight, he was unclassed as a novice but his fearless approach to kumite was appreciated by his Sensei. So when a team member cried off sick Tony got to fight. He made a good go of his first competition and made the quarterfinal bout where he was beaten by a club colleague, so his own disappointment was eased with his team mates win. He was aching all over, even where he had not been kicked or punched. Bruises were forming on his forearms where the simple approach offered to him was followed.

"Just block and counter, let them make the first move and then you can take them out with a counter punch" his team mates had advised. "None of the Bruce Lee shit, keep your feet on the ground." Tony agreed to do as he was bid, it worked well for several bouts up to the quarters.

Tony and his girlfriend knocked on the door, he had left his keys on the window ledge, Teddy opened the door without saying anything at first. When they had closed the front door and were going through the lounge door Teddy spat out his position.

"Now you tell your Mother why you left a load of sunscreen oil all over the sunchair!"

"I didn't." Tony simply answered. Teddy was erupting with rage at this set back. He leapt up and went for Tony, fist raised for intimidation. Tony seeing the approach and being programmed all morning to block and counter, made a simple left arm preparation stance, right hand tight against his hip. This infuriated Teddy.

He stormed off muttering curses and threats of 'I'll fuckin' kill yer'. Tony realising that severe violence was imminent if he stayed, grabbing his keys and said to his Mother.

"What is all this about?"

"You made a mess on the sun chair, according to Carlo."

"No I didn't. I haven't been in all day." As he heard his Dad rummaging around outside the kitchen in the small shed, he decided to leave quickly. Telling his girlfriend to come with him he left. As they walked the short distance to where he had left his car, he heard his Dad shouting. They both turned around to see Teddy holding a lump hammer in his left hand and a hand scythe in the other.

"If you fuckin' come back here again, I'll cut yer fuckin head off!"

Tony was the third one.

Chapter 43 The Man

Tony left home the day of the argument and never lived at 382 again, he was eighteen. He saw his Dad regularly, but they didn't speak. The Boundary pub was the local drinking place for all age ranges. It was near enough to the two big estates of Dovecot and Huyton, but far enough away from the notorious pubs just inside the Huyton boundary. The Eagle and Child was a bloodbath on most Saturday nights, with the coppers attending there every week. The Boundary was genteel by its standards. The lounge bar was called the Gaiety Lounge and they occasionally had live music playing. Tony had used the boundary for some time taking his then girlfriend along or going with Leo for a pint.

Teddy had taken up the same spot at the start of the bar in the Gaiety since they had lived in Dovecot. His drinking buddies varied over time. He had people join him for a chat on their way in, before they found their own seating for the evening, or on their way home. He no longer sold the football tickets for cash or frozen chicken prizes. His days as an unofficial banker were long gone, no one gave him their money to hold for safe keeping anymore. He was becoming an old man at the end of the bar, the spot gradually taking on older groups of men as time went by.

One night a stranger caused quite a stir of comments in the Boundary. He never spoke to anyone but the woman he was with. He had walked in the Gaiety with the lady on his arm. A big man with an overcoat on and he wore a large statement hat, a Borsalino Fedora. As hats go this was shouting out look at me, I am on someone's head that is very different. The man looked for all the world like Humphrey Bogart from the Maltese Falcon. He was built like a fighter. Chiselled chin, steady eyes. No one would want to pick a fight with this guy. As he walked in there was one person he did communicate with, if you could call a slight nod of heads and fleeting eye contact, communication? He saw Teddy at his bar end post and in the lingua franca of Liverpool, he 'let on to' Teddy. He gave a slight nod. Teddy returned the miniscule gesture and held his gaze for a second or two. Everyone in the pub saw this exchange. The stories started straight away. They became sillier and more outlandish as the night progressed. Who was the big gangster like fella that knows Teddy the Barra Boy. How do they know each other. Leo was drinking with his Dad at the time, he stood next to him and saw the man and woman enter, and the exchange. He waited a while before asking.

"Who was that?"

"Wisht! I'll tell yer later." Replied Teddy indicating that whatever the connection, it was not to be discussed in the pub.

Later that week Leo called to 382 and was chatting with his Dad.

"So, who was that Fella in the Boundary the other night, the big fella with the hat?"

"That was Charlie. Charlie Connolly from Huyton." Leo was none the wiser. His face said so. "I was in Walton with Charlie a long time ago, yeah, a long time ago" he added with a faraway look in his eyes. "He was framed for the Cameo murders and got away with eight years"

"That's not getting away with being framed!" replied Leo.

"It is, if the alternative was being hung. Like the other poor sod, Kelly."

"What happened?"

Teddy then related to Leo what had happened back in the late forties and his encounters with both men while working as the prison barber.

Tony and his Dad were still not speaking several months after the outing from the family home.

He still saw his Dad in the Boundary on some nights. His girlfriend had encouraged him to make peace with his Dad. She came from a loving family where no one ever got hit or even a cross word was spoken, that was a very different environment for Tony to find. He wanted to be part of a family where people were civil to each other all the time. He accepted her suggestion to make it up with his Dad, but how? That was the question. He might swing for him in the pub, that would be anathema as he *would* fight back. When his girlfriend's Mum was told the tale of Tony's outing, she was aghast, not at the weapons he had armed himself with or the real threat to kill him, but that Tony had 'raised his hand to his Father'. That was a family crime too far.

Tony decided on a peace offering, a glass of whiskey. He bought the drink and carried it to Teddy's spot at the end of the bar. Placing it down in front of Teddy he said.

"Here yer are Pah" he used Teddy's preferred paternal pet name. Teddy thought that 'Dad' was too soft for a hard man to be called, unless it was a daughter using it. Teddy looked at his son, the one he had chased away from the family home with the hammer and the hand scythe, because he had not controlled his temper that day. He didn't say a word. He did give the faintest hint of acceptance in his eyes, just a bout. Sorry was not a word he ever used, so no sign of error or misjudgement on his part could be shown either.

Tony returned to his own seat by the band's stage to his girlfriend.

"How did it go?" she asked all wide eyed and naively hopeful of a hugs and kisses reconciliation.

"OK" was all that Tony said. He didn't enlarge on the exchange despite her insistence on knowing what happened.

Mary had always wanted a bigger kitchen. Both Aldwark Road and 382 had long thin galley kitchens. She had seen the possibilities of having a big square lay out kitchen. She had been saving up her wages. As she had the pay packets she was in control of the money. Her savings tin was hidden away from Teddy, just in case. Teddy had little opportunity to remind himself of his previous prowess. He was now a kept man, dependant on disability pension and Mary's earnings. He did have the Boundary cronies who he entertained with his tales from the past, but those stories were old hat now. He still had faith in himself and his abilities, given the chance. So he decided to build Mary her big square Kitchen.

He was going to build an extension to the back of 382. It would make the kitchen square and massive. It was going to be the biggest kitchen on that stretch of the main road. Mary would finance it and Teddy would project manage it with labour help from the lads Leo and Tony.

The plot was about six wide by ten foot long. The footings trench was dug by Leo and Tony. Tony was welcomed back without an apologetic word from Teddy. Both boys had worked at labouring jobs and knew their way around digging trenches. It took just a day of their digging by hand spade to reach the depth required. The footings went up equally quickly by the brickie Teddy had sourced.

Mary didn't like the mess in her kitchen but was accepting it as a price worth paying for her dream kitchen. The exterior walls soon reached the roof height, a single-story flat roof was going to finish off the extension to save money. Then the job stalled for a while. The big ten-foot span required two rolled steel joists, known as RSJs. These were going to be expensive to buy new, so Teddy was waiting for a deal to fall into his lap. Meanwhile Mary's kitchen was permanently dusty from the supports holding up the back of the house where the final breakthrough would eventually take place.

Teddy waited for the windfall RSJs in his usual window seat at the bay window. Mary went to work every day and stopped asking after a while how he was getting on sourcing the RSJs. It seemed to go on for weeks. Teddy appeared to be in no hurry. He enjoyed sitting watching the World go by his window. He loved to spot the police radar traps on the main road. They would be parked by the new buildings being built opposite, that were once the prefabricated estate, caching speeders. He had a friend who worked in a local minicab firm. He would telephone him and use their local jargon of 'mousetrap' for a speed trap on the main road.

One day he saw an altercation opposite. He was like a child again back in Bidder Street in his excitement watching a street fight. He had to wait what seemed like ages to tell someone else what he had seen. Tony had called in to visit to see how the extension was going. Teddy eagerly recounted what he had saw that morning. Tony was puzzled to see his Dad in such an excited mood as he told the tale.

"I was looking out the window this morning and two cars pulled up quickly. Three fellas got out of the first car and went over to the other car to give the driver a hard time. He got out of his car and just like that, bam, bam, bam. Floored the three of them. He never said a word, just got back in his car, drove off and left the three of them lying on the ground. It was great!"

Tony looked at his Father. He had not seen such life in those eyes for some time. He had watched him slowly wind down in everything, the second heart issue had been the start. The loss of the barra and his local status had waned in line with the life in his eyes. Tony felt that he was really missing being someone, someone of importance albeit relative.

Tony's thoughts were stopped when Sharon arrived at the house. She was the youngest and only her and Carlo were still living at home by them. Teddy adored Sharon and she reciprocated his feelings. She had been spared the worst of his anger while she was growing up. Teddy's anger driven beatings of the boys had slowed right down, partly due to them getting bigger and also to his softening as he got older. He had not beaten Tony since he stopped squirming away from the lashings of the cane as he brought it down across his buttocks and back. The pivotal time was when he had finished administering a beating to Tony. When Tony said.

"Is that it?" he was not crying or even seemed to be put out by the beating. It was then that Teddy realised he could no longer control him with the fear of the cane anymore. He would need to change his way of influencing behaviour.

Sharon was excited about the Christmas preparations and had bought several items for the house decorations. That stopped Teddy's reminisces of street fights.

"Hey, go into the kitchen and see what we have got for Christmas Dinner." Sharon went into the dusty kitchen and screamed. A large turkey still with the head and all the feathers on was hanging from a hook.

"Oh hey!" she exclaimed "You could have warned me!"

Teddy was smiling from ear to ear at his joke.

Chapter 44 The Big One

"Jesus, Mary and Joseph!" Mary exclaimed as a shiver went through her shoulders. She was not averse to animal slaughter for food, it was just that she didn't want to see it in her kitchen for the week before Christmas. Its head was lolled over to one side as it was suspended, a small bird tongue just protruding from its beak as its last call was frozen in time with the severing of its spinal cord. Eyes that no longer saw looked at her as the small oscillations of the head described ovals in the horizontal plane. Taking her mug of tea into the lounge she put the image out of her mind.

"What on earth did you get a turkey like that for?" she demanded of Teddy as she took her usual place on the sofa.

"That is a great turkey. I got it from the farmer in Tarbock, he said it was a great bird for a big family dinner."

"We are not going to have that many for dinner next week, it will have gone off by the time we get around to eating it!"

"It's maturing as it hangs. They all hang for about a week before you cook them, it's just that you don't see them hanging."

"Well I don't want to see it hanging there all bloody week. It's putting me off the idea of Christmas altogether!"

"You will love it when you eat it. All succulent white meat, hmmm!" indicated Teddy with pursed lips.

The room was sparsely decorated for Christmas. A tiny tree was stood, slightly wonky, on the meter cupboard in the corner behind Teddy's window seat. All told it had about ten miniature baubles suspended from the green plastic boughs and an equally tiny star at the apex finished the meagre effort off. A string of Christmas cards was looped along the long wall of the lounge. Various seasonal scenes stared out to the opposite, fire grated wall. Stars, camels, Arab dressed bearded men and lambs were on almost all of them. Teddy suffered the nonsense for Mary's sake, he still wanted a quiet life, and this was a small compromise to allow.

Mary sipped her tea, the turkey still swinging, ever so slightly, with its blind eyes watching her from the kitchen through the glass panel in the door.

"And when are you going to finish this bloody kitchen? Its driving me mad, as well as that bloody bird!"

"I have told you that the RSJs are hard to come by. They are a big size and most yards don't have them. I have asked around and I will get them just as soon as they are available. I have told you that before!" he added with a side to his voice. Mary heard the warning and left it for now. She was not really in the mood for another row this close to Christmas. He was always in a bad mood on the run up to Christmas with all 'the shit' that goes with it in his mind. He always enjoyed it when it came though, strange that she thought. It might be the drink and that everyone tended to be happy, at least for a while that is. Like most families the Kelly's had rows due to too much 'togetherness' at Christmas.

"Don't blame me if you get dust in yer dinner from them holes in the bloody ceiling, either!" was her parting shot that just came out without her thinking it through.

"If there are, it will go in the fuckin' bin!" Shit thought Mary I have overdone it now. She leaps up and decides to finish her tea with the turkey in the kitchen. At least it was just looking, not shouting.

The remainder of Monday was uneventful, apart from the news that evening that St John's precinct in town had caught fire. Teddy went to the Boundary just after nine and was back for eleven fifteen, or thereabouts. He was in bed a midges before midnight.

Restlessness meant he was sleeping fitfully, tossing and turning. Disturbing Mary. He woke to a dry mouth sensation. Twisting around for his water bottle at the bedside, an old glass lemonade bottle with a screw cap, he took a few sips of stale water directly from the neck. Returning it to the floor, he turned again on the bed. Then the same pains made themselves known again. The tightness formed just under his left armpit and started a slow, tortuous journey along his arm. Almost immediately the pain spread through to his back, high up near the shoulder. He wanted to clamp his chest to ease the pain. He began to sweat. A sticky consistency liquid not like the normal runny stuff of physical effort or summer heat. It clung like a ghostly sticky spider web to his face and neck. He knew this one was different. It was the most pain he had felt in his life. He was worried. He was not ready to die.

Mary woke and realised that something was really wrong. Teddy could not speak clearly, he laboured a few breaths, if that's what you could call them, between clenched teeth. Mary rushed out and down to the phone in the lounge. She picked up the handset and in the soft glow of the sodium street lights of the road pressed 999 on the base unit. The man on the other end of the line was calm, he asked her the details and she gabbled them out as he requested. He repeated that she should remain calm and that an ambulance was on its way.

The glow changed to a mixture of blue and yellow as the Bedford ambulance arrived outside 382, just about eight minutes later. Sharon was up and at her Dad's bedside uttering comforting words to the unconscious form on the bed. The two men walked calmly up the stairs turned right at the top and into the bedroom. They did their usual paramedical checks and announced that they would take him to casualty at Broadgreen straight away. A small buggy like wheeled chair was produced from the customised Bedford and Teddy was seated in it, unconscious. The two men carried him effortlessly down the thirteen steps to the front door and then wheeled the buggy chair out the gate.

Mary and Sharon were still in their pyjamas.

"Shall I get dressed and come with you?" asked Mary. The senior of the two replied.

"No. We will be quicker if we go alone." He didn't want a weeping widow on his hands. "The hospital will call you with any news. You try to relax. Have a cup of tea while you wait for news. I am sure you can go and see him in the morning." He was a wise technician and he had a soft spot for widows.

Broadgreen hospital is only a four or five-minute drive from 382. In that time the rear crewman recorded his vital signs check on the clipboard. As the Bedford pulled up at the A&E bay, he made the last amendment to the transport notes of the case. In large upper-case letters he wrote in a slanting direction across the page. DOA.

Mary and Sharon waited together for the call. The phone didn't ring, but the doorbell did. A policeman had called to tell that Teddy had died on route to the hospital. Mary was devastated as was Sharon.

Shortly after the policeman had left, clear thinking arrived in Sharon's head. She had to step up and help her mother to cope with the news, she had to stifle her own grief. The clock showed six thirty, was it too soon to call everyone? No she answered herself. She used the red faux leather phonebook on the telephone stand to start letting the family know.

Leo was up when she phoned, he was going to work and always was up around six. He gave an animalistic roar of denial when she told him. After he recovered from the shock, he enquired about his Mum.

"How is Mum taking it?"

"She is really upset, and you should come here as soon as you can" advised Sharon.

"I'll be there in ten minutes!"

Sharon called Maureen with the news. A similar exchange took place with the emphasis on how her Mum and Sharon were coping.

Tony was next for the call. He was in bed, not due to get up till just after seven for his trip to work in St Paul's Eye hospital. He was staying at his fiancée's house in Wirral.

"How is Mum?" he asked when Sharon told him about his Dad.

"She is OK now, getting used to the idea."

"Who is there now?"

"Leo, and our Maureen is on her way too. Are you coming?"

"Yeah. I'll be there as soon as I can."

Tony made the journey across the Mersey and out to the east of the city to 382. The door was opened before he got a few step down the pathway.

"I am glad you are here" said Sharon.

"What's happening now?" asked Tony.

"We are all just sitting around not knowing what to do" replied Sharon.

On entering the lounge Tony hugged his Mother. She was crying on and off, her eyes were wet all the time. Sharon was the voice of reason when Tony arrived. He saw she needed to be useful and he resisted the urge to take control. He was the calmest of all the Kelly family. Sharon answered the phone when it rang mid-morning.

"OK yeah, yeah. I will do. Thank you."

"What was that?" asked Leo.

"They said we need to formally identify his …" she couldn't finish the sentence for crying.

Tony knew that now was the time to quietly take control of the situation.

"Leo do you want me to come with you?"

Leo looked uncomfortable and said.

"I can't go and see him!" he gasped for breath between sobs.

"OK then I will go. Where did they say to go?" he asked of Sharon.

"At the mortuary" she managed to utter.

"Does anyone want come with me at all?" No takers for the short trip to Broadgreen were forthcoming. "OK" added Tony. He was willing to make the journey alone.

He drove a full circuit of the hospital site locating the mortuary and to find a parking space. He rang the doorbell. A medium sized man opened the door.

"Yes?"

"I am here to identify Edward Kelly. He was brought in early this morning"

"OK, come in." Tony followed the man down a green tiled passageway to a waiting room. "Wait here please." He left Tony in the waiting room and returned a few minutes later to collect him. Another short walk down the same green tiled corridor led to a small room with just a wheeled trolley in the centre. On it the obligatory white sheet covered the shape lying on it. Another man had been waiting in the room. He held a clipboard in his left hand, a biro in his right.

"Are you ready?" asked the new man.

"Yes."

He turned down the sheet to uncover the face of Teddy Kelly, the barra boy. He had a set expression on his face as if he had been biting his lip when death froze him in time. Tony looked at the face for a few seconds. He was not sure what he was supposed to say at this point. He had come to terms with the death in the short space of time that had elapsed since Sharon had called earlier that morning. He was a pragmatic character.

"Yes, That's him. Edward Kelly." Tony felt awkward as soon as he had said it. He didn't feel any emotion, just a little confused on what he thought they wanted to hear or see. He was saved from further thoughts when the clipboard man offered him the board.

"Sign here please." Indicating a signature line on the one page. "And here too, for his belongings."

On cue the first man gave Tony a small clear plastic bag with his Dad's pyjamas, wedding ring and gold coloured watch, with an expandable strap.

"Thanks" acknowledged Tony.

"This way please" hurried the first man. Tony followed as instructed, back along the green corridor and out the door into the winter afternoon sunshine. The days would be different for everyone from now on thought Tony.

Chapter 45 The Peace

Tony had returned from the formal identification process at Broadgreen. Calm had descended on 382. The main emotions now were shock and grief. There were many arrangements to be made for the wake and the funeral. That afternoon as the fire brigade continued to dampen down St John's Precinct fire the spectre of Teddy's death hung over the family with mixed feelings. Sharon was still crying at any mention of her Dad or when she had flashbacks of times with Teddy. Carlo was putting on a brave face, saying even sillier things than usual. Tony was the quiet watching one, trying to see if everyone was actually OK. Leo was unusually reserved, he adored and hated his Dad almost in equal measure. Michael was Michael. Maureen helped her Mum to start seeing the spiritual side of Teddy's passing. Mary was in a quandary.

"What funeral directors are you going to use?" asked Tony of his Mum.

"Oh. I don't know" replied Mary. She looked at Maureen for some inspiration.

"There are quite a few in the Swan. Why don't we get the phone book and have a look?" suggested Maureen. The BT large phone directory was produced, and the adverts scanned for funeral directors. One was found in Old Swan and the number called out for Tony to call them. An appointment was made for the following day.

He was tall and dressed in an appropriately dark sombre suit. He was well versed in talking quietly to bereaved family members and the range of emotions they brought to his office. Despite his empathetic manner he was always looking for upselling opportunities. Offering the more expensive coffin with the brass handles over the simple pine one with the plated ones. One more car to ensure late arrivals could travel with the family, preservation treatments for the body. He ran through the formalities of name dates of birth, and death, quickly. How they were going to pay? This was his inner sigh moment. He thought by the way the two were dressed that it was going to be a budget affair, what they said confirmed it and so he truncated his range of services to the minimum. Moving on to the allied services he asked.

"What religion was Teddy?"

"He was an atheist" stated Tony. Mary nodded her confirmation as she wiped another tear from her eye.

"So what are we thinking about an official? Who will officiate if you don't have a priest or vicar?"

Mary looked at Tony, her eyes red and pleading for a solution.

"For now we won't have one. But if it changes can we let you know?"

"Of course. I have a few people I can contact, and they are very good at catching up on the life of the deceased and delivering a fine eulogy, at short notice."

"OK, thanks."

"Now we have a slot at Springwood this Friday, late morning. How does twelve o clock this Friday sound for you?" Mary looked to Tony he nodded.

"Yes that is fine with us. The sooner the better really." He nodded sagely and noted down the details on his pad. After a few more functional questions as to where the body was now and if they wanted to have Teddy at home, or the chapel of repose in their premises, the arrangements were completed. Teddy would be brought to 382 the following day for the wake and they would return with the hearse, and one following car, at around eleven thirty on Friday for the short trip to Springwood.

The wake was a rolling affair of comings and goings. The kitchen, still in its long galley configuration with Acro supports holding up the load bearing timbers, housed the younger mourners, mostly extended family. Tony had decided. He went back into the lounge and started a thread going about the lack of priest.

"How do you all feel about him not having a priest at his funeral?" there was the briefest of delay before at least three women started speaking at once.

"I think it's outrageous!" said Mary's sister Annie.

"Yes, it is" added Molly, Teddy's youngest sister. "I know he hated priests. Especially after our Tommy as I said, but c'mon? No priest at a catholic funeral," her expression added the question mark. Mary let a deluge of emotional tears fall as she scrambled to catch them in a tissue, which was a permanent fixture now. Tony had the support, and the rationale, he needed to make the executive decision. Teddy was dead. He was an atheist, had no belief in any form of afterlife, as people believed. When he was dead, he would just be a big piece of meat, like at the abattoir, was what he had said on many occasions. In fact he had wanted his body to go to 'medical science'. Tony had enquired, but as he had under gone a post mortem examination that was not possible.

"OK. I will sort it" said Tony determinedly. Mary beamed a look of thank you to her middle son. The gathered sisterhood, from across both sides of the family, voiced a communal thank you too. Tony took the phone out into the small hallway, running the wire under the door as he did so, to make the call to the sombre suited man.

He returned into the lounge and replaced the trim phone and associated wire to the stand.

"All done. He will get a priest to call you for the details later." Tony decided that he would release the information to Leo gently to minimise any emotional fallout.

The remainder of the afternoon and evening was more of the same. Conversations about his exploits as a young man stealing to get food for the family, getting caught and going to prison. Fighting bullies and so on. The women were circumspect in their chats about his exploits, they didn't want to upset Mary with inadvertent mentions of his other women.

Tony had broached the subject of the priest to Leo. He was not happy. Tony used his best calmly spoken logic to let Leo see that in Teddy's beliefs, and both of theirs too, there was no afterlife, no essential Mumbo jumbo required. He was gone, and it was the people left behind that they had to care for now. Mum was the most important. If she felt better with a priest to ease her concerns, that was the most important thing for them to do. Eventually Leo acceded and agreed that it was best for his Mum to have a priest.

Mary was trying to see how the future would be, without his shouting and 'ever so' criteria for anything she had to do for him. The money side of things was not going to be as bad as some would have thought. She had made provision for this event. She had an insurance policy with Royal Liver Insurance. That would cover the funeral expenses and leave a little over. The mortgage that Teddy had taken out to buy the council house, was going to be paid on his death. Her job was going to see her through. The extension was only part built and the money for that was already set aside. For now she didn't think about how that would get finished. In amidst the tears and commiserations she could see light at the end of the tunnel.

Friday morning saw Leo's 26th birthday and his Dad's funeral. The morning was a bright December one, cool but clear. A range of cars had been assembled outside 382, all parked down the road a little to allow the funeral cars to pull up outside. Old funeral practices were bandied about like closing curtains and covering mirrors. Some were done others were pooh poohed away as being daft. The foreman undertaker took control of the lone car loading, instructing the private follow on cars to keep up with the cortege and to park in the main car park at Springwood.

On arrival the young men of the extended family carried the pine coffin with plated handles into the chapel and laid it on the rolling bars, the foreman positioned it into place and indicated for the bearers to be seated. Tony sat on the second row back behind his Mum and sisters, Carlo sat next to him. The entry music had ceased, and the frocked priest began his performance. Hands outstretched, his arms resembling bat wings as the colourful garment fell in folds below them. He started his monologue making eye contact only with those he could see were of his persuasion, he knew he would be wasting his time with the likes of Leo and Tony. Tony sat watching him perform. He was sad that they couldn't have adhered to their Dad's wishes and not had a religious service, but as he had explained to Leo, it was for Mary's sake they had allowed it.

After the soulless speech from the priest. The assembled mourners took their cue from the increasing music and the rising tone of the sky pilot, tears and sobs began to grow louder. The modest curtains that formed the border between the here and now and the afterlife, slowly opened. Sobbing increased. The metal runners started to spin, and the pine coffin began to move forward. The final music volume increased again, it was as if it didn't like to hear the sobbing grief. The priest stood to one side as the final part of his choreography, accepting handshakes and thanks from mourners as they passed him by. They emerged into the weak sunshine outside and the informal gathering while the allotted time was used up, before the next group of mourners sent their loved one through the veiled portal.

Many people offered their commiserations to Teddy's family in the small area outside. Handshakes, hugs and tissues were offered accordingly. Mary had not wanted anyone to go back to 382 and the kitchen mess, in fact there was no formal 'after party'. Leo had offered to meet people in the Boundary that afternoon for drinks and a wet send off for Teddy. Leo was happiest in the company of men and men's talk. Tony decided not to go to the Boundary that afternoon but to return back to his adopted home in Wirral and his fiancée. He had not asked her to join him just in case the funeral was a sparky affair, as it happened it was quite genteel.

Mary went back to 382 with Maureen and Sharon and a few other women. Tea was made, and comfort given to all who needed it. Michael carried on drinking whiskey into the evening and made the usual show of himself, as the expression goes. He did however give Mary permission, in his outrageous talk, to think about herself and her future without the yolk of Teddy's controlling behaviour. She sat and thought about that. It was exciting and scary at the same time. She had been controlled by him for so long, she was unsure of how she would cope now she was free of it. She *was* free of it. Thoughts filled her mind. She began to see herself as the woman she once was, happy and outgoing with a flash of risqué round the edges.

On Saturday she woke in an empty bed. His smell was still there, in the room, in the wallpaper she thought. I will decorate this room she decided, after Christmas, and all the dust has settled. I will wash his bad temper right out of my house and out of my mind.

That Christmas was a busy one as all her kids made the effort to fuss her. The boys plucked the turkey in the garden, Michael officiated over the cooking of the monster bird. Laughter and good humour had started to fill the rooms of 382 again, without the risk of a raging outburst to shatter the spell. In fact 382 never saw another violent event for the next thirty odd years while Mary lived there.

In the following spring Leo took control of getting the extension finished. He called on a variety of men he knew, from the pubs he drank in, to source the elusive RSJs and the final pieces of materials for the flat roof. Mary was pleased to see her boys and their cousin Frankie complete the kitchen extension, and when Michael had decorated it, she was delighted that eventually her dream kitchen had arrived.

In the few months that had passed she had started to replace bingo with going dancing, a treat she had missed most of her life with Teddy. He never danced. He was jealous at the thought of Mary dancing, and that she might find a better man than him in the process. He preferred to keep her close, and well controlled, with threats of violence to those she loved. He was quite a sad man she reflected over the years. She rediscovered that she was a person in her own right, and not a 'do as I tell you', controlled, non-person.

She was free. Free to live her life now.

The end

Printed in Great Britain
by Amazon

10464782R00258